Dream of the Dove

To Judith + Charlie

Bruce Graham

Bruce Graham

Pottersfield Press, Lawrencetown Beach, Nova Scotia, Canada

National Library of Canada Cataloguing in Publication
Graham, Bruce
Dream of the dove : a novel / Bruce Graham.
ISBN 1-895900-56-5
I. Title.
PS8563.R3143D74 2003   C813'.6   C2003-900378-7
PR9199.4.G7D74 2003

Edited by Julia Swan and Lesley Choyce

Cover design by Dalhousie Graphics

Pottersfield Press gratefully acknowledges the ongoing support of The Canada Council for the Arts as well as the Nova Scotia Department of Tourism and Culture, Cultural Affairs Division. We acknowledge the financial support of the Government of Canada through the Book Publishing Industry Development Program for our publishing activities.

Pottersfield Press
83 Leslie Road
East Lawrencetown
Nova Scotia, Canada, B2Z 1P8
To order, phone toll-free 1-800-NIMBUS9 (1-800-646-2879)
Printed in Canada

   Canada Council for the Arts / Conseil des Arts du Canada

To
John & Edrie,
George & Jack
And our kin

Author's Note

ream of the Dove is a fictionalised account of the life of Captain James Allan Graham. Fictionalised in that I have added between the lines of his letters and logs to put meat on the bones of his story. I have also taken great liberties with romance and high adventure. Where possible, I have given accurate times, dates and places. To the best of my knowledge, everything concerning the *Dove's* last voyage is accurate. I followed the ships log page by page and relied on stories passed down from those involved. All of the names of the *Dove's* crew are accurate. With the exception of the *Celeste* and possibly the *Treasurer*, I have put Captain Graham on the ships he was on at the times told in the story. I know when he was a night watchman in New York and when he was making regular runs between Cuba and New York. Otherwise, the story is fiction and should be considered as such.

There are many people who helped me in my task.

The story would have been impossible without the assistance of my cousin John Graham who owns the logs and letters of our great-uncle and who was most generous in letting me borrow and copy much of the research material.

I owe a debt of gratitude to his late sister, Edrie, who was for many years the custodian of the Graham family history.

Beatrice Wickett of Ottawa, Captain Graham's granddaughter, told me the story of the operation in Great Village and supplied me with other stories and materials as well.

Merna Perry of Springhill, the granddaughter of Jacob Campbell, donated much of the material of her late husband, Garfield Perry, who had done considerable research on the ships built in Lower Economy.

I thank my publisher, Lesley Choyce, of Pottersfield Press for his support and assistance in bringing the story to book form.

I also wish to acknowledge the valuable contribution of editor Julia Swan, for her many notations and helpful suggestions.

Helen Wasson, who has a nautical heritage herself, read, re-read and proofed the pages, making helpful suggestions in turning a thousands scraps of paper into a book. As with my first novel, Helen's assistance goes beyond words. To say thank you, Helen, is never enough.

It has been one hundred and eighty-five years since James Graham first swung his axe to fell that first tree in Lower Economy. The Grahams have lived on that piece of land ever since. The three houses of the three brothers are still standing, although our Great Uncle John's house was moved many years ago to Central Economy. My cousin John and his wife Virginia live in our grandfather's house. Below them stands what was the home of Captain James Allan Graham. This is his story, the story of the brave men who served with him and the story of all who follow the sea.

Prologue

James Graham felled the first tree at Lower Economy the day after he arrived, on November 9th, 1818. Before he took his first swing of the axe, he walked the few steps to the bank and looked out over the water. Two canoes with Micmac Indians were coming around the cove. He thought about waving to them but didn't. Nor did they acknowledge him, or even look his way. He turned back to the small knoll where he planned to put the cabin. Much remained to be done and winter was at hand.

It was not the way he planned it. Not the way any of them planned it. They had already been in Nova Scotia a year and he had built one cabin in the Cobequids by the steep banks of Gondola Mountain near the village of Five Islands. It was discouraging to start again but he had no choice. The land at Gondola was too swampy to farm and it had taken all spring and summer to get a new grant. After two trips to Halifax, they had finally given him this point of land jutting into the bay. He was still by a mountain, less steep than Gondola but bigger. Rising out of the morning mist, its base swept into the Bay of Fundy in a great circumference of timberland and fertile fields.

It had taken a year of discomfort but he was well satisfied with what he saw. It would be better this time. Fish and game were plentiful, the soil good for potatoes and turnips.

He kept the children busy as best he could. They wanted to explore the shore and he warned them of the tide, how it could silently encircle them so they would be unable to reach shore. The oldest boys would help him cut the limbs after he felled the trees. When he had cut enough they would all work on the walls, the children packing mud between each log. He pledged to do better with the fireplace and this time make the chimney higher, less smoky so they wouldn't have to leave the door open in winter.

He had brought his bellows from Scotland so once the cabin was finished and some game hanging, he would open a shop in Five Islands. And that's what he did, paying careful attention to all his accounts.

A few years later, he and his sons sawed boards by hand to build a house next to the log cabin. Slowly, painstakingly, the clapboard walls began to overshadow the small cabin, making it look more like a hovel.

It was in the "new house" that I was born on April 3rd 1846. James Graham was my grandfather. My father was also James, and in the 1870s he built another house on the same knoll next to the new house. That's where my brother George lives today. Another brother, John, built his house on the far side of the orchard and I built mine down the knoll in the glen. Three brothers, three houses and it all started with that first swing of the axe on the morning of November 9th, 1818.

What does it matter, you ask?

It matters because this is not a singular experience for me or for you. We are all connected in some mysterious way. We face the same fate. I am facing mine now. An old dog at the other end of the spy glass looking down over his years, the seasons – even the moments. We are all merchants at times, taking dusty articles off the shelves to examine and evaluate. It is the inventory of our lives.

Scoff if you will, but one day you'll turn around quickly and in one blinding moment you'll see yourself for the first time. The whole truth awaits you.

My inventory day has come and nothing I can do will stop it.

Chapter One

They had nothing in common except a common name. The first name of one, the family name of the other. That's as close as they ever got. Two men moulded my life. With a shared name and a total dislike for one another.

Captain Thompson Densmore marked me early as my mentor. Captain Will Thompson has marked me lately. Today they both left an impression. One of them by going into the ground, the box lowered by taut ropes sliding through sunburned hands. Murmured prayers and bowed heads.

One captain gone into the gaping hole. The other staring at it, disapproving of its mystery.

Disapproval had hung heavily in the churchyard. I could feel it through the pine box and the black coffin. I could feel it in the stiff, arched back and square shoulders. Half blind, I can see more. Half dead, I can feel more. Feel the living and the dead disapproving of me. The funeral has only added to the complexity of my recent inventory, this digging and examining I am going through. It started years ago deep inside, finally springing to the surface on my way home from the west, drawing closer to the outside accompanied by the clickety-clack of the train. Hour after hour, mile after mile as I moved farther away from Laura. Memories started to seep out of my skin, an old dam no longer able to withstand the pressure.

When I arrived home and found Will Thompson dying, the seepage increased. Small streams started to break through and trickle down, further weakening the wall I had built around myself.

Maybe this is natural. I know I am moving closer to my day of judgement. Not the judgement of the men I sailed with or the women I loved. Not the judgement of some higher power. That will come but it is not my concern. This is different. It is my judgement. It will be me and me alone who unravels my life, unties the knots and straightens out all the complexities.

When the service was over I wanted to walk home along the water and take stock of the gathering storm. A man of my years should have tranquillity but there is too much swirling inside me. There is an anger I can't identify. I could have stood up in that sweltering little church, clenched my fists and screamed at the top of my lungs. But what would have come out? What righteous indignation would I have brought on that startled assembly?

I can't find categories to fit things. My memories are a jumble. Small details of conversations from fifty years ago and I remember every word. Deeds of last year or yesterday are gone. Still, it is more than that. I am perplexed by the kind of man I've become. Maybe that's what I would shout.

"I can no longer identify myself! I can't tell the bad from the good, nor am I sure there is a difference."

Maybe that's what I would do. I would stand up and point at his coffin and yell at the top of my voice, "This occupant refuses a definition."

Will Thompson was never my friend but believed he was my superior. Not unusual for a man who believed he was everyone's superior. Today watching him go into the ground, I know my visits were not out of compassion. I had been studying him, for to better understand him is to better understand myself. He refused to give enough of himself for me to learn much. Even while he was dying, he defied death.

Thompson Densmore, on the other hand, gave enough of himself but has taken it back. He was my teacher and my friend in my early life.

But he has retreated and now holds me at arm's length. I loved him like a father, respected him above all men. Now I receive only his cold stare.

Perhaps he is a little daft like the rest of us.

Why am I trying to fit together pieces of my life? What is the point? Why try to bring to the floor long-dead dancers when the music has stopped?

Will Thompson would never take such stock of himself. He would scoff at such attention. To him life was a game where people could be changed and cheated. Consequences were of no concern to him and perhaps of too much concern to me. I was repelled by his tactics and refused to follow him. Did it make any difference? We both ended up alone. Old men with brittle bones, sitting in dark houses listening to the rain.

His wife died from some dreadful disease they say he brought back from the south. That's probably rubbish. So many stories! They made him out a monster because he would not bow down to them. He had no shame, never hid his dallying with whores. Why try to hide it when you come from this shore where the men you live with on the water, you live with on the land. There is no anonymity at home or in foreign lands.

"We are the only captains who travel the world with the people next door," Captain Densmore would say as a way of warning his sailors. Whatever they did thousands of miles from home would get home. Often before they did.

Under Thompson Densmore I learned the sea. He taught me to read the face of water, to watch the waves for an ocean change, to know the dip and fall of fair and foul omens. He taught me the winds. The trades are the mariner's most important friends, where they blow and how to catch them.

"Get in a good trade wind and she can take you home."

He taught me how to square off a ship during a wind change to keep the sails full as a nor'easter blew around you. He handed me my first sextant and taught me the heavens. The Dippers, Orion, the North Star.

"Walk the roadway of the stars," he'd tell me.

When I became his mate there were the other things. How to run a tidy ship and how to read a crew, for no two crews are alike. Change one man and it changes the ship's company.

He was my mentor and I was the only person with whom he shared his secrets. Sail with a man for long and you know him well. Too well! Shared confidences can congeal and harden in time. The secret itself becomes a burden on both parties.

In Thompson Densmore this afternoon I felt the disapproval of the living. In Will Thompson, I felt the lingering ridicule of the dead.

Will Thompson's ridicule should no longer affect me. Captain Densmore's quiet condemnation is more difficult to digest. I was uncomfortable from the moment I stood next to him and his wife.

When I came back from out west I went to visit them. It was uncomfortable then too, our talk strained. In the cemetery this afternoon he gave me an officious nod.

"So he's gone," was all he said, looking off over the fields.

Silence.

His words sounded harmless but I felt more – an almost undetectable stiffening of his spirit, as if he was pushing me away with invisible arms. Was this the captain with whom I had shared so much? We had been hurled into the gunwales together, clinging to each other to stay alive. We had been on the same sinking ship, its deck listing into the Atlantic. We had been prisoners in a hot, Charleston harbour. We had shared the heartaches of seeing a good man fling himself overboard, made crazy by the sea, and we had also shared the happiness of a cool breeze on a warm tropic night. This was no ordinary man who stood before me, his body rigid, his jaw firm, eyes never flickering. This was the man who confided his deepest despair to me and I never told his confession to a living soul. I kept my trust. Yet he is unfriendly, his presence packed in ice.

Words from his wife filled the air. Her thin lips took up the slack.

"Has Laura returned?" she inquired, knowing full well Laura won't be returning.

I replied that no, she had not returned and followed her husband's gaze across the fields, trying to catch a glimpse of the bay. I waited, wanting more from him. There was nothing. Soon Will Thompson would be in the ground and we could all go home.

The death of an old sea dog should be short on ceremony. He already experienced the heavenly glow of tropical sunsets and the raging hell of lashing gales. Pray for him, but don't sing his praises. Will Thompson needed many prayers but deserved little praise. Of course, he got the opposite of what he deserved. Praises that were a pack of lies and not enough prayers to buy him a glass of warm piss in the depths of hell! No one gave a damn. God rest his soul, Amen!

Then into our wagons to gossip about the deceased all the way home.

Not kind things either. No, not in his case.

His dying wasn't a shock. He had been sick the past months, coughing, spitting up blood. Rubbing his stained handkerchief into his face with his chest congested and heaving. His lungs rotting away. I watched him die bit by bit, day by day. I was one of the few who visited. I endured his criticisms as he was dying as I had when he was full of life. Little did I know he could pull a final trigger even after death, as he was sliding away in his new pine box.

It was only a simple reflection but it was enough to blame him for it. There are moments when a man turns a corner in his life and sees himself as he really is. Who can withstand such truth?

A strange day all around. The first of May but the heat of summer. Before the service the sky darkened and a squall came up the bay, carried by billowing black clouds that looked like horsemen draped in flowing robes. Those in the churchyard noticed but said nothing. They were still scared of Will Thompson. People went inside as the squall brought hammering, hot rain that ricocheted off the roof and walls. The little church, already humid, now reverberated with the thundering sound of the sky and sea. How appropriate. North Atlantic rain and the rising vapours of the tropics. Who else could die and order his own weather? He would have loved watching the steamy people sing their hymns of praise.

Laugh, you bastard, laugh!

The young pastor's light brown curls were sticking to his forehead by the opening prayer. He is a pale, willowy lad who knew nothing of Will Thompson, so he used the standard words, of course. The same said last month for Alvin Berry and the month before that for someone else. They didn't fit Will Thompson and the more the pastor talked, the more the wind beat and the windows rattled as if in complaint for the falsehoods spoken inside.

It is customary to say something good about the deceased and in truth that's why so many had come today. To hear what good could be said of Will Thompson. They loathed the man, hated his nonconformity, his sneering at their pettiness and principles. They sighed and shook their heads at stories their sons and husbands brought back of his gambling, drinking, women and worse.

"He was a man of extraordinary stamina," the pastor droned.

Extraordinary stamina? What the devil does that mean? That cold body in the box, was he laughing? Who could blame him?

Extraordinary stamina? It sounds more like lustful praise from a satisfied young wife than a eulogy for a pirate.

I listened for any hint of a snicker. Were some next to me holding their breath, smirking? Presbyterians don't smirk or snicker even if they want to. Some of the more pious were saying prayers. Not for Will Thompson but for their young pastor who surely must answer for such whoppers.

Before the end of the service the rain stopped as suddenly as it had arrived. The full sun broke through the clouds, making the afternoon again unseasonably hot.

Then a short walk to the cemetery and around to the grave.

"Into thy hands we commit the spirit of our brother."

Then he was gone – finally. No, not yet!

Another prayer as the box is lowered. Another prayer for a man who never prayed. Kind words for a most unkind man. The pastor closed his Bible and looked toward the heavens, knowing he had tempted fate.

Now we enter the awkward stage. Everyone wanted to dash off but instead stood around and waited in a final show of respect. The bereaved, his elderly sisters who seldom visited him had suffered enough of his slings and arrows. There are cousins from somewhere and a young son. All huddled in a mass, they crossed the cemetery together low and slow, like a hermit crab draped in distress. The rest of us mumble to each other about the weather or something. Meaningless exchanges. A cemetery isn't the place to involve yourself.

Much around me is just a blur but by closing my left eye and squinting I look for shipmates. He never kept a crew long. For most sailors once was enough. I pick out two or three. Old men with leathery faces who fidget in their ill-fitting suits. Their bony fingers already in their pockets around a plug of tobacco. Old men who have outlasted their ships. Who have outlasted sail.

My suit smells of wet wool as though I'd been shearing sheep in the rain. Damp, heavy sheep who are pulling me down. I need air! Not the air inside a carriage but sea air. The air of the entire sky. I had accepted a ride over the mountain but declined offers to be taken further. I wanted to walk home along the shore.

"Are you sure, Captain Graham? Can you see well enough to walk alone?"

"Oh yes," I replied, "I can see fine most days."

I see too much. My blindness blurs the present yet I still see too much. Even in the past I see clearly except the parts I'm searching for. Where are they? It is the past that haunts me. Will Thompson and Thompson Densmore are part of it.

As I walk, I see that box going into the ground. My days will be longer without him. Yet now that he's gone I may understand better why I was drawn to him. What am I searching for?

His final insult was Monday, the day before he died.

"For all good purposes your life is over too," he said to me. "Face it, man. There's no more work for you, and your blindness is only going to worsen. They can't make you see again."

"No," I mumbled like a small child humiliated by a bully. "No, they can't."

He had a way of being right that was dreadful. Who wants the truth tossed at them? Only he had the strength to face it. Maybe that's why I went daily and sat by his bed. I was looking for that same strength.

And then the insult hurled from his grave. A simple reflection causing a vibration in my knees, travelling through me until it pounded in my chest and set my teeth chattering.

The afternoon squall had enlarged the puddles in low patches along the road to my house. At the edge of one of the larger pools the bright sun threw my image back at me. In a startling instant I saw an old man. Whiskered, hard-eyed and haggard in his own ill-fitting suit as his body shrinks inside it. Half blind I could see the struggle, the agony of a man trying to put his memories in order. Memories are half forgotten and slippery things, refusing order from a man who wants order. The reflection showed me a man who knows he has missed something. Something valuable that got by him.

Nothing is worse than seeing the truth. Breathing hard, I stopped and watched waves out in the bay. Each wave lit by the receding sun. Squint just enough to see crystals, and the bay is a shimmering chandelier.

I have seen the world from end to end but this is the place I love. This road. This bay. The place of my beginning and my end.

The beginning was wonderful in its warmth, marked by sweet memories of the noise and commotion of our kitchen. My mother, sisters and brothers. Me the oldest boy, ruler of a small roost. My father coming in from the barn, sitting in his chair by the window, telling stories of Scotland and his own boyhood by the River Nith.

We always had company in those days, people coming and going, a different number for supper ever night. Friends and family; neighbours from along the shore; kinfolk from Parrsboro, Port Greville and Kirk Hill. I remember the smoke curling from Captain Densmore's pipe as he sat in our kitchen talking to my father. When he wasn't at sea he was a regular at our house. He and my father would talk by the hour. Politics, of course. The reformers and the losing grip of Westminster, the land grants handed out by the Whigs. The American states and trade. When they talked about people they would start close to home. People along the shore. First Economy, then Five Islands, Bass River and Great Village. They knew every man, woman and child. Knew their business, their trials, successes and failures. From what stock they came. Once they had finished with people, they moved back to trade and charters. What was going where, on what vessels and who was captain. Who was building and when the newest brig would be launched. What ship had been sold recently, or lost.

Thompson Densmore was fifteen years my senior. He was a master mariner by the time I was five. When there were no chores to finish, I would sit on the floor by the stove and listen to him. With my father's prompting he would tell stories of things he had seen – the markets and customs of exotic lands or the sweet smelling jungles of tropical islands. He was not a braggart. His stories were woven around other topics. But it was those rare tales of far away places that swelled my imagination and pointed me toward the sea.

At that time, the voyage that changed him and caused his nightmares had not happened yet. Nightmares are common in old sea dogs. So much danger. Battering storms and lashing ropes and broken bones. Even Will Thompson had nightmares, except he laughed at them, refused to let them scare him even with the grim reaper at the door. He would wake up in the darkness covered in the pungent sweat of an old man, that mixture of decay and sulfur, to lie in his wet sheets refusing forgiveness.

That was not the case with Captain Densmore. He prayed mightily for forgiveness. It was a prayer that went on for years. He would stand by the wheel on the mate's watch, looking across the dark water. We were accustomed to his spells. When the wind died, part of him seemed to go with it. If I was at the wheel he would come and stand with his hands folded behind him, looking out into the blackness.

One night without warning he confessed. By then I was mate and knew his moods, but this was unexpected. Why had he chosen me? Maybe it wasn't a choice at all. Maybe it was just the time and place and he could no longer contain it. We were on the brig *Allandale* off New York. In the calms, waiting for a good wind to take us up the East River.

It began almost casually as if he was talking to himself. Alone on the dark deck of a still ship. He said they repeated the same words over and over like a chant. It sounded like, "Main-ga-boo-ee, main-ga-boo, na-tay-sue, ma-tay-sue." They would keep it up hour after hour. He expected they were praying for deliverance. It unnerved the crew so much that finally the mate beat on the hatch and yelled at them to shut up. There wasn't a day, he said, that he didn't regret that charter.

That night off New York he told me everything. Details, smells, curses, fears. He talked hour after hour, never asking if I wanted to hear about his torture. He asked me for no opinion and I gave none. He was my captain.

His story started when they were held up in Barcelona in early '59 on the Halifax barque *Murray S. George*. Things had gone slack all over but in Barcelona at least the crew didn't drift away as they did in Liverpool or New York. A glut of vessels lined the wharves waiting for charters. Finally he got word from the British consulate. The owners had arranged a charter in Rabat on the African coast. The instructions were, "Take only if you can find nothing else."

"I didn't much fancy going down the coast in 1859. Pirates had burned a British frigate three months earlier and the whole region was rebellious. Ships get caught in local disputes and small violent wars."

Captain Densmore was a Presbyterian but he couldn't find a Protestant anywhere in Barcelona, so before leaving he brought a Roman Catholic priest on board to bless the ship. It was the only time he did such a thing, he said, because the omens were so strong. The priest spoke Spanish and not a word was understood by the crew. His presence and his prayers unnerved men already edgy and argumentative.

He made one last try to find a charter that would have taken him to England or America. Reluctantly, on the fifth of April he put the *Murray S. George* to sea. They left Barcelona without a notion of what charter awaited them. They took on water and food in Gibraltar and the captain tried again to find a different charter. On May 12th, the *Murray S. George* sailed past the Pillars of Hercules into the open Atlantic.

Things were bad on board. Before they left Barcelona, a sailor name George Smith had an infected hand. Even though the cook lanced it, the swelling got worse and Smith couldn't go aloft or work the rigging. Nor was he much help on the deck pulling the fore and aft sail on the mizzen. Less than a day after starting down the African coast a man named Fry accused another sailor of stealing a pair of boots and they got in a fight. The mate pistol-whipped the pair of them and the captain put both in irons for twenty hours, docking them a week's pay. When they were released, Fry complained of headaches, was sullen, refused to eat and stayed aloft when he was sent to the rigging. When his watch came the captain finally ordered him down. He climbed slowly towards the deck, picking his way like a long-legged spider walking the web. When he reached the deck, Able Seaman Francis Fry, without a word to anyone, jumped over the side.

Two men down. The crew dour when they hit the whipping, hot devil winds carrying the sting of the desert across the ocean. The hot winds burned their eyes then shifted to the west and blew off the water, turning cold and raising goose bumps on their bare arms. Hot and cold, clashing in great gusts of shrieking gales that stopped and started again. Men running up and down the rigging, onto the yards, pulling and tugging the reef lines, lifting sail with a blast furnace in their faces. Down they came onto the deck, sprawled, breathing hard. Another change and up they went again.

They were too tired to complain or fight and Captain Densmore was thankful for that. But it was not the shifting wind that he felt on his face and hands. It was something else. A strange foreboding deep inside him added to the rancid stench of evil.

Big breakers rolling in on the long yellow beach at Rabat. Sea birds and fig trees, gold sand and black rocks. The old walled city north of Casablanca hasn't changed in a thousand years. Narrow streets criss-cross in an unending catacomb of butchers, bakers, spice sellers and carpet merchants.

The captain's troubles continued. A dispute ties up the harbour and they can't get a pilot. They anchor offshore and wait in the boiling sun. The ship is an oven. The crew sleeps on deck. In daylight the mates keep them busy. There is always work on a ship. New bunt lines needed, top gallants to be replaced, one of the courses needs mending. Always work and always better to have the men working.

The captain goes ashore and comes back every night more distressed. He knows the charter. I can imagine his appearance coming back to his crew: ruddy skin turned chalk white with thick eyebrows knit in a gathering storm.

They would see the displeasure in his eyes that I saw today.

I'm sorry now I didn't accept a drive to my house. I am amazed how long it has taken me to walk these few miles. My knee is bothering me. Just ahead is a pile of poles George's boys have cut for the weir. I'll sit on them and rest a bit. There is no hurry. No one is waiting.

Already the moon is coming up, calming the water. Dusk. The bats are out, one swoops by my head on its way to the meadow. They drift and glide, catching insects with a freedom denied us mortals.

Ah yes, mortals. I can close my eyes and drift back to my own voyages to Rabat. The noise from the ships with every flag waiting for the spice trade to improve before loading, whether for England or the American states. Ships full-rigged, brigs, barques. Sailors dancing the hornpipe and mates cursing. Merchants of many tongues, voices piercing the morning air. Black bowlers from Liverpool, the flowing robes of camel drivers from Marrakech. Turks in pointed slippers and pantaloons, veiled Arab girls and Berber women with the mark of their tribe tattooed on their faces. Sailors, sellers, Mediterranean, European, African. Dark, light and white.

I can imagine Captain Densmore's grief as he pushed his way past the hawkers on straw mats calling out the quality of the wares or holy men saying their prayers. Pleading and praying in mystic languages. How alone he must have felt. Not because of Rabat. He was accustomed to exotic lands and mysterious dialects. Alone because he faced a great burden and he was a good man and a good captain whose ship, the owners and crew, came first. He had responsibilities and could not walk away.

It was near midnight, he said, when he first saw them. Dark forms marching along the dockside and up the gangplank two by two, chains jangling from their tethered legs. The men with pistols roughly pushed them in the forward hole – a place for lumber and coal or salt cod and tobacco.

The other hole was filled with bags of spices and wooden crates of colourful pottery from Spain. They took on provisions of dried meat, fish and water and were finally ready for sea.

All except George Smith, whose infected hand by then had the odour of rancid meat. A dark-skinned doctor told him the hand would need to come off.

"Not on my mother's grave am I letting that black butcher take off my hand," he raged as men will in such circumstances. With bloodshot eyes he stood before his mates cursing and asking, "What good's a man without his hand?"

"If it gets worse, we'll be cutting it off at sea," said Captain Densmore. "Then you'll be praying for that black butcher."

George Smith refused to have his hand cut off and he refused to be left behind. Captain Densmore refused to wait. He wanted to be gone from that place. His mate had looked for sailors to replace Fry and the stewing Smith, but the captain was not satisfied with the dregs brought aboard and refused to hire them.

"Pray for a good voyage, Mr. Goodman. We're putting to sea."

The forward hatch was opened twice a day – mornings for water and bread and at night for beans and water. At first there were just muffled noises, though it was an oven down there. On the second day they started what the captain called "the chanting." There was a crew of nine on the *Murray S. George*. They had seen slaves sold in the market in Havana and working in the fields of the big plantations. Cane cutters. Black men bound together on the dusty roads. Sultry guards with guns nearby. The only noise was the jingle of the chains.

"On the second night, things started to get bad," he said.

His mate at the time was a man name Goodman. A big profane fellow who wanted to keep his distance from them, but the chanting got on his nerves so badly he would rage and scream as if he was losing his mind.

"Ease off, Mr. Goodman," Captain Densmore would say. "They can't understand a word you're saying any more than you can understand them."

"They'll understand the billy, by the Jesus, if they don't stop. I'll bring it down on every one of them."

After hours of chanting the captain finally told Goodman to open the hatch. The stench made men ill, sailors staggered back it was so foul. They were much agitated in the hold. Crying and screaming in a mess of their own bowels and bladders. He ordered Goodman to bring them on deck. Up they came, rancid, stained and crying. Thirty-three of them. Mostly men, but a few women and a boy of maybe ten. It had been night when they were brought aboard in Rabat by men in wide-brimmed hats with pistols in their belts. Captain Densmore didn't realise how young they were, many of them little more than children, wide-eyed with fear.

He remembers two of them especially, a man and a woman. Violently shivering, their teeth chattering.

The mate grumbled about them being on deck and in the way, but most sailors kept their distance.

"Keep the hatch off, Mr. Goodman, and throw some lye down there." Turning away from his crew he looked out to sea and whispered, "God forgive us all."

He let them stay on deck for an hour and gave them extra water. They went back without complaint, and after that he let them up every day until the weather turned as it can only in the South Atlantic.

The crossing from Rabat to Havana took fifty-seven days. By that time the shivering man and woman were dead. He didn't know exactly when they died. They just did. Several others were sick. In Havana, other men with pistols would curse him for not dropping the sick into the sea. He buried only the dead. Wrapped them in old blankets and weights and said prayers before letting them slide over the side.

"Into thy hands, oh Lord."

I can remember most of what he told me. His dark form still and steady, his voice low. He would stop talking when the steward brought coffee or a sailor on watch walked by. I looked at the sky and wondered when the wind would come up and take us into the East River. I remember him lighting his pipe. There was water on his cheek. He had been weeping as he went back to the beginning of that god-awful voyage.

"We started across with the devil wind," he said, "all sails running until late afternoon when it turned into a gale. We furled the royals and reefed the courses and gallants. She was hitting us hard by then, the ship pitching and labouring in the heavy sea. Water rolling over the deck, driving us into deep troughs that would bury the bow. All night the ship rolled in the frothing darkness. When the winds didn't howl, we could hear their cries."

They were being knocked about and tossed, their chains slamming against the hull and their bodies ramming into each other.

"There was pitiful crying, the sounds of hell. Low moans and high screams. We opened the hatch at first light when the storm passed. I was trying to get us back on course before we lost the stars when the third mate came to me."

'Awfully hurt, Capt'n, three of them. Four or five others knocked about some. All is sick. All is in a bad shape, but three of them is real bad.'

"Goodman was overseeing the pumping, for we had taken a lot of water. I sent him to investigate. Grumbling, he obeyed. They were mangled, caught up in the chains. One woman was dead, one man had a broken leg. Two women had broken arms."

In Rabat the agent had given Captain Densmore brutal instructions. They were his charter, his responsibility. "If they're sick or have broken bones, throw them overboard and it's your loss."

He could never do that, never. It was all bad enough carrying them from one place to another, but to put people over the side? He would never again be able to take down his family Bible.

The dead woman was bound in a sheet and weights. He would say a prayer later and put her into the sea, but he had to look after the living first. The injured women and man were carried on deck. The cook made plaster and the captain set their bones. He offered whiskey. They would not take it. The young women were shaking violently as he knelt beside them. They were girls really, fourteen or fifteen. Crying, in convulsions and choking on tears.

One at a time, Goodman and the cook held them while the captain set their bones. The crew, white-faced and numb, bruised from being knocked about, watched. He needed two more sailors to help hold the first girl. She was so terrified two men could not keep her still. As the captain put his hands on her arm she looked at him, her eyes wide, writhing in pain. As he touched the arm near the break, she fainted.

"Is she dead, Capt'n?" asked a sailor.

"No," replied the captain, "but she probably wishes she was."

There was less of a struggle from the second girl. She cried softly and only screamed when he actually put her bones together. It was a bad break.

The man offered no resistance. He lay on the wet deck looking up at the gathering light of the morning sky. The broken bone in his leg was below the knee and difficult to bring together with so much swelling. The captain could see the struggle raging inside the man. Young, proud, he would not cry or utter a sound. A warrior maybe, or a leader.

No, not a leader. The leaders had conspired with the slavers, taking profit for their people who were then run down in the bush, caught in nets like fish, twisting and flipping.

He patched up the rest in order of seriousness. The last was the boy. His lower lip was cut badly and there were bruises on his shoulders where he'd become tangled in a chain. He wondered if the boy's parents were on the ship. The lad seemed alone. There was a cold fury in the boy's eyes. But it wasn't just a fury of hate the captain saw. There was something else. The captain stumbled through his explanation, with long pauses and false starts. He was searching for words. Something that he felt was important for me to understand. In the boy's eyes, fused with the fury, was what he thought was surprise. The outraged disbelief that such misery had struck him so mightily and he had not yet turned his twelfth year.

They buried the dead woman. Mr. Goodman was prepared to throw her in unceremoniously. No, they would offer prayers. Some sailors doffed their caps while others backed away. There was a strange stillness.

In the afternoon a sailor went delirious, claiming he had seen Francis Fry climbing over the side. The captain put him in chains.

The sea was calm. In the evening when the bell brought on the next watch, the moon had lit the ship in a silvery glow.

The three with broken bones could not be put back in the hold. The two girls huddled together under a blanket the captain provided. The warrior man was a little way off, still staring at the sky. At midnight the wind came up, the crew was called aloft and all sails unfurled. The ship was making seven knots. They were forty hours out of Rabat.

When the mate's watch was on, the captain went to his cabin. He told me he sank down and prayed. Prayed for his ship, his crew, his slaves and mostly his own eternal soul. Then he wrote a long letter to his wife, the quill scribbling furiously across the parchment. He told me the gist of it.

> *My Dearest Myra:*
>
> *I trust in providence this letter finds you and the children safe and in good sprits. It is my deepest desire to be with you. I am saddened to be so long and so far away from you all. There is not a day you are not on my mind. I hope there is enough firewood for you and that the horses are fine and the roof is not leaking.*
>
> *Myra, you may recall a conversation we had one day a few years ago in our meadow. We talked of when a man needs his wife more strongly than he needs air or food. Not in comfort of the flesh but in comfort of the soul. You agreed that you too felt the need. You said you prayed for*

*me in those times with extra effort. Dearest, for me this is
one of those times. We are moving away from Africa toward Cuba so this letter will not reach you for considerable time. The writing will somewhat console me, for I
am closer to you with this quill in my hand and my mind
on you in such a deliberate way. This is a trying voyage
and I feel so very far from all I hold dear, particularly you
and the children.*

When he wrote the word "children," his hand froze. He thought of
his son asking a thousand questions that defied answers and of his
daughters sitting by the fire and taking turns combing each other's hair.
He pictured them doing their tables and spelling by the lamp, the girls
planning to be teachers themselves. An awful misery hung over him.
He put down the quill and prayed again. Later he wrote of other
matters.

*From the captains in Barcelona and the English
newspapers they bring from Liverpool, things sound bad
in the American states. I hope the conclusion of this voyage will not be held up by those troubles. I will attempt to
find a charter to New York or Boston and from there to
Nova Scotia. When I return, I may stay at home awhile. I
will write more tomorrow.*

At three in the morning he was still at his desk, neither asleep nor
awake. Suddenly Gibson, the second mate was knocking at the door.

"Capt'n, we need you on deck."

When he got there, all the sailors on watch were looking over the
side.

"What's wrong?" he commanded.

"It's the man, Capt'n, with the broken leg," replied a shaken sailor
named Fowler.

"What happened?"

"He's gone, Capt'n. He jumped – just got up and hobbled to the
gunwale. Didn't look back or nothing. Just went, just like Fry. Just went
over!"

The captain looked into the water and swung his lantern back and forth. There was nothing. A man with a broken leg. If he didn't drown, how long before the sharks came? He took the lantern and stood above the two girls. The one who had fought so hard was asleep but the silent one gazed up at him with a look of unspeakable things. He told me he felt at that moment that he understood her. That she was pleading with him.

"Why has such pain and misery fallen on me?"

The captain bowed down and touched her cheek. "It's all right, my dear. It's all right."

Young Fowler was still looking into the dark water, not realising the captain had moved away.

"He just got up and went over, Capt'n."

Fowler then came and stood by the captain's side. The girl's expression unnerved him even more.

"Jesus, Capt'n sir. I wish she'd stopped staring like that. I wish I wasn't on this ship at all, Capt'n."

The captain put his hand on Fowler's shoulder, nodded and, without a word, went back to continue his letter.

He hadn't written of the slaves, not a word to his wife. He would never tell her. Never tell his daughters. Never, never!

When they were tied up in Havana he wanted to say something to his passengers. That's what he wanted to call them – passengers. Except he knew better. They were not passengers but prisoners, locked in a hold and tied with chains. He wanted to apologise in some way for Mr. Goodwin, for himself, and for the entire evil world of which he had never felt so much a part. He wanted to apologise for their tribal chiefs who had sold them and the white men who had bought them and the plantation people who would use them. Of course he didn't. The prisoners were brought up out of the dark hold, blinded by the harsh glare of the West Indian sun. Still chained, they were marched off the ship as they had been marched on three thousand miles away, their heads bowed, limp and lost. He watched them go until they disappeared in the bustle of a hot Havana morning.

Only the boy looked at him. His young face, already preparing to be gaunt and haggard, looked at him with the eyes of an old man. The child had aged in some indescribable way.

"He didn't look at anything or anybody but me, as though the two of us were the only people on earth. As if I was solely responsible for his troubles."

The boy's look carried such fire, such a piercing repugnance and horror, that it haunted the captain every day of his life. The boy was the age of the captain's son, Ambrose.

"God in heaven, what became of that boy?"

In Havana he told the buyers the girls with broken arms had died at sea. The big man with the scar snarled at him.

"Six, you lost six of them?"

"It was rough. We took a pounding," the captain replied.

"Less money for you," the big man snarled again.

Near Boston a month later, black churchmen holding a meeting were startled by an interruption. A captain entered and entrusted two girls into their care. He never forgot them and never stopped supporting them. I know this because years later, as the one who shared his secret, I went with him to the christening of a child in a church outside Boston. It was a first child, a boy. She had named him Thompson.

Chapter Two

I have been to that place where men leave humanity behind and get down on all fours to become animals. The line is reachable for all. Take away food and water and see how long you last. See how long it takes your respectability to wash away.

Those dark days in '72, weeks without a sign of the sun.

It still makes me tremble. Our ship was pitching but the waves were no longer crashing over the deck. The storm had blown itself out and left us exhausted, after beating us to pieces. A tin cup from the galley rolled back and forth, toward the poop and back toward the bow.

His back was to me when I first saw him. Crouching on his knees as if he was praying. My mind was playing tricks, presenting the jubilation of jumping into the sea as more appealing by the hour. Nine days without water, longer than that without food. The tongue swollen and thick, a strange creature in a dry hole.

As I limped toward him, I realised it was he who had gone into the galley and brought the cup out to the deck. I touched his shoulder but he paid no notice and I pressed until he looked up. I hardly recognised him.

"Stand up, man," I said. "Stand up. Come on, let's go back to your bunk."

"I'm so hungry, Capt'n. Just a little more then I'll go back," he said as he dug his knife into the deck again, prying between the planks. Still I pressed him.

"No, let's go. You can help me walk John and Isaac."

"No, not yet. Not yet!"

He was going about it madly. Digging, digging, digging! I thought of us as boys, haying in the big field. His father driving the wagon with Isaac on top of the hay, Jim and I forking it up.

"God help us all!"

I left him there and went to see my brother.

"Bring him back safely," were my mother's last words. I was failing her. Failing all the parents, failing all the families. I'd had a chance and I turned it down.

I looked back at him. The tin cup was rattling along the deck again, striking the raised poop and rolling back toward him. He didn't notice, intent on his task.

Jim Wilson saved me once, and I saved him the same day. We saved each other from certain death. We were coming around the tip of Cape Breton heading for Montreal and the winds were howling and shrieking. Our brig was rolling in heavy seas and the deck was awash. A big wave knocked me off my feet and carried me over the side. The life saving net known as "the sailor's friend" had washed away. When the icy water hits a man's balls, he's paralysed. His chest locks up as though his lungs are caught in a steel trap, his legs go stiff and then there is no more. Jim grabbed me just in time. He saved me and half an hour later I got a fist full of his hair as he was going over the side and hauled him back on deck.

That happened when we were young sailors. I went to sea with Jim Wilson for many years after that. We never spoke of saving each other that day off Cape Breton but it built a bond between us. Doesn't matter. When a man is thrusting a knife between the planks, digging in the deck and ready to eat a speck of dirt or even the dried carcass of a dead insect there is no pact. When a man has reached that stage, even the bond between lifelong mates isn't strong enough. Not when a man has gone on his knees to survive.

Chapter Three

Captain Thompson Densmore delivered two girls with mending bones to Bostonian churchmen just before the bad autumn of my life. The autumn of 1859 followed a hot summer in Nova Scotia. Our crops were dry and the leaves on the apple trees had turned brown and spotty. Even the usually cool mud flats were warm underfoot when I tended the weir. Father was fussy about the weir. He had built the fence of fishnet tied on long poles. The two arms of the weir gradually came together into a circle of poles and here the net covered both the sides and top. The fish going out with the tide followed the fence and once in the circle couldn't find their way out. Twice a day at low tide I collected the fish, gutted, salted and dried them before they went into wood barrels in our cellar. I always tried to get to the weir early while the receding tide was up to my ankles. If I was late, the water was gone and mud flats gave you the sensation of walking on boiled pudding just off the stove. Being late also meant digging in the mud with your toes until a flounder squirmed and flipped.

My brother John never came with me any more. A year earlier he had been badly stung when he stepped on the barb of a strange looking fish. Our father said it was a ray. John suddenly had too much to do to tend the weir. Mornings he collected eggs and filled the big wood box by the stove. After school his chores included cleaning the hen house and the cow barn. I worked the fields and livestock with our father and cut wood for the winter. After John stepped on the strange fish, I also tended the weir twice a day.

There were ten of us. My parents, three boys and five girls. A happy house full. Mary was the oldest. She looked the most like my mother. That's what people said. She had the same oval face and dark piercing eyes. Mary was twenty, ready to marry and move away as her friends had done. She was not unattractive but her slightly plump roundness irritated her. Teasing Mary would make her sunny disposition quickly disappear. She was like my father, very loving when kindness was called for, but strong-willed and stubborn when riled. Once Mary had her mind made up, no one unmade it.

Martha was eighteen. She was tall and pretty and only nine-year-old Maria with her black ringlets and ivory skin might challenge her for the distinction of the prettiest sister. Martha was lively and boisterous, constantly on the go, much to my mother's displeasure. Mother said Martha might have a regal bearing if she could only stand still. My father playfully called her "Your majesty."

Susanna was sixteen, less plump than Mary and less pretty than Martha. She had the chore of looking after three-year old Rachel, six-year old George and nine-year old Maria. Susanna had more patience with the young ones than Martha and more time. She was the quiet one, as my father called her. When the small ones played by themselves or were sleeping, Susanna would curl up in the parlour with a book.

So there was my family, Mary in the kitchen baking bread with Mother. Martha yelling down the stairs asking if anyone had seen her hair combs. Rachel hanging on to Mother, George and Maria playing in the barnyard, Susanna in the parlour reading Swift, John filling the wood box and Father and I putting a new wheel on the wagon.

We weren't rich by any means but we had friends and family around us and there was an air of contentment in our lives. Only Mary had been unusually quiet that summer. She hadn't sung much while kneading bread or making molasses cookies. Mary had been mulling over many things. Martha said she was worried about becoming a spinster. Even though she had a kind disposition and a charitable heart, few men had come calling.

"You have time," I once heard my mother tell her.

"I'll not settle for less than I want," Mary replied.

"Nor should you," responded Mother. "But you might be too fussy. You might want too much in a husband."

Then came the cough, a tickle in the throat, with something unusual in the sound. Mary's eyes watering as it grew persistent. Other things began. A stricken look in my mother's face as Mary stood by the stove, her shoulders hunched and her long chestnut hair shaking. She could not clear her throat.

Then reports started from all over the shore that diphtheria had come again. They said it was carried on the boats from the tropics. Any cough could be its beginning. A girl in Bass River was said to have been struck down a week earlier and there were rumours of cases in Five Islands and Portapique. Nobody knew for sure. Across the bay they said people had already died.

Soon Mary stayed in the bedroom she shared with her four sisters. In my own bed across the hall I could hear her laboured breathing and the heavy rattle in her chest. Day by day, a despairing look settled into my parent's eyes. We now knew. Mary was coughing up gobs of phlegm that filled her chest and throat. She was wheezing heavily, her shoulders vibrating as she struggled to draw a breath. Neighbours came in the evenings after they heard the old doctor's noisy cart leaving our farm. They brought pies, bread and venison stew.

A solemn quiet settled over my family. A stillness, void of any singing or laughing. We spoke in hushed tones. Martha now had the responsibility of helping in the kitchen and John helped Susanna look after the younger ones.

"Get them out of the gloom," my mother said, looking at my father. "Keep them busy outside."

Looking back on it, my father is the one who should have been kept busy. He grieved for Mary's state of health and the farm work fell more and more on my shoulders. Susanna cared for Mary as much as my mother, for it took two to wash and bath her, read to her and bring her meals, although she ate little and coughed through the readings.

Susanna became the stronger by the ordeal. She worried about us all. One sunny afternoon she suggested I leave my work and hook up the wagon and take her, Martha and the little ones for the last picnic of the year. I knew we would be a glum bunch without Martha so we finally convinced Mother to let her out of the house. My mother told her to go, mind the young ones and don't get wet in the tide.

Everyone cheered when Martha walked to the wagon. We needed her. She was the funny one in our family who could always make us laugh. It was time for a little relief.

Martha always stood out in a crowd. There had been suitors at our door since she turned fourteen, boys with scuffed, dusty boots who had walked the three miles from the foot of Economy Mountain. Hopeless, sweaty boys driven by desire. Instead of the smiling face of my sister they often met the solemn glare of my father. Suitors showed up in the rain, their hair matted over their forehead as they tried to stammer a coherent sentence in front my father's cold stare. Some passed his approval and made it to the parlour, some were driven back in our wagon from whence they came. Others returned to the dusty road without a glimpse of the prize they sought.

But suitors will not be denied. As Martha transformed from a girl into a strikingly beautiful woman, even my father's sternness could not stop them. A few months earlier there had been a fight at a church social. News of it got around the shore. John heard about it at school. He proudly told Martha she was as famous as Queen Victoria.

Alvin Berry and Noah Marsh were strapping, broad-shouldered farm boys who both wanted to drive Martha home. Noah had his father's new carriage pulled by a pair of fine greys. They were fitted with hand-tooled reins and a new bridle. He thought Martha should go with him.

Alvin was ahead of him and had already asked. Martha wasn't sure she would even be permitted. While she was asking Mother, an argument began between the boys that led to them pushing each other. Martha was promptly driven off, leaving the suitors standing in the empty churchyard. The last they saw of my parents was the withering glare of my mother who did not conceal her disapproval of bickering in front of the house of God.

The boys remained still, tight-lipped with fists clenched until my parents were out of sight. Then, where twenty minutes earlier they had sung of the healing of the Jordan, the universal love of God and the Golden rule, Alvin Berry and Noah Marsh proceeded to punch the living daylights out of each other. Long before my parents and a pouting Martha reached Economy Mountain, Alvin and Noah had their church-going clothes ripped to shreds. Noah's sleeve was torn completely off the frock coat his mother had brought back from the Boston States. Alvin's bottom lip had a deep split that cascaded blood down his torn and tattered shirt.

Being a spinster had never crossed Martha's mind.

The day of our picnic Martha took our minds off the troubles. She did her impressions and impersonations, first of the old doctor and then of her schoolteacher. We laughed and skipped rocks in the tide and helped George built a sandcastle while Rachel dragged a piece of driftwood that she said looked like a rabbit, along the beach. We hadn't brought a true picnic because we knew it would cool very quickly in the afternoon. We did lay out a blanket and have molasses cookies and some oatmeal cakes the neighbours had brought. We told stories and John said if there was war in the United States he was going to join up and fight for the North. We had races on the beach, me giving the others more and more of a head start and still almost catching up with them. Rachel stubbed her toe and started to cry and Susanna said it was time to go.

It was an afternoon I always remembered as the last happy time at home.

We were packing up getting ready to go the first time Martha coughed. It was Mary's cough and suddenly everything stopped. The sea, the sun, the birds in the air all froze and the only sound was my sister coughing repeatedly, until her eyes watered. Maria and George started to cry and Rachel, seeing them, cried also. In Susanna's eyes I saw the desperation that haunted my mother. The incoming tide lapped around the toes of my boot and a chill went over me.

Martha was brave.

"Oh dear," she said, trying to clear her throat. Rachel and George had put their small arms around Martha's legs.

"Don't get sick, Mart, please don't."

"Oh, don't be silly. I'm not going to be sick at all. Come on, let's go. The sun is cooling and Father will be looking for Allan and John to finish their chores."

As I drove the wagon up the beach Martha sat next to me wrapped in the blanket we'd used for the picnic. Susanna was crouched down behind the seat with Rachel in her lap. John and the others had their feet dangling off the back of the wagon.

"Martha, I want to sit with you," Maria said and scampered along the back of the wagon until she reached her sister.

"You'll have to sit still," replied Martha, raising her voice just enough to be heard over the wheels clacking along the stony beach. She started to cough again. I took her hand and squeezed it. At the back of the wagon the others had stopped talking. I could feel a strain in my heart.

"Please don't tell Mother and Pa," Martha asked. "I'm sure it's nothing and they have enough worries. I feel guilty leaving Mother as it is." She lowered her head and whispered, "Oh God, please, please!"

I continued to squeeze her hand and Maria had tears in her eyes. We went home without speaking another word.

Martha could not hide her secret. That evening as she and Susanna were clearing away the supper dishes, her coughing started again. It came on her so fast she couldn't flee the kitchen.

There was a look in my father's face I could not describe. My mother went pale and reached for the back of a chair to steady herself.

"Did she do that today?" Father asked.

"Yes, at the shore."

"God help us," he whispered and sank into his chair.

Within two days, Martha was in bed. My sisters' coughing tore through our house and people came from up and down the shore. My mother was in and out of their room all night. I would wake past midnight and see the light from her lantern under my door. The girls would both be coughing. Little George would cry and John would lay in the moonlight wide-eyed and unblinking.

My other sisters were moved out of the bedroom. Susanna and Maria slept in the parlour and Rachel went in with my parents. Nights were the worst. Trapped in my bed I would bury my head in the pillow and pray there would be no coughing. Pray my sisters would be sleeping. Pray they would get well.

Their coughing permeated our house and our spirits. It was infectious. Callers fell silent at the sound of two pairs of lungs straining. What pleasantries can be spoken between gasps? Hopeful words are banal, interrupting coughing fits that ricocheted through our saddened rooms to confront the caller face to face. What was there to say? Diphtheria had no cure, except – except sometimes people did recover. Sometimes when God was in your corner. Go to God, they would say.

There was always hope. Go to God, for there was nowhere else to go. They left our house shaking their heads for our sorrows.

Old Dr. Pace shuffled through our house. He had been thrown by a horse and as a consequence dragged one foot that made a strange sound on our stairs. We waited in the kitchen as the uneven step brought his daily dreaded report ever closer.

"God, spare my daughters, spare my daughters."

Then he would be at the kitchen door, large jowls and white hair. A messenger from God, his news was worse every day. He would shake his massive head and tell my parents that Mary was slowly suffocating and Martha's condition was worsening.

"Mary's case is critical. Her breathing passage is increasingly clogged. The only thing now is to administer a caustic acid."

A wheezing groan came deep from within my father. He knew. Burn the mucus and burn his daughter's throat.

"It will give the poor girl a chance," sighed the doctor.

"But," my mother said. There was a pleading in her voice.

"Yes," the doctor replied. "It will burn her. But there really is no alternative, the phlegm is suffocating your daughter."

It was a night that still brings ghostly visions to my dreams. A night of hollow-eyed children numbed by days of despair, now listening to their parents tearing themselves asunder like strained animals locked in combat. Mother defiant, tear-stained, refusing. Mary was suffering enough and she would not let her daughter be burned.

"Caustic acid has never saved a life. I will not. I will not!"

My father had lost the strength of a stubborn, strong-willed man. He was so distraught his hands shook. He told us all to get on our knees and pray as we had never prayed before.

"Pray until your heart breaks," he ordered.

We knelt by the kitchen chairs. Mary and Martha's coughing mingled with my father's plaintive voice.

"Spare our children. Spare our children, we beseech Thee, oh God!" The younger children were crying and so was I.

That night Mary had a high fever and her neck started to swell. She was getting weaker, the continuous coughing sapping her strength.

The next morning my exhausted mother relented. She called it "the blackest chapter during this dark time."

I went to Five Islands and fetched the doctor. He brought a contraption to hold open Mary's mouth. He would drop the acid down her throat. My father's brother Thomas lived along our road and he also came to help. He took off his coat, draped it over a chair and rolled up his sleeves. His arms were sunburned and powerful. The three of us, Uncle Thomas, my father and myself, would hold Mary down, pinning her flailing arms and legs to the bed.

"It will be uncomfortable. Very uncomfortable," the doctor said.

The acid was foul smelling, and burned our eyes. Mary tried to be brave but when the acid dropped into her throat and smoke came out of her mouth there was a mighty lunge as she tried to throw the three of us off her. Even though her strength was gone, it took all we had to hold her as her struggles drew the acid deeper. She was on fire. Oh God, the smell, the smoke. Muffled in our arms she silently screamed. From across the room, Martha watched, pale and frozen.

"Poor Mar, poor Mar," my father repeated and I whispered to her that I was sorry.

Mary cried and stopped coughing. Wet with tears and perspiration, gasping air, she finally fell asleep. The wheezing accompanied each rise of her chest.

My father had always been talkative, more outgoing than my mother who went about her business with a quiet determination. She still did, but my father stopped talking.

He would come in from the barn without saying a word and sit in his chair by the window. You could see the bay from that window but he didn't look. He put his face in his hands and sat there. Then he'd go back to his work. Every afternoon my mother would read to Mary and Martha, a sentence or a paragraph between coughs. She kept her composure in front of them. In the evening I would read the Scottish poems of Burns that Mary loved and Susanna read stories from the newspapers that came from Halifax.

Most of the time Mary was burning up. Dr. Pace shuffled into our kitchen and told my parents it was now only a matter of time.

"A day or two, I'm afraid."

"She'll not get better, then?" my mother asked.

"No, she will not."

"The acid did no good," Mother said.

"It helped for a while. Maybe her condition was too far gone." He started to leave then turned back.

"I'm sorry, but I would not be doing my duty if I didn't tell you. I recommend Martha be given the treatment at once."

"No," cried my mother. "No. Never!" Her usual softness was gone.

The doctor limped away and my father sat in his chair. Our house was still except for my sisters' wheezing.

My mother refused to believe the prognosis. She prayed more earnestly. She went to her bedroom with the big family bible my grandfather had brought from Scotland. Through the wall she could hear the laboured breathing of her daughters.

If company came, she would not come down until she had finished reading. The callers, ill at ease, would sit in the kitchen near my father, who stayed hunched over in his chair. Susanna would make them tea and force herself to bring them up to date on the girls' condition. Except there was no news. No good news, anyway. When my mother finally entered the room she was serene. Only the dark circles under her eyes revealed her agony.

Outside the house I would find George or Maria in some out-of-the-way place, usually crying. They would turn up in the flour bin or the chicken house or the top of the haystack. John would take his rifle and go for rabbits, finding a safe place in the woods. Maria would cry in my arms.

"Why is God taking them?" she asked.

"I don't know, Maria. Maybe he won't. Maybe they'll get better."

As September passed into October Mary fought on. She held my hand one Sunday morning before Father took us to church. Mother would stay home. Susanna, who had been up most of the night, was asleep.

"Come here, my brother." Mary spoke in a leathery voice I didn't recognise. When she took my hand I could feel the fire in her fingers.

"You look after Mother and Father." That was all, nothing more. She closed her eyes and Mother touched my shoulder.

"Go now, let her rest."

In church that Sunday Rev. Rose asked the congregation to pray for the Graham girls. "Two young women in our community stricken with diphtheria."

My father pressed his hand against his knee to stop his shaking. I do not remember the hymns we sang that day but I remember the feeling of gloom that hung over us.

Little George would soon be six, young enough to break away from grief, for there is a world out there. Maria appointed herself George's guardian. She told Mother she would look after him. Just three years older than George, she had always guided him, first through the house, then through the yard and barn. As George got bigger, they would go to the fields and woods. Maria seemed to understand George needed to be shielded, yet he was full of puzzling questions no one could answer.

"They will be angels," Maria explained as they sat on the fence by the vegetable garden.

"But I want them here," George protested.

"Yes, but God wants them to be with him and He's bigger than you, Georgie," she said, lightly slapping his knee to emphasise her point.

"But Mummy is sad. She cries all the time and she isn't nice to me now," he complained.

"George McBurnie Graham! That is simply an awful thing to say."

At seven o'clock on the fourteenth, as the morning sun was making its way across the barnyard, promising a warm October day, Mary died.

Mother and Susanna were with her and Martha looked on from across the room.

My father had started working early that day. We were in the far pasture where the fence was broken and one of the cows had fallen over the cliff to the beach below. We saw John coming through the fields. Just a speck at first, bobbing in a sea of green. He was walking slowly, hands in his pockets.

"Maybe Mother wants us," I said.

My father sighed. John walked right up to us with his head down, staring at his feet. Then he looked up sharply, straight at Father.

"Mary has gone. Mother wants you."

That was all. He turned around without another word and walked back towards the house. He was eleven years old, carrying the message of a man. He did it in a manner that made him seem much older than my father.

I never forgot the sight of him walking back towards the farm that October morning. For some reason some images stay burned in your mind.

Many things happened in the next hours. My father sent me to tell Mrs. Soley, then the family gathered in the bedroom to say our goodbyes. Each of us in turn, kneeling by Mary's bed and saying a prayer for her, then a kiss on her cheek. Martha was first, carried by my father. She kissed her sister lightly.

"See you in heaven, I hope," she whispered.

Father and I rolled Mary's body in her bed sheet and carried her downstairs to the parlour. Mrs. Soley, Mrs. Berry and other ladies arrived and closed the parlour doors. They changed and washed Mary, combed her long chestnut hair and put her in her best dress. There she lay in our parlour as people came to pay respects and my father sat in his chair. My mother was brave and I was very proud of my sister, Susanna.

Unlike Mary who fought for weeks, Martha succumbed quickly. She died the day of Mary's funeral. None of us were with her. We hadn't expected the end so quickly. There was even hope. God would not take two, would he?

Mrs. Berry had come to stay so we could give Mary a Christian burial. The church was packed. I held Rachel in my arms. I don't remember much about it except that at the cemetery, my mother leaned against me. Rachel clung to my neck while my father remained ashen and quiet.

Mrs. Berry was on the front steps when our wagon drove into the farmyard. She stood twisting a handkerchief and weeping. We knew. Each of us knew. Statues, just sitting in the wagon as she ran in front of us.

"She has gone. No more than half an hour ago. She could not breathe. I held her hand and we prayed. Prayed for all of you, prayed for Mary. She closed her eyes and the breath would not come."

My mother got down from the wagon with help from my father. The two women embraced and my mother slumped, falling through Mrs. Berry's arms. Father pulled her from the ground. He hugged her while we stood with them.

Stricken and silent, we came in the house and went upstairs.

Mrs. Berry had washed Martha's face, combed her hair and folded her arms. My beautiful sister wasn't coughing any more.

"She suffered less than dear Mary," Mother said. "The diphtheria was swift with her."

"One is a tragedy but to have two daughters taken? It's unfair." My father had hardly spoken in days. His voice was shaky, weak, and yet still defiant. We all felt his awful rage.

My mother remained mute for the rest of that day and the ritual was repeated. Father and I gently rolled Martha in her bed sheet and took her to the parlour. We laid her body on the wooden table. The ladies came, washed and dressed her.

For the second time in a week, the second time since Sunday, the good folks along the Economy shore put on their best clothes, hitched up their horses and drove to the Presbyterian Church in Five Islands. Another Graham girl had died.

She wasn't the last. A few weeks later, when they thought diphtheria had gone from the area, Maria was struck. She died on December 3rd.

The night of her death I sat on my bed listening. There was weeping in every room. That was the bad autumn, that autumn and early winter of 1859.

I was thirteen.

Chapter Four

I got them up. Isaac first, then John. Ruphus would have to stay. I ordered them on deck. Wearily they staggered into the dull light. When Isaac saw his brother he shuffled towards him, fell on his knees and tried to take Jim's knife. The others watched.

Ten days earlier they had surrounded me with hope in their eyes. Healthier then. Battered for sure, but not yet broken. Ruphus had stood in front of me, his eyes red and swollen. Behind him was my brother, ragged and pale.

"Bring him back safely," my mother had said. Against her wishes I had let him come. She had lost too much, she said. At the door she transfixed me. "Take care of yourself, Allan, and bring him back safely. He is not you. He's not a sailor. Bring him back."

What would she say? How could I tell her I refused the opportunity to save him? It was only my word they waited for. Phillip stood at my left, Jacob a little farther off, then Jim and mate Landry.

They waited.

When you are a captain no man is your friend and no man is your equal. You and you alone are responsible for ship and crew.

A sailor has premonitions of storms and wrecks in his future. A captain can see them too. But the captain's duty is to the day. To react to situations as they are, not as they might be. A captain who was ruled by "what might be" would never go to sea because the worst will happen. Storms will come. Sailors will die. Ships will be lost. Stay home in bed if you want a safe life. A safe life is not on the sea. Ten days ago, battered and beaten as we were, my ship was manageable. Our tattered sails could be mended. Our bruised crew could be healed and no captain can surrender. Even if he eternally hates his weakness for not believing his own premonitions there is no choice. The sea is the sea. Taste the surge and the urge of its daring or stay on land.

Chapter Five

Captain Densmore sailed up the coast determined never again to haul human cargo, no matter what the circumstances. From Havana he got a tobacco charter to Boston where he said goodbye to the African girls. He didn't wait around. The *Murray S. George* arrived empty in Halifax where he resigned his command and told the company he wanted no more to do with them. His failure to find a charter in Boston cost him wages but he didn't care. He returned to the Economy shore and shut himself up with his family.

He seldom came to visit during that time. While coming back from the weir I would often see him walking along the beach with his daughters.

In the early evenings he would come to the shipyard in Faulkners Cove where DP Soley was building the *Allandale*. I spent time myself watching the giant timbers go in place as the hull gradually took shape. Captain Densmore closely followed the progress. He talked to the night watchman and climbed over the staging, inspecting the ribbing. They consulted him on the placement of the masts. It was natural that DP Soley offered him command. Where was there a more able captain, practically standing on his doorstep?

The *Allandale* was a small brig, meaning she carried square-rigged sails on the front masts where men worked from yardarms high above the deck. The mizzen or third mast was shorter and schooner set, with fore and aft sheets raised and lowered from the deck.

I had little experience but Captain Densmore hired me perhaps because he knew the hell my family had been through. To be truthful he was reluctant to take me away from my father and the farm. The dreary winter had been depressing, all right, but my desire for the sea was more than an escape. I wanted the water, the adventure, and new lands. I wanted to tell my own stories of the world. I wanted it all. Walking the new deck of the *Allandale* sitting in its cradle, I couldn't wait for the sea to be under me.

The *Allandale* was launched in late summer of 1860. DP Soley predicted a propitious time for charters. He was right. Within a year, the American States were in a full-fledged civil war and business was booming. We'd carry lumber from Parrsboro to New York, where the waterfront along old South Street was so busy you could see the rigging of four hundred ships. I had never seen a forest of masts, flying flags of every sea-going nation on earth. New York, with painted women, frothy beer and hot summer breezes that lifted a million tons of horse dung off the streets into a swirling storm of toasted shit. The dried dung was coarse enough to cut your cheek and burn the eyes out of your head. If you cried out it got in your mouth and all the spitting in the world didn't take the taste way.

From New York we'd take a charter south to Cuba or to the big plantations in Jamaica. Then we'd fill our holds with salt in Grand Turk Island and come back up the coast, selling the salt to the fish plants along Cape Breton.

My sea legs were slow. On the third day out I was hanging over the side, sick as a dog while the rest of crew took great delight in my suffering. It made me feel somewhat better when Mr. Corbett, the first mate, told me he was sick his first three years and still at times felt a mild dizziness. As a greenhorn, I got plenty of ribbing and had plenty of tricks played on me. Captain Densmore paid me little attention. Mr. Corbett was my taskmaster. When we weren't on watch, we'd be cleaning, scrubbing or mending. There was always sail to mend and two of my fingers bore the marks of my mistakes.

My first big wind up the yardarms was so terrifying my needle-poked fingers bled and I was hanging on for dear life as the ship pitched and bowed.

"You can't reef with one hand on the life line," the sailor next to me said. "Hang on with your feet and don't look down."

We reefed standing on a rope forty feet off the deck. It appeared more like four hundred feet. The ship looked like a speck from the yards and every roll was so violent my stomach let go and my breakfast dropped to the deck. The ship pitched and we were swaying over the ocean and back to the deck and it awash as if the masts were coming out of the ocean. No ship – just men and masts.

Gradually I acquainted myself with the ways of the ship or thought I had, until I faced the terror of my first winter gale off Cape Hatteras. The wind roared with such force it pitched the deck perpendicular, throwing men into the aft cabin, masts and each other. There was a "sailor's friend" near the gunwales to catch crew swept over the side.

Work depended on the wind and the wind was always changing. Eventually we settled into a pattern as predictable as possible on a ship. We stayed away from southern ports in the United States because of the federal blockade. Although blockade runners could make a fortune, neither Captain Densmore nor DP wanted to risk the ship so all offers to go to Charleston were refused. There was enough business elsewhere but try as we might we couldn't avoid the war. People at home never realised how much of that damn war was fought on the water. Confederate ports were starving for goods and blockade runners were everywhere. Choking the southern ports choked the Confederate cause and the Union navy was everywhere too. There were pitched battles and we'd often hear the cannon on quiet nights off the Carolinas.

The *Allandale* was a fine brig. Except for the usual storms and shipboard accidents things ran smoothly until July of 1863. We left New York carrying flour, foodstuffs, wine and laths for the plantations in Montego Bay, Jamaica. In peacetime flour was a cargo that would come from Virginia, but demand was high as many of the farms and fields had been destroyed and the workers had gone off to the war.

Several miles off North Carolina I was standing the mate's watch with Mr. Corbett when we saw a flickering light off our starboard, orange and yellow flashes in the distance. We could hear the low thud of thirty-pounders.

All hands up the rigging. We needed to work fast, for a good wind was taking us closer to the flashes. Thud-thud-thud! Red and orange explosions. The bow of the *Allandale* was turning when a tremendous explosion came off our starboard. It was followed by the deadly buzzing whoosh.

"Jesus," said Mr. Corbett as the deadening hiss went over us.

I've never been sure whether I actually saw that ball in the darkness or just felt it. Some of the rigging flew in the air and the lower topsail twisted on the main, cut by the ball. Over the years people have told me a black whirling cannonball in a black sky is impossible to see. A holy man in Baltimore once told me I might have seen it with my soul, what he called "my mind's eye."

The captain yelled, "Ship ahead." Out of the darkness came a Confederate ironclad, its stacks billowing, its iron-plated sides laden with cannon. We'd seen Union warships tied up in New York but never one spoiling for a fight. Those of us aloft froze as if we were covered in ice. The ironclad crossed our port close enough to read our name.

"*Allandale*. Stand by for boarding."

Captain Densmore ran to his cabin and came back with his revolver. Grappling hooks were flung over our gunwales and the sorriest lot of ragtags I'd ever laid my eyes upon were soon over our side. There were seven of them, wild looking boys and old men – wrinkled, haggard and hard. Their clothes were ripped and shredded as if they had fallen in a thrasher. Only two of them had rifles and they didn't point them at us. Mr. Corbett called me down from the rigging to take the wheel while the others stayed aloft. Only Mr. Corbett, the captain and myself were on the deck. A longboat brought one of their officers and the ragtags helped him over the side. Unlike his men, he was dressed in a smart gray tunic with high leather boots. A scarlet sash adorned his midsection, giving him a festive look as if he'd just come from a social. The contrast with his men was so remarkable Mr. Corbett whispered, "Right out of a haberdashery, ain't he?"

Captain Densmore hardly waited for the young officer's feet to touch the deck. Clutching the revolver in his belt, he proclaimed in a loud voice, "We're under the British flag."

"I see that," the officer sniffed, trying to look unruffled. He could not hide the fact he was a boy, milk-fed, fair and rosy-cheeked. A boy with a lieutenant's rank and an aristocratic manner, just a very young Southern gentlemen with flared and formal speech. He didn't smile or seem overly interested in us. Instead he kept looking away at the fiery flashes, now close enough to distinguish two Confederate ironclads firing on a Union gunboat, already ablaze and listing badly.

"We are here to escort you to Charleston, Captain. I take it that is your destination."

"No, it is not. Our destination is the Indies and you have no authority to board this ship," the captain replied.

The boy lieutenant sniffed again. "What's your cargo?"

"Flour and foods for Montego Bay."

For the first time the lieutenant looked at the men hanging and waiting in the rigging. He tapped his boots on the deck then told one of his men to signal the major. A torch went back and forth.

"Now about your British flag. England in the past has been a friend of the Confederacy and we are in great need right now, especially of flour."

"You'll not be taking my ship," the captain replied, never taking his eyes off the young officer who for his part tried not to look ruffled by this defiant, slightly rotund little man standing threateningly in front of him.

"This isn't for me to decide. If it was I'd take your ship and cargo."

By this time I'd sailed with the captain for three years and I'd witnessed his moods, including his quiet ferociousness. He spoke with a tone that would curl the hair on a corpse.

"You're not man enough to take this ship."

The lieutenant put his hand on his holster while the other members of the boarding party stepped back. One of the two rifles was raised toward the captain. He ignored the rifle and glared at the lieutenant.

As if he had the upper hand, Captain Densmore said, "A petticoat around your waist doesn't give you authority over me or this ship."

Some of the ragtags snickered while our boys in the rigging laughed aloud. In the light of the torches I could see the lieutenant's stance change as if the captain had slapped him with a glove. The young lieutenant glared at his ragtags and tried to keep his voice in control. It came out high-pitched and boyish.

"Perhaps you'd like to spend this war in a Confederate jail?"

The captain ignored him and ordered Mr. Corbett to have the men in the yards reef the sails and come down to the deck. We dropped anchor and stood around our captain watching the cannon fire. The Union gunboat was on its side and burning brightly. Suddenly the wet timbers of her bottom started hissing and spitting steam. The cannons stopped. Sprays of steam put a mist around the dying ship. Another victim of the war on the water.

The Confederate major was a slender man of forty with sharp features and a pockmarked face. He studied us for a full minute after he boarded, putting up his hand for silence when the lieutenant tried to speak.

"So Lieutenant," he finally said, "what have we here?"

When the boy lieutenant gave his vainglorious answer filled with haughty self-righteousness, the major looked at Captain Densmore, who had continued to shake his head through the young lieutenant's description of how hostile these men from Canada were. We "surly agents of the Union."

The major asked, "How much flour are you carrying?"

"She's two-thirds full one hold. Two hundred barrels."

The major nodded thoughtfully and paced back and forth.

"Captain, has not the British government and the Confederacy been offended by the *Trent* incident? Our representatives kidnapped off a British ship by a Union gunboat. Are we not brothers in this struggle to give the South its own destiny? I'm sure you understand we need flour to keep our army going. We'll purchase your flour, Captain. We're not pirates, Captain, you'll be paid."

"Paid?" the captain almost yelled. "Paid with what? Your money is no good in the Dominion."

"No, perhaps not right now but when this war is over, Confederate bills will be honoured everywhere in the world. Including your Canada."

"Not if you don't win."

"We are winning," the major declared with a sweep of his hand over to the burning Union ship. "Are you not paying attention, Captain? The great battles we are winning. Winning them all."

He looked away again at the flickering images the fire spread on the dark water. Licks of gold and yellow.

"This is war, Captain, and flour is urgently needed. There are many mouths to feed. We'll put a towline on your bow."

"You'll have to kill me first," the captain said, and the boy lieutenant drew his pistol.

"Are you disobeying a direct order?" snapped the major.

Captain Densmore was fearless. He took a step towards the major.

"Captain, no!" shouted Mr. Corbett, who stood directly in front of the captain, shielding him from the pointed rifles and pistol.

The major spoke. "Alright, Lieutenant, take over."

The captain was overpowered but it took almost all the ragtags to do it while the others held their rifles on us. Finally he was overcome, picked up, rigid and hard like a stick of wood, and carried to his quarters. I don't remember much about the rest of that night except the boy lieutenant didn't have the slightest idea how to tie a towline.

"These men aren't sailors," Mr. Corbett whispered. Our small anchor was down but we were still being dragged closer to the smouldering wreck. George McBurnie and myself were ordered by Mr. Corbett to assist on the towline. Off in the distance there were more cannon flashes. The towline went taut and McBurnie whispered, "The *Allandale* is now a prisoner of war."

We were sent aft to our quarters. The captain was under guard in his cabin. After working a ship, being in your bunk makes for a long day. A long hungry day! The Confederates barely fed us, just gave us a few apples and porridge.

"Hardly surprising," Beaton our cook said. "Don't look like they feed themselves. Did you ever see such a bunch of soldiers? Boots and clothes must be in short supply except for officers."

They kept two armed guards on board and we got to know them. They weren't sailors or even enlisted men but they were militia, farm boys and merchants, the last batch available for service. They were starved themselves and let Beaton go into the galley, where he made some bread and found some dried meat he'd hidden, not from the Confederates but from the crew. When the cook sleeps, food disappears.

The tow was going slowly. The ironclad was constantly leaving us adrift to go after an unidentified ship. On our third day, one of our guards, an old fellow named Christopher from some place in South Carolina we'd never heard of, told us the tow was going far too slow.

"Could be you'll be up them yards pretty soon letting out the sails."

Christopher's words were prophetic. The next morning the major was back on board, doubled the guard and ordered all hands, except the captain, on deck. The *Allandale* was twenty miles off the coast and there was a good wind. The ironclad stayed directly behind us. Mr. Corbett gave the sailing orders while a Confederate boy with an old rifle stood by the captain's door.

"The captain, I hope he doesn't blame me," Mr. Corbett said.

The *Allandale* cut the water and a warm wind blew on my face.

So many memories! It all seems like a dream now, the dream of an old man with a bad knee, blurry eyes and creaking joints. Our houses are directly ahead of me. The white clapboard sitting on the hill was built by my father and now owned by George. John's house is farther up in the field, behind the orchard. Mine is in the tiny glen at the foot of the rise before George's. Three brothers, three houses with the sparkling waters of the bay at our front and the muted green of the mountain at our back.

I will rest a minute. There is something confusing about 1863 that won't come straight in my mind.

Charleston was the centre of commerce for the Confederate government. Much of the merchandise for the rebel cause came through the city. It was breathtaking. We could smell war. Coming into the harbour with the ironclad behind us, we passed French men-of-war, captured Yankee traders, square-riggers, Confederate packet boats, brigs, barques, full rigged ships, and schooners. Swinging booms were unloading cannon. Crates and small wooden boxes lined the jetties. Soldiers, wagons and horse teams were everywhere, an array of business, commerce and capitalism. Yet there was sign of a sullen dismay, not victory. The war was turning. Some already knew it and others just felt it.

Captain Densmore wanted to send a wire to DP care of the British consul in Halifax advising that our cargo would be paid for in Confederate bills. The Confederates agreed, then said no. They said we would be unloaded within the week.

We stayed in the middle of the harbour. Ships were coming and going, their men in the yardarms occasionally waving. We waved back and waited while the crew worried about their wages being paid in Confederate currency. A fight broke out and Mr. Corbett put Victor MacKay in chains for twelve hours. The captain was finally allowed to leave his cabin. With so many ships going by, he posted a double watch to ensure we weren't rammed.

On the fifth day the boy lieutenant came on board looking very pale and tired. His sash was gone and so was the neat press of his uniform. He told the captain he required half a dozen men by tomorrow at dawn. This was not a request, he said haughtily, trying to live up to rank.

"This is an order. Have the men ready at daybreak."

Sitting on the deck we drew lots, all of us wanting to get off the ship. I was picked along with my friend Marshy. George McBurnie, Victor MacKay, George Berry and Rector made up the rest of the chosen men.

"God knows what they'll have you doing. Just keep a straight head on your shoulders," the captain said.

We were waiting on deck in the early morning mist when the steam tender came alongside. Once on shore we were ushered into an open wagon and driven through the streets of Charleston just as the sun was beginning its climb over the buildings on Front Street. Charleston was already moving with wagons, riders and soldiers. We noticed the number of one-legged men sitting against buildings, waiting.

"No talking!" shouted the boy lieutenant sitting next to the driver. One old soldier rested against the back of the driver's seat with one old ball and power musket.

"We need as many hands as possible. Do a day's work and we'll put you back on your ship tonight," the boy lieutenant said, half turning in his seat.

"Are we gettin' paid?' inquired McBurnie.

"You are not."

Away from Captain Densmore the boy lieutenant was considerably braver. He said we were considered non-combatant neutrals.

"What the hell?" said Victor MacKay.

"You are not prisoners. You are here as a matter of trade and we are pressing you into emergency war duty. There will be no payment and you will do what you are told. Is that understood?"

His words were lost in the noise and dust of passing wagons. A city at war is a city that never sleeps. We turned on to a street where several soldiers were unloading boxes and stacking them on the wooden sidewalk. They had several wagons involved and the congestion forced us to stop. A mule team, driven by a black woman, came up behind us while soldiers picked their way past us.

We finally came to a stop at the crowded Charleston train station. The structure was large and enclosed by a wooden roof with open sides for the trains to come and go. It was already hot inside despite the ventilation. We were marched onto the platform. Men and women, soldiers and civilians stopped their talking and when ordered, made a path for us to the very front. In a few moments the novelty of our presence wore off and people resumed their talking. Men and women stood in small clusters, others mingled in a larger group. The constant buzz of human voices filled the station. Bits of a dozen conversations floated by – politics, generals and recent battles, but mostly the losses in those battles, boys left in the battlefield. There were no trains and as the hours passed the morning heat intensified. Wagons arrived and people pushed closer together. Two sweaty men in frock coats and derby hats smoked cigars in front of us, absent-mindedly kicking dust at stray dogs that weaved through the crowd. A man and woman stood silently to our left. His face troubled and burned brown by the sun. They wore the rough cotton of rural farmers. He seemed far off somewhere, absent-mindedly playing with a piece of rope making full and half hitches. She stood with her arms folded in front of her. The war was written on their faces.

We finally pieced together what was happening. A train was coming from somewhere carrying wounded. There had been great battles, they said, and it had been bad for both sides. It wasn't clear from the snatched conversations whether the Confederates had won or lost. Nobody seemed to know. Nobody acted like it was a victory and nobody talked about winning the war.

By late morning the boy lieutenant told us our job was simply to carry the dead and wounded to the wagons. He separated us into pairs and gave each pair a homemade stretcher, a piece of canvas tacked to beanpoles. Marshy and I were standing next to each other and were assigned to work as one pair. We had seen many things together as boys and men. That hot day, we stood in the train station with a stretcher and looked at each other and the scene around us. Strange, where the sea takes you.

The hours ticked by. Long hours with nothing much happening. There wasn't a train in the station but the smell of burnt coal and cooked grease permeated the air. A boy was playing a banjo somewhere behind us. A saucy girl was talking back to her mother and she got a slap for her cheekiness. A boy, bitten by a mangy dog he teased, received a cuff from a soldier as well. A fight broke out down the platform, with much cursing and shouting. The soldiers broke it up and dragged one of the combatants away, not too kindly, by the scruff of the neck. The crowd of several hundred people turned sullen in the heat. Cigar smoke hung in the air. A man accidentally spit tobacco on my boot, tipped his hat and said he was sorry. A woman said the odour of train grease was making her ill.

"Keep your back up," her male companion said.

It was at that very minute I saw Sadie Muise for the first time. She has haunted my memories all these years. Maybe that's why everything about that day in Charleston station looms so large in my mind while other details are so distant and blurry.

I paid her no particular attention at first, except to notice how tall she was. As the hours wore on my eyes kept going back to her, possibly because she was a more interesting figure than others around me. As the crowd continued to press, packing the human mass together, she kept getting pushed closer to us. She was thin and pale, not beautiful in the normal way but striking in other ways, her height and distinctive hue. She carried the colours of the Caribbean. Eyes that matched the green waters of the islands and hair like the sand, yellow with fine grains of amber. She had a full bosom for such a thin frame and a face that could not yet hide the traces of childhood. I guessed she was not from the wealthy class. She did not have the puffy cheeks of the certain set of young ladies who could not refuse the rich soufflés and heavy cream desserts of Southern dining rooms. She wore a little blue bonnet with small yellow flowers. I could detect a thin diagonal scar on her chin. Once, as the multitude shoved and jostled, our eyes met. In that brief second I felt I knew her, that we had shared something somewhere. It wasn't recognition as much as an instinct. It was the first and only time I wondered if we could live past lives as other people.

Soldiers were coming through; we were pushed closer, almost touching. I nodded to her. It was rude, I suppose, for a gentleman to do such a thing but there was a desire in me even then to let her know I was there. She caught my gesture and with her eyes she acknowledged me. Then there was a press of people between us and she was lost from sight.

By two-thirty a hush fell over the station. There had been rumours every hour that the train was near, but now we could hear something. A low rumble like far away thunder. Then the rocking cars and the mashing of steel, the steady rebellion of the wheels on rails; then smoke and the smell of hot iron and hissing steam and the high pitched scream of brakes.

The white and smoky vapours streamed off the boiler. The engine hadn't stopped sizzling when the heavy odour of iodine and camphor hit us. The air carried the pungent steam of a newly butchered cow.

"It smells of death," a woman whispered.

Marshy and I lined up in front of the boy lieutenant who had us in a line. He and other officers forced the crowd back and with our stretcher we walked into our first car. There are things that stay with you, images that burrow into your soul and creep out years later, only at night. Scenes and odours mingle in my mind – of urine, blood and straw and men crying softly and others cursing and calling out names. This wasn't just looking at war as we from the Dominion had done in the past. Unaffected and unconcerned, we would stop our work to gaze at a big man-of-war as it sailed past. We would stand on the sidewalk of Fifth Avenue as Union troops marched by and people cheered and waved. That was war to us, but the train had delivered the grit, the guts of battle. There was no cheering in Charleston.

The window shades on the railcar were drawn but even in the poor light we saw enough. Low moans from bloody bandages. The seats had been removed and the floor was littered with bodies on straw mattresses. Filthy mattresses, filthy clothes, delirious chatter, make-believe conversations. When we put up the shades we could see many were already dead. Above all else, those alive wanted water. They pleaded for it. People on the platform stuck their heads into the car when the soldiers weren't looking. They gagged on the stench of dying flesh and stale body fluids.

"Why did they bother bringing them?" Marshy whispered. "Some must have been clearly dead when they loaded the train. Look at this poor soul, half his stomach missing. Looks like a cannonball went through him."

I didn't look. I didn't want to see. I didn't understand what it was all about. I didn't see what they were fighting for.

We started with a young fellow in a blood-soaked shirt, carefully putting him on our stretcher. He was very pale but alive. We took him to the car door but it was impossible to move outside with the press of people pushing up to the train. The few soldiers could hardly clear a path for the stretchers without the crowd filling in again. Clergymen made their way through the throng and brought water to the wounded. The noise and commotion drowned out the weeping. The constant bellowing of two belligerent sergeants was heard above everything.

"Leave the dead till last."

The boy lieutenant suddenly hovered over us. He had no interest in lending a hand, just giving orders.

"Be careful there. Easy, easy now. Never mind him, he's dead. Take this one."

The wounded soldiers were packed so tight it was difficult not to tramp on a hand or foot. Three dozen cars in two trains were unloaded that day with wagons taking away the dead and wounded. I'm not certain how many men we moved.

When the wounded were gone we went back to the first car and took out the dead. We stacked the bodies three deep on the wagons until a family showed up frantically looking for their son. Every time we left the railcar the crowd pressed around us to see if the boy on the stretcher was one of theirs. There were sudden harsh cries up and down the platform. A mother fainted on finding her son on our stretcher. There weren't enough wagons for the bodies and we were ordered to stack the bodies. Then another woman found her son among the stack and she went into hysterics. After that the sergeant ordered us to put only three bodies on a wagon, which meant we often needed to wait for more wagons, meaning the job took longer.

"My God, Allan, are we going to get out of here?" Marshy asked.

"Keep working there," the sergeant bellowed.

With the dead and wounded gone, we removed the mattresses. Those that weren't too bloody we took to the two back cars and piled them up. The ones wet with blood and urine were piled in a wagon for burning. It was the dirtiest job of all.

Finally the Confederates let us sit on the platform with a bucket of water. Somebody brought us some apples.

Our last job was to mop down the floor of each car. The mop water was soon red. Our only thankfulness was that our homes hadn't been touched by a war where sons were wrapped in bloody bandages crying for their mothers.

It was past six in the evening. We were covered in blood, straw and dust. I longed to be on my ship under full sail. There would never be enough sea air to make me forget this awful day.

Four more days we stayed in the middle of the harbour. The ship below decks was like an oven. The crew became extremely agitated, the captain said there was no berth to put our ship, no stevedores to unload the flour, so we'd be handling the cargo ourselves. That made our foul mood even darker. Charleston was rife with rumours. A man and his son pulled up to our ship in their little skiff and told us the army was short of men. The captain said that was why our guards had been removed.

Captain Densmore was furious. Many in the Dominion favoured the Confederacy and Mother England herself still smarted from the wounds of the revolution from her colonies in America. "Why are they punishing us?" he muttered walking back and forth, smoke streaming from his pipe. "If they're going to rob us, rob us quickly, and let us be on our way."

We knew he wanted to make a run for it. The ironclads with their steam engines could easily catch us, unless of course we chanced on a good wind and put a fair distance between us before they discovered we'd fled.

But the risk. Their cannons. We had no defenses.

On the evening of our eleventh day in Charleston, the lieutenant came on board again. Another work crew was needed, not for tomorrow but for right now.

"We are taking men from every ship in the harbour, including this one."

We refused. Bored and resentful, we challenged his authority.

"My authority is the war! I want the same men as last time and I want them now."

Rifles were aimed and when Victor MacKay was impudent, a musket butt punctured his lip. We left.

This time there was no waiting at the station. The train was there when we arrived. There had been a great battle somewhere in Pennsylvania and the wounded from field hospitals were being evacuated to Charleston to make more room for the latest casualities.

I remember that the wounded on that train were in better shape. There was less screaming and crazy talk and only a few were dead. The station wasn't nearly as crowded. The Confederates put torches in the railcars and along the platform, giving the place an eerie, almost festive atmosphere. It appeared as a ghoulish carnival where the winning prizes were finding your son alive with his limbs intact. Marshy and I were trying to keep a big man with a missing leg on the stretcher. He wanted to get off, calling hysterically that he was fit for duty and ready to fight. I looked along the torches and suddenly there she was again, walking slowly toward me.

She seemed almost serene in the midst of the human ruins around us. My mind could not grasp how she could remain disconnected from the blood and bodies, the crying mothers and hectoring sergeants.

Then a man with a shabby coat ran up to me asking who was in charge. "In charge?" I asked.

"No one is in charge," Marshy replied. "This is just chaos."

I hadn't seen an officer, only people looking for loved ones and other people being pressed into service, struggling with the wounded.

Back from the wagon where we had turned the struggling one-legged man over to an army private who carried on our struggle, I wiped the sweat from my brow. When I lifted my head, she was right in front of me. There was a hollow look in her beautiful eyes. I realised it wasn't the nonchalance I had seen before, but bewilderment caused by some awful shock.

"Ma'am, are you alright?" I asked, raising my voice enough to be heard.

"Why yes. Yes, I think so. Right as rain. My brother is back there. He will live, so I will only have to go to my mother and tell her that two, not three, of her sons are dead."

"I'm sorry," I replied. "This is such a dreadful thing."

"Your accent sir, are you a Yankee?"

"I'm from the Dominion of Canada. Our ship was commandeered by the Confederate navy."

"Canada," she said softly, pondering my answer as if she couldn't quite fathom what I had said. "Canada, how unfortunate for you."

Her reply riled me. Were we not seeing the stupidity of this conflict? Were not the blood and the bones before us?

"Not as unfortunate as these lads, Miss," I replied.

She looked as men on stretchers passed us but I couldn't tell the meaning of her expression.

"Where was the latest battle?" I asked.

"Some place in Pennsylvania. It can't be very important, nobody's ever heard of it," she replied. Then the snobbish boy lieutenant was back telling us to get moving. When we came out of the car with another victim I could just see her making her way through the crowd. Then she did something I had not been expecting. It was my first taste of her unpredictability. She turned to me and waved. The next minute she was lost in the crowd. I watched, trying to catch another glimpse of her when a soldier in a passing stretcher grabbed me by the hand and hung on.

"Please help me, sir," he pleaded. "I'm dying. Please help me, please."

A portion of his midsection was covered by a stained bandage. He was shivering and I never again felt quite as helpless as I did standing there. A clergyman came from somewhere in the crowd and spoke to the soldier.

"My dear man, these kind gentlemen will take you to the hospital and to doctors who can help you." The clergyman touched the soldier's face and softly brushed the hair from his forehead. The man died right there before me and a final look of peace settled over his face.

People hurried every which way, paying no attention to one another. A soldier with his arm shot off was quoting scripture, "*Yea, though I walk through the valley of the shadow of death,*" and then he broke into crazy shrieking laughter that sent shivers down our backs. Then he started to cry.

I was feeling dizzy but the boy lieutenant kept pestering us to keep going.

Many parents praised us when they found their boys on our stretcher, alive with all their limbs.

"God bless you sir, God bless you." A well-dressed woman spoke. "May I inquire your name sir, so I can say a prayer for you?"

"What are you doing?"

The boy lieutenant's high-pitched angry voice ordered us to move on and the lady gave him a harsh look plus a good dressing down.

"You need not use that tone with me," she snapped and the lieutenant, his face failing to hide his astonishment, took a step backwards and didn't say a word.

She turned to me. "My name is Mrs. John Prepper. That young man needs a good whipping and if he talks to me like that again, he shall get one. However, I'm feeling charitable today." She frowned at the lieutenant and continued to talk as if he wasn't there. "If we had lost Gordon – well, I couldn't tell you." She was gone with her family and the boy lieutenant grabbed me by the wrist, propelling me toward the railcars.

"Get to work you two," he bellowed and I wondered what the consequences might be if I struck him soundly.

It was almost morning by the time the tender took us back to the ship. Marshy was the last up the rope ladder. Just before jumping over the side he looked down and expectorated a great gob of tobacco juice on the young lieutenant's hat.

"What do you make of her?" Marshy asked me later as we sat exhausted on the deck. I knew which "her" he was referring to. In the midst of all those bodies and blood, I knew.

"She waved at me," I replied.

Then he gave a tired little smile. "Allan, for a farm boy you can be gallant sometimes. Must be all that book reading."

The sun was coming up when we stopped talking and crawled into our bunks. Bathed in the pale pink light of dawn, Charleston looked serene.

Ah, Captain Densmore. He may be stiff and formal now, but then, well, he could be a driven man. He got the most from his men, but not by bullying. He was not a man to use the whip or harsh words. His secret was that he believed in his seamanship and his belief was contagious.

We could see the winds and torrents of the storm developing in him. He never stopped checking the sky. He'd walk the deck every hour studying the sea, looking at the horizon. He made us nervous and there was constant discontent and comments that running would mean our death or spending the remainder of the war in Libby Prison, which would be worse than death. Mr. Corbett stayed in close quarters with the captain. There was a sense of something about to happen and it riled the men up something awful, until Mr. Corbett threatened to smack a few lads down with a belaying pin.

A few days later, the captain called us aft for a meeting and we were a grim-faced lot.

"There's a big cloud bank blowing in and the wind's coming in good from the nor'east. I'm ready to make a run for it. No one has to go with me. You can make your way to shore in the dory as soon as it's dark, but I'm going and I'm going tonight. You've got an hour to make up your minds. Those who stay, stay. Those that go, go and there'll be no more said about it."

Everybody started talking at once and he held up his hand for silence.

"Captain, what if they catch us?" inquired Moses Randall, a big strapping lad who had signed on in Parrsboro during our last call home.

"If we can get into open sea under darkness with a good wind, we've got a good chance, even against their ironclads," said the captain.

"They'll blow us out of the water," interrupted McBurnie.

"No they won't," the captain replied. "I believe it to be a bluff. Neither Britain nor her colonies are at war with the Confederate States. These Southerners are constantly trying for better relations with our government. They're desperate for support. It's one thing to take our cargo, but to fire on a queen's ship?" He slowly shook his head. "I don't think they will fire on us." He paused a moment and searched our eyes. "My responsibility is this ship, the owners, its cargo and crew. If we're caught they will deal with me as master. But if we don't run, we lose most of our charter and that's our profit. The war has turned and the South is crumbling. Look around you. The Confederacy has lost authority over the sea. Union gunboats will be blowing up this harbour any day. There are no guards on our ship because every man is being pressed into the campaign. Boys are being sworn in."

He pointed to the harbour. "They leave us in the middle of the channel with flour they need. Not because they have no place to store it, but because they have no wagons to carry it, no spare trains to put it on and, God help them, no cooks to turn it into bread. The South is being decimated."

He paused. "That is my responsibility and I've made up my mind. Any man who wants, can take his chances making his way north."

There was silence and the captain walked away. Then at the hatch-way he turned. "I'll only give the order to go if the wind is right and the moon is concealed."

He was gone and the crew began arguing and grumbling amongst themselves. There was no question of anyone leaving. On other ships maybe, from cities like New York or Baltimore or the Boston States, but not a ship from the Minas Basin or the Parrsboro Shore. It wasn't the vessel that tied us together, but our common geography. We were not a crew from far-flung places. We were neighbours, knew each other's families, played and prayed together and the bones of our ancestors rested in the same graveyard. If any man left the ship, he would be for-ever marked along the shore as the man who left his mates when they needed every hand. There was grumbling all right, but it was all hollow talk. We were tied together by common roots.

In the pitch dark of Charleston harbour and in low tones, Mr. Corbett called for all hands topside. "Silence now, as quiet as you've ever been."

In the distance the buoy bell broke the still night. Up the yards we went, working by feel. I was ordered right to the top, working next to Step and A Half Rector. As a young sailor he had fallen off the upper yardarm. They couldn't set the leg right and his limp earned him his nickname. But he was adept at clearing the reef tackle and the leech lines and in no time we untied and cleared the bunts, let down the roy-als and top gallants. The sheets rippled in the strong breeze and flut-tered, then came full with a snap. Step and a Half and myself slid down to the lower topgallant and repeated the work. Then down to the deck to help hoist the boom on the fore and aft on the mizzen while others turned the capstan to bring up the big anchor. The capstan is always noisy and it screeched in complaint as the anchor chains clattered over the deck. There was no time to look over our shoulders. The nearest ironclad was half a mile down the harbour. It had been tied up without a sign of life since we'd been in Charleston. It seemed empty and we could only hope and pray it was waiting for repairs.

The *Allandale*'s sheets were snapping as the captain brought her round. When the brig came directly into the wind, she lurched as the stiff breeze filled her courses and lower topsails. We were underway.

Somewhere a fire bell began to ring.

"Are they on to us?" Logan asked.

The Charleston harbour channel narrows at one point, made so because two derelict ships were anchored there. We veered so close to shore at one point there was danger we would run aground since the buoys and markers were lost in the darkness. The captain proved why he was a master mariner that night. He took us so close to shore we could see the foggy outlines of derelict hulls, jetties and sheds. A wagon went by somewhere on the East Battery and we heard the horses. The fire bell kept ringing.

The *Allandale* left the mouth of the harbour on the lee side of Fort Sumter and hit the open sea under full sail. Our masts creaked under the pressure and the power sent a strange sensation through us. Never before had we run from anything.

Moving away from Charleston, our sense of elation grew. Jovial feelings echoed along the deck with low laughs and backslapping until Mr. Corbett told us to hush.

We were constantly at the sails. The captain wanted everything we could get. A double watch was posted but nobody slept. Our course was set due east, as if we were heading straight across the Atlantic. The captain reasoned the Confederates would tack south, knowing we were heading for the Caribbean. His plan was to make a much wider arc than they expected. It would take more time but was safer.

We remained on deck, filled with nerves. Our spirits were rising with every minute. At midnight the watch changed and the routine of the ship started again. Daybreak began with just a sliver of orange on the horizon. We watched and waited with nervous excitement. As dawn opened the sky and ocean, our hopes faded. Off in the distance just visible was a speck, a speck with a plume of smoke. Black smoke and running at top speed. Our wind was still strong and we were far ahead but little by little the plume got bigger. Hour after hour the ironclad drew nearer. By mid afternoon it was less than a mile away.

The captain stayed at the wheel. Mr. Corbett kept the glass to his eye.

"We'll have an early night. If we can keep going we can lose her in the darkness."

"We didn't lose her last night, Capt'n," replied Mr. Corbett.

"No, but tonight we will."

It was the longest day of our lives. We worked at the rigging at fever pitch then hung over the side watching as the ironclad, ever so slowly, drew closer. Mr. Beaton made some biscuits. We had hot coffee and some dried beef Mr. Corbett had hidden. We ate on deck, never far from the wheel or the captain. In early evening the ironclad fired a ball at us. It landed in the water a quarter mile behind us. We frequently changed course, tacking so we cut into the changing wind.

At dusk they fired again and again. By this time the balls whizzed past, whirling iron above our heads. We would cringe and duck sometimes, they seemed so close. One ball went through our lower topsail on the main'sle, sending a vibration throughout the ship. We put on a port tack. The cannon balls were all around us.

"I thought the captain said they wouldn't fire," said McBurnie as we were sliding down from the yards after a ball whirled so close we could feel the air from it.

"Oh, God help us!" Rector replied.

There was consternation on the deck now and McBurnie put the question directly to the captain.

"Captain, sir, you said they wouldn't fire on us."

The captain had been at the wheel for twenty-four hours with his pipe clenched in his mouth and he didn't take his gaze off the sails. He simply said to McBurnie in an even voice, "I was wrong."

Darkness came and all we saw from the ironclad were flashes from its cannon. The last ball ripped our rigging on the starboard at the base of the foc'sle. We worked all night putting a patch on the sheets, working from the yardarms in the dark. Two men stitching with big canvas needles, two more trying to steady the canvas as best they could. Others repairing the rigging, all while the ship was in full sail.

We were exhausted, numbed by a day and night on the run. Suddenly it was dark. The cannons stopped and the only noise we could hear was the wind.

A good ship can sense its destiny and the *Allandale* was a good ship. It was cutting through the darkness with every piece of cloth we had. Even the studding sails were employed. At two in the morning the captain ordered all hands at the rigging and we made another change, due south this time. The moon was coming through the clouds. The ironclad could see us. I was so tired I nearly fell asleep and the swaying of the ship from high in the mast made me dizzy and sick. Rector fell from the yard of the lower topsail and lay unconscious on the deck until we could help him. Even Beaton, the cook, was up the yards. We were running, and running hard.

At dawn we were alone on a great golden ocean. There was no jubilation, just weary sighs as men slumped down on the deck and fell asleep.

I fell into my bunk and was immediately asleep. In my dreams, the tall woman with the small scar on her chin and beautiful eyes was waving to me before disappearing into the crowd at Charleston station. In my dream though, and it is the one dream I have remembered all these years, she runs back to me, puts her arms around me and all the oceans of the world give up their dead. Every wrecked ship is made whole. There is no war, no misery and the world is right in every respect.

Chapter Six

I dreamed of the *Dove* last night again. Dreamed of leaving Parrsboro, proud as a peacock in my new captain's uniform. Nothing can change a proud man as quickly as the sea. Having a humbling experience is not unusual but when the humiliation burrows into your soul and stays there, then you are out of reason with the rules of nature.

I dreamed of being forced back to Liverpool less than two days after departing for the open Atlantic. I felt, after all these years, the sharp sting caused by the faint smile of the harbour pilot. The only words he spoke as he let the little boat cozy up to the jetty were, "I guess I'll be takin' ya back again."

He didn't ask questions. Our damages were evident. He turned his steamboat around and went off. That little hermit crab of the harbour, whose life means scurrying back and forth between the buoys. What did he know of the sea? Why is it that the knowing look of a know-nothing is always the greatest offense?

I didn't dream of the nor'westerly gales. I didn't have to – they are always with me, as is the lightning that turned night into day. I can still see the great flashes that lit up the sea as if our ship had sailed into a place of God, where all will be judged. A captain's first crossing is the ultimate demonstration of his ability to handle ship and crew and we had been beaten back, our sails in tatters.

I don't know if I dreamed further or just listened to the rain outside and remembered more in my waking moments. Walking the waterfront in Liverpool, feeling cursed and cold. The dampness of the docks seeped inside me, right into my bones. It was late afternoon. The sky was grey and the streets were empty. Far up the hill I saw a steeple. I was in despair. The pride I had felt weeks earlier had festered and turned raw inside me. I climbed the wet cobblestones, higher and higher.

An old woman came out of an alley. She was selling ribbon trinkets. One of her ears was partially chewed off, the work of rats. I shook my head to say that no, I didn't need anything and passed her but something pulled me back. I bought one. She tried to pick one that wasn't wet and I said it didn't matter. The colour had come off on her hands, red and blue wrinkled fingers handed me a trinket and I held it in my closed hand and continued walking up the hill. I purchased it to show myself I wasn't proud anymore. There were people worse off than I was and self-pity is as much a sin as pride. Yet self-pity isn't essential to a ship. Pride is.

Then there was Yarmouth where people whispered and pointed as I walked by. I went to the inn and took off my captain's uniform. I didn't want to be recognised. I didn't want to be known as the master of the *Celeste*. Out there, off the coast, sitting on a rock like a wounded bird punctured by an arrow. They were working on my ship and I faced the indignity of questions and an inquiry. When I folded my captain's uniform that day in Yarmouth I knew my career was over. I slowly rubbed the brass buttons. It was the last time I put it on until the inquiry.

If you care about yourself, your ship, your crew then pride must be part of you.

It is the curse of contradiction. If you don't give a damn about anything there is no pride, in your crew, your ship, no pride in getting your charters to port on time, no pride in being called dependable. Pride and captains go hand in hand. A captain's pride is the fluid that greases the workings of a ship. A captain puts his reputation on the line every hour his ship is moving. Captains aren't home, hiding under the bed. They are out there challenging the powerful, unpredictable sea, doing battle with enemies who are the elements – wind, tide, rain, hail, hurricane. Frailty is always there. Sail long enough and the sea will humble you. Live long enough and life will humble you.

Chapter Seven

My dark house is just ahead at the end of the drive. Up the hill the lanterns are flickering in George's windows. So many memories up there. On summer nights the laughter of George's children are the sounds of my own brothers and sisters enjoying a few minutes from lessons and chores in the twilight, the farm children's ritual at the end of day.

It has been hours since the funeral and these few miles have taken me a long time. I don't have the breath anymore. My knee pains with every step. There is a chill as I open the front door.

I recall how Laura had laughed when I carried her across this threshold.

"Put me down, you silly," she said, kicking but not really trying too hard to have her feet on the floor. "Put me down, Allan. Right now."

Why bother lighting the lantern? I can get about unless Mrs. Marsh has moved something. I'll make a fire and put on some tea or maybe have a glass of rum to take away the chill.

A very strange day today, where everything seems to be coming to an end. Yet all I did was go to an old man's funeral and walk home. There is an emptiness now. I won't have Will Thompson to visit tomorrow. Captain Densmore is too far away and we're uncomfortable now. Shared secrets at sea bring forth a brotherhood that on land becomes a wedge between the confessor and the listener. Will Thompson didn't believe in secrets. I think he was right.

The rum burns and warms at the same time. George has brought down the mail and stayed to talk a few minutes. He lights a fire in the stove. There isn't much news so he doesn't stay long. Being a strict Presbyterian he approves of rum.

I have another dram for Will Thompson. Owls on the mountain are hooting again and I'm sitting in my dark kitchen thinking of Sadie Muise and my mind is drifting back to the *Allandale.*

Nine days from Charleston on the run with good winds brought us into the rolling breakers of the Windward Passage. Through the glass we could see the coast of Cuba. The tang of burnt sugar hung in the air. Small dolphins plowed the water at our bow. There was a great relief on board. I remember. We had made it. Two more days and we were off Montego Bay.

Victor MacKay caught a small shark and Beaton cut it up for steaks. At the mouth of the bay we reefed our sails, waiting for a pilot boat. Through his glass, the captain studied the harbour and didn't like what he saw. It was empty. The only ship was a big man-of-war with white flags fluttering off its stern.

"A warning," Mr. Corbett said. "Don't go near."

Eventually a tender came out with a port official. The nervous little man kept his distance and yelled at the top of his voice. There was a sickness on board the British ship, HMS *Rover.* Many of the crew were ill, and so were people who had been in contact with them.

"You best drop your cargo at Kingston."

The captain was of no mind to do that and besides we needed provisions. Big Logan and I rowed him ashore to consult with the Maxwell plantation. Big Logan was a giant of a man. In exchange for no brains God had given him extra muscles. Even before school, Big was big when he was supposed to be little. We tied our skiff by a freight shed, across the bay from the stricken man-of-war. It had cannon from its gunwales to the waterline. Miles of rigging ran between its three masts with not a sign of a sailor anywhere. No sign of a man, woman or child along the entire harbour. Ghostly quiet too, only our oars disturbed the silence.

"You stay put," the captain ordered, "and that means here. Don't go near that ship."

Logan and I sat on the jetty smoking, watching the captain walk up the long hill to the Maxwell plantation. The sweeping lawns ran all the way down to the dusty road. They were separated from the road only by huge flowering hedges. At the far end of the lawns, half a mile away, stood the Maxwell mansion. White pillars, arched portico and a great Roman hall. The road between the waterfront and the plantation ran in a wide half circle to the far side of the bay and the small village. Banana trees along the road were picked clean. Great long-legged birds fed in the reeds and shallow waters at the edge of the shore.

We'd been there an hour when a man approached us. A leather satchel was slung over his shoulder. His hair and clothes carried the dry dust of the tropics. He was a white man with copper skin, wrinkled and dried by time in the Jamaican sun. His accent was English. He said most of the people around the bay were keeping away from the British ship and the waterfront in general. That's why it was so quiet. He told us the sickness had only claimed one life but many of the crew were in their bunks. No one knew the cause of the illness, but a rumour had spread great fear among the Jamaicans that it was the return of the plague.

He was a talker, this man, jumping from one subject to the next, about Jamaica and the trouble on the island. Suddenly he said, "Is there a chance I can sign on with you? I want out of here."

Big Logan had no authority to speak for the captain but he did so anyway.

"You cannot. We've a full crew."

The dark Englishman wasn't taking no for an answer and asked Logan if he was in charge. Logan bristled a bit but conceded that no, he was not.

"We're waiting for the captain," I replied.

"Then I'll wait too."

He said his name was George William Cook from Manchester, England, but he was twelve years in Jamaica.

"Things aren't good here," he said. "Jamaicans by nature are a fine people but they are very unhappy now and who can blame them? They were promised their own land by the Crown so they could farm for themselves. That promise was never kept. The plantation owners fear they'll have no workers. They fought against it. It's in an awful state now and I expect trouble."

He lit a clay pipe. "That's another thing," he said. "Who do you think is going to unload your cargo?"

"Stevedores," Big Logan answered rather hesitantly.

"No they're not," Cook replied. "Do you see anybody anywhere near this place? The sickness has scared them off. It will be yourselves who unload."

"We've done it before. What of it?" Logan snapped.

"Ah. But you see, I know people and I can bring them around to unload your ship. If I tell them it's safe they'll believe me."

"And you'd be willing to do that in exchange for signing on," I said.

"That's true. Even if I couldn't get any stevedores, you'd have another pair of hands to unload."

At that point, the captain returned with a glum look.

"No stevedores," he said. "They won't work because of the sickness. Maxwell is even having trouble getting his own wagons down here."

George William Cook held out his hand as the captain was stepping into the boat.

"My name's Cook and it's more than the sickness bothering people."

As we untied the skiff, Cook quickly put his proposal to the captain. He said he'd been before the mast and knew the duties of a sailor.

"I'll consider what you say," was all Captain Densmore replied. As we rowed out to the *Allandale* I kept looking for a sign of life on the massive man-of-war. Far off, on top of the hills there were more plantations, white castles in the lush green of the hills.

Few places in the world are more beautiful than Montego Bay, with its dark mountains sloping green to the shore. Sheds and jetties were just breaking through the tropical jungle and pointing with wooden fingers into the water. Pink and white sea birds gliding over a hazy green sea. Something else too, little fluttering white flags on a big British man-of-war gave the bay a ghostly emptiness that chilled you on a hot day.

It is part of the life of a merchant sailor that often he works as a stevedore. In ports like New York or Boston stevedores do the work. Try to unload a ship in those ports and you get your skull cracked, unless of course the captain buys his boys into the stevedores. Hand out money and stevedores will look the other way. In Montego Bay the Jamaican stevedores were under the thumb of the plantation owners, the big merchants and the governor. They were under everybody's thumb, but no master matched the fear of the plague.

The captain wanted the charter unloaded so we could get to Grand Turk Island for salt. Salt would take us home. It was always in demand at the fish plants in Nova Scotia and he wanted to be away from the sickness before it touched his ship. But he was loyal to the crown and HMS *Rover* was a British ship. As we rowed him back to the *Allandale,* he said it was our duty to assist in any way possible.

The next morning, the pilot boat pushed us into the jetty directly across the bay from the man-of-war. We started to unload at once. George William Cook was signed on and sent to locate half a dozen Jamaican stevedores.

By the end of the day we were burnt red from the sun. Cook returned with a handful of Jamaicans but he said they wanted extra pay because of the danger of getting sick. The captain had gone to the village to see about provisions and Mr. Corbett was in charge. He refused their demand and when the captain returned, the stevedores put their demands to him. They wanted their daily wage doubled and us to stand aside and let them unload, for this was their business. Captain Densmore steadfastly refused. We were already delayed due to our troubles in Charleston and he was in no mood for negotiating.

By mid afternoon the next day the Jamaican heat began taking a toll. A water barrel was brought from the plantation after Big Logan jumped over the side to cool off and screamed as the salt water burned the water blisters that had bubbled up on his back. We poured fresh water to cool our burnt backs and Mr. Beaton mixed up some goose grease to apply to the blisters.

A wagon with three Jamaicans from the plantation helped us with the flour as we boomed it over the side. While we worked we could see the stevedores behind the small sheds across the wharf from us. They talked to themselves, sometimes quietly and sometimes excitedly as they continued to watch us. One of them was clearly the leader and he kept shouting at the rest of them. He hectored and scolded the Jamaicans from the Maxwell plantation but they didn't answer back.

As the afternoon wore on, the stevedores kept moving closer until they were right behind us, forcing those of us lifting barrels of flour to walk around them to the wagon. I accidentally bumped the big fellow who was the leader. He pushed me hard and with the uneven weight of the flour, I stumbled onto the loading pallet and struck my head.

I was stunned and angry. I knew the words of the Good Book, turn the other cheek when someone wrongs you. That's what I should have done. However, I got up and cuffed the man, hard, with my opened hand. He clenched his fist and punched me, shaking my jaw with a blow that spun me around. Again I landed on the pallet.

Marshy, Logan, McBurnie and Rector jumped off the ship. Victor MacKay, who was working on the jetty with me, was in such a rush to get at them he tripped over a loading rope and sprawled on the jetty. The plantation workers had become increasingly nervous by the taunts of their countrymen. They wanted no part of a fight. Their horse and wagon went galloping down the dock. We gave a fair accounting of ourselves, standing toe-to-toe with the stevedores even though we were outnumbered by three or four.

Cook, who had not been seen for a couple of hours, suddenly appeared and started yelling at the Jamaicans in their language. Captain Densmore fired his revolver into the air and the fight was over. At the same time, a horse and carriage came at full gallop down the long driveway from the Maxwell plantation.

The stevedores disappeared behind the tiny sheds.

Sir George Maxwell was a plump little man impeccably dressed in a white suit and wide-brimmed straw hat. His carriage had shiny brass fittings and was pulled by two beautiful white horses. On back were three men with long rifles.

Maxwell carried an ebony cane with a silver handle. He tipped his hat to the captain as he stepped from the carriage and weaved his way through us as we were picking ourselves up and examining our injuries.

"I shall post an armed guard to make sure they don't return," he said as he came up the gangplank.

"That won't be necessary. We can look out for ourselves," the captain replied.

My ear was ringing, I was spitting blood and my face was on fire. I wasn't at all sure we could look after ourselves.

We unloaded the next day while an armed guard from the plantation stood by. We posted double watch at dusk. Sir George had been generous with food. Beaton's back was so covered in blisters he was ordered to stay in the galley, so he roasted a small pig with apples and fresh melon. The next morning, the wagon from the plantation brought us baked hams, bread and more fruit.

Despite his promise, George William Cook didn't lend a hand with our work. After the fight he told the captain he required time ashore to attend to some remaining business before our departure. He did not return until dark and by then we were getting suspicious. For a man who had gone to sea, he was dumbfounded around a ship.

"Best keep a keen eye on our new shipmate," said Mr. Corbett.

On my watch at four the next morning, I was standing by the poop when a dark form came out of the aft sleeping quarters and crept along the port gunwale. He was moving slowly, making his way to the gangplank. I was certain it was Cook. Big Logan was on deck with me. He delighted in grabbing the crouching figure and lifting it by the scruff of the neck. He was holding a fidgeting George William Cook.

"God Almighty, man. I'm just taking some air," Cook gasped as Logan held him a foot above the deck.

"It's not your watch and the captain says no one leaves the ship. And just why are you taking your satchel for some air?"

Mr. Corbett was called and young George Berry came up the gangplank

"Trouble?" he asked.

"This man was going ashore without permission," Logan replied, still holding Cook in the air.

"Now why would you be doing that?" Mr. Corbett asked.

"Just to get the night air. My goodness, what's wrong with you all? Are your nerves on edge?"

"And is your brain not working, Mr. Cook? Were you not there when a fight broke out with them stevedores?" Mr. Corbett took a step closer to the squirming Cook.

"Tell me, Mr. Cook. For all your sea time, what knot do you use to tie down the royals?"

"I'll not be tested by the likes of you," Cook sneered.

Mr. Corbett pressed, "Answer the question."

"I'll do no such thing! The captain signed me on, not you."

"Aye, that he did, believing you'd assist us. You haven't filled your part of the bargain. No stevedores and no help unloading."

"Mr. Corbett," Captain Densmore was behind us his voice low and firm, "take Mr. Cook aft and see that he stays there."

In the morning, Cook was gone and we were given a good roasting by the captain. However, there was a general sense of relief. Sailors can smell trouble. Many men walk off a ship after signing on because they sense the vessel will be lost. They are often right.

In the Jamaican heat we smelled plenty of trouble.

Another day of hard work and we had boomed the last of the flour then began working with the big flagons of wine.

Meat from the plantation helped make our evenings more pleasant, but we wanted shore time. The captain was apprehensive but came back the next evening to inform us the entire ship's company was invited up to the Maxwell plantation. Half of us could go one night, and half the next night.

"This is not a calm place. You're sure to go into the village and meet up with them stevedores. Make do with the plantation and take shore time in the next port."

It was not a request on his part. We grumbled to ourselves as sailors will do but then we caught a glimpse of the Jamaican stevedores between the small sheds. The next day they threw rocks at us. The man with a flintlock posted near our gangplank raised his rifle and they fled.

I was talking to him at the end of the gangplank when my mates came back from their night at the plantation.

"Good rum up there, Allan," George Berry said as he was coming a little unsteadily up the gangplank. The next night the rest of us poured fresh water over each other and slicked down our hair then walked up the long, sloped driveway.

The truth of the tropics is an everlasting truth. The soft lushness is a lie. Close at hand, everything is baked hard by the sun. The deep green grass of the large lawns is sharp and brittle. More than one young sailor after many weeks captive on a ship has followed his urge to run barefoot across the lawns only to find he was on nails sharp enough to puncture his skin. Up close the palm leaves are like leather, tanned and hardened by the sun and beaten by the hot winds. The jungle is not soft and fragile but is hard and enduring and grows over everything. The grand old house was losing the fight. Jagged cracks along its face, green and yellow grasses growing in tufts where given half a chance. Mildew, and mossy green leaves, a solemn, slow decay.

The captain walked with us. He regularly ate with the Maxwells and he went in to dine with the family through the great front door. It was held open by a butler who bowed to him. The rest of us went behind the mansion to the cookhouse used by the cane cutters. There was an entire industry going on behind the mansion. A dozen whitewashed buildings and sheds and outdoor cooking fires. The smell of sweet cane was everywhere. The dark cookhouse we were ushered into had long wooden tables. Sullen black women served us dark pungent rum kept in crockery jugs. After a few glasses we were served mutton stew, yams and roast pork with steaming bowls of brown rice. Our cook, Beaton took a good deal of ribbing as we compared his food to this meal. He had a good deal of rum by then and didn't mind. In fact, he was quite agreeable to the suggestion we leave him in Jamaica in exchange for the women who had done the cooking.

"A fair trade."

"I'll stay," he declared.

It was an enjoyable evening and made us remember how good life can be. The captain didn't let us linger too long. Amid much grumbling about no shore time again, we headed back to our ship.

The next morning we were awakened at daybreak to a low drumming coming from the man-of-war. Marines led by fife and drum in full parade dress, muskets on their shoulders, were marching off the ship. They carried two wrapped bodies to a waiting wagon.

As they were putting the bodies on the wagon a dozen horsemen rode up. They were yelling and swearing at the marines but didn't come too close to them. It was obvious the horsemen didn't want the dead buried on the island. They refused to let them move until the marines leveled their rifles and marched away on either side of the wagon.

Captain Densmore had already gone to the stricken ship many times and had arranged supplies for them.

"A rule of the sea," he called it. "We help any ship under British flag."

He told us the British sailors were recovering and things were much better. We could see the people moving about on the man-of war by that time.

A day or so later a British officer from the *Rover* walked around the bay to our wharf.

"We're very short of water again, Captain, and our quartermaster is having a hard time of it. The merchant's wagon drivers still won't come near. Rumours are everywhere that to approach the *Rover* is to die. We certainly don't have the plague. Most of the officers and men are feeling stronger by the day. The ship surgeon thinks it may have been bad meat. We've thrown all our tinned meat overboard and with so many men regaining their spirit we're continually short of rations. There's been nothing from the plantations in four days."

Captain Densmore told the officer some of the plantation workers had run away to Kingston. There was great unrest everywhere. The rule of authority was breaking down.

The officer listened and nodded. He was thin, with an angular, bony face. He wore the three-cornered hat seldom seen at that time in the British navy.

"Anarchy is on this island," he said. He thanked the captain for all his help and dropped a leather bag containing pound notes for provisions on the dock. He waited for us to pick it up. Half a dozen Jamaican stevedores were behind the small sheds.

"Allan, look there," Marshy said, pointing between the buildings. "It's that damn Cook."

I wasn't certain at first, but yes, it was him in the midst of the stevedores.

"Troublemaker," said Marshy.

Captain Densmore undertook the gathering of provisions for the *Rover*. George McBurnie and George Berry went to the village with him in a borrowed wagon from the plantation. That afternoon we carried meat and fruit and rolled barrels of water up the *Rover*'s gangplank. There were pasty-faced men about and many good cheers for our work.

"God bless ye, mate," they called in weak voices.

Captain Densmore came back from dinner at the plantation with a wagon full of dried fish and meat for our homebound voyage. The Maxwells also guaranteed adequate food for the *Rover* with the remaining money the officer had dropped by our gangplank.

As we were preparing for sea, word came of trouble. Several Jamaicans had been hanged in Kingston. There had been a rebellion and workers were walking away from the plantations all over the island.

"Mr. Corbett, prepare for sea." Little did we know that our leaving Montego Bay would make news all over Jamaica and the world beyond it.

All rations and water were stowed. The little steam tender was standing by to nudge us into the channel. Just as we were untying the lines, the Jamaican stevedores walked from between the sheds carrying clubs, their faces set in violent expressions. George Cook, looking very officious, was leading them.

"They want their money, Captain," Cook declared, showing his authority.

Some of them raised the clubs in the air and shouted.

"Money you took from these men by refusing them their rightful work," Cook went on louder and louder. "The double pay you wouldn't give them for working near a ship with the plague." He pointed across the harbour to the man-of-war and they gave a rousing yell. "They want it now!" Cook raised his hand and waved it back and forth as more men appeared carrying lighted torches. There were two dozen standing near our ship.

"These men are to be taken seriously. If you don't pay, I can't say what will happen."

Many men misjudged Captain Thompson Densmore. Maybe it was the mild manner they mistook for weakness. But when faced with an adversary the captain was all grit. He had escaped the Confederates, delivered his charter, been paid in British sterling and he was leaving Jamaica. No wind, no storm, no man was going to stop him. He had his revolver in his hand and his voice turned icy cold.

"By God, I'll kill you where you stand if you try to burn my ship!"

He ordered them to stand away. They didn't move as we grabbed anything we could find, belaying pins or brooms. Big Logan had an axe, McBurnie a bucket and Mr. Beaton, stooped by his water blisters, came out of the galley with his iron frying pan.

"Move away from my ship!"

The captain's voice echoed across the bay, sending the pink wide-winged birds squawking from the marshes to nearby bamboo trees.

Before the cries of the birds faded the captain fired a warning shot close to the feet of the large Jamaican I had fought with. The man jumped back. The captain fired again, closer to his feet and pieces of wood stung his skin. This time he jumped back and hurled his torch onto our deck. Other torches followed and we were busy trying to beat out the flames. The captain fired once more, forcing them back.

"Mr. Corbett, on my cabin table there's more shells. Get them now."

As Mr. Corbett raced to the cabin, other Jamaicans appeared with torches, throwing them on the deck and into the rigging around the courses and lower top sails. The captain took aim and yelled at the top of his voice.

"Back. I'm warning you. For the last time, back."

A tall man with spindly arms and legs ran between the sheds, his torch blazing brightly. His body half turned as he readied himself to throw. The captain ordered him to stop but he kept running faster and faster, his arm drawn back and ready to hurl his torch high into our rigging.

"Stop!" The captain's cry could be heard around the bay.

The man bent his body back about to throw and the captain fired. The spindly man dropped his torch and spun completely around and took an unsteady step. His long legs turned to rubber. One long step. He tried another and dropped face down with no attempt to break his fall. The remaining men, noisy and menacing a minute earlier, disappeared. A silence fell over all of Montego Bay.

For a minute we waited and watched, unsure if the stevedores would return. The man sprawled on the jetty was still. The captain ordered George McBurnie to see if he was alive.

"He's living, Captain."

"Mr. Logan, run up to the plantation and tell them a man needs attending to."

"With them out there, sir?"

"Blast it, man, take a rifle."

"Captain, I'll go," said McBurnie.

"No, I'm not sending anyone else," replied the captain.

Big Logan, without his usual bluster, ran off holding the musket in front of him. The captain reloaded his revolver while McBurnie and Mr. Corbett tried to stop the man's bleeding. The bullet had gone through his chest and out his back. He was losing blood and began to groan. His groans became weaker. McBurnie put a blanket over him for he was shivering even though it was a hundred degrees in the sun. The man said something that McBurnie did not understand. Pleading with McBurnie about something.

The captain was inspecting the damage and doctoring the crew. He put goose grease on the new burns caused by the torches. They had accomplished nothing that would prevent us from sailing.

Then the stevedores were coming again with more torches. They were running toward us and then something different occurred. The sound of fife and drum pierced the air.

"By God, look," shouted George Berry. A dozen marines were marching from HMS *Rover.*

Seeing the reinforcements, the stevedores fled and the little steam tug was signalled in to our stern. The captain ordered our lines untied and we were pushed away. We dropped anchor a way off and watched as Maxwell's carriage and a dozen riders arrived from the plantation. The tender delivered Logan, who said the man was still alive and we finally set sail. When all sheets were full we looked back at Jamaica. Through his glass, Mr. Corbett said the plantation workers and British marines looked to be lifting the wounded man.

We could see other things from our vantage point, hundreds of fires burning in the hills above the bay.

We sailed under a warm West Indies wind but we were restless and irritable. There were two fights on board before we got to Grand Turk. The captain took no action against those involved.

"Goddamn it, to hell with the sea," was the way Rector put it after a fight with Victor MacKay. He swore he was finished with the sea. Sailors always say that then come back and swear the same thing again.

We got shore leave upon arriving in Grand Turk while the captain arranged to buy salt. By the time we tied up at the salt dock, we were talked out on the subject of the shooting and what, if any, consequences might come of it and whether the man was alive or dead.

"Dead is what he is. The bullet went right through him and messed him up plenty. He's dead, I'm telling you. Dead," George McBurnie said.

But Mr. Corbett said he'd seen men survive worse wounds.

Big Logan, the worst complainer about no shore leave, now complained about shore leave in Grand Turk, "Why can't we be some place else but this big block of salt? I'd like to see some women."

"And what would you do if you saw one?" Marshy asked. We were sitting under a thatched roof, watching an old woman with huge arms fry fish.

"Would you rather be in Charleston or Montego Bay?" someone asked.

"Charleston," I heard myself say, snapping out of my dream. They looked toward me and Marshy just smiled.

After loading we made ready for sea. Provisions were all aboard and we were rolling the last of the water barrels across the deck when the captain called a meeting on the poop deck.

Two Boston ladies would be making the voyage north with us. He said they'd come in on the *Marion Dawson,* a barque that ran aground off Grand Turk two weeks earlier. It needed extensive repairs so the crew and passengers were finding their own way home. The ladies had offered to pay extra to be taken to Boston, but the captain refused.

"We're bound for Nova Scotia and that's where we're going." They could take a schooner from Cape Breton to Boston quite easily.

However, he did give up his cabin.

"I expect every one of you to be gentlemen," he told us. "These are ladies of refinement and manners. There will be no rough talk or ill will. And no tobacco juice when they're on deck. I want no complaints. Is that understood?"

The next morning we were sea-ready when the ladies arrived. They were sisters, Miss Agatha Young and Mrs. Glenford Manning. The Mannings were living in Cuba where Mr. Manning worked as an engineer. But Mrs. Manning couldn't tolerate the hot season and her sister had come to accompany her home. They were tall, slender women. Mrs. Manning was older and rather stern looking; Agatha was younger and very thin with beautiful blue eyes. She had a hooked nose and a long chin. However, her eyes lent such a pleasing feature to her face that you almost forgot she was quite homely.

As we were pulling up the gangplank, two policemen from Kingston arrived with a paper and placed Captain Densmore under arrest. He was charged with the murder of one Wilmit Hanshall. The policemen said they were taking the captain back to Jamaica for trial. The captain took the news calmly and read the paper very carefully. We all attested to his innocence until one of the policemen held up his hand, signalling the end of our complaints. After packing his kit, Captain Densmore came on deck in his best uniform and gave final instructions to Mr. Corbett.

"You know the orders. Take this charter to the fishermen's dock in Sydney and let nothing stop you. I'll wire DP informing him of my predicament."

Captain Densmore marched to the gangplank with a policeman on either side. He turned and said goodbye to the crew. Then he said to Mr. Corbett,

"Mr. Graham is your mate."

So in that state of bewilderment I got my first sea-going promotion. It was a poor time for it. The mood on our brig was awfully sour.

"We shouldn't leave the captain," McBurnie said. Others agreed, wanting to go back to Jamaica.

Mr. Corbett shook his head firmly. "No," he said loudly. "We've got a charter and our job is to deliver it promptly."

The final preparations for sea were conducted in a state of general unhappiness. We were lashing down the water barrels when Marshy tugged my arm.

"Allan, isn't that the *Rover?*"

Coming into harbour towering above masts and spars was the British man-of-war. There was great excitement. Surely they would have news of events in Montego Bay. What had happened after we left?

Mr. Corbett made a decision to delay departure until evening. When the *Rover* was tied up, he sent me to find out what I could learn.

"Ahoy, *Rover*," I shouted up to the big ship. "I'm from the *Allandale*. We were tied up across the bay from you in Montego Bay. Brought you water."

After a few moments an officer invited me on board. "You're safe now," he smiled. "Our illness has passed."

It was my first real look at the man-of-war and what a ship it was! Two-hundred-twenty-feet long, three masts and miles of rigging. She carried forty-eight large cannon, twenty-four to a side on three gun decks. One-hundred-twenty men, including a company of thirty marines.

I met the bony-faced officer who had dropped the coins by our gangplank in Montego Bay. He introduced himself as Lieutenant Hanson and greeted me warmly. He took me to his skipper.

Captain Lawson Donaldson was a different matter altogether. He was not a man to trifle with. As we approached he was dressing down several midshipmen in a manner far worse than anything I'd ever heard from Captain Densmore. Donaldson was a powerfully built man, well over six feet with shoulder-length grey hair tied at the back by a black bow. He cursed and belittled his young officers, who cringed in his presence. All I saw was a ruddy faced bully who enjoyed drinking claret and belittling those of lesser rank. Finally through yelling and berating the midshipmen, he turned, smiled and thanked me for our assistance in Montego Bay.

"I am very sorry your captain finds himself in such a fix for defending his ship. It might interest you to know I have already sent a letter to the governor on his behalf."

I thanked him and said our acting captain would appreciate any particulars he could learn for our ship's owners in Nova Scotia.

"Perhaps your officers will dine with me tonight," he said. "I'll send an invitation to your captain and mate."

"Sir, I am the mate."

Captain Donaldson raised his eyebrows and even the young midshipmen looked surprised. "You are?"

"Yes, sir. Acting mate, sir."

"Well," he paused and then smiled. All officers around him followed his example and smiled or smirked at me.

"Very good. Bring your captain and dine with my officers and me at seventeen hundred hours."

Mr. Corbett was fit to be tied. We had no proper uniforms for such an invitation. I kept a black suit for church socials and to meet decent people away from the roughness of the waterfront. I shined my leather boots, dressed and Mr. Corbett and I went off to the *Rover*.

Old sailors, gnarled and tobacco-stained, looked at us in our Sunday suits and starched collars. Our hair wetted down to defeat the cowlicks that kept springing up despite our efforts. Mr. Corbett had just turned twenty-one and I was all of eighteen. I suppose we looked like country bumpkins out for the night. Who else was walking around in the heat of Grand Turk Island in black suits? We were piped aboard the *Rover* and treated with the utmost respect. The midshipman of the watch ushered us below decks where several officers were enjoying a glass of sherry. I have always thought sherry lacked the taste of good rum.

At the conclusion of our second glass a steward informed the officers that dinner was served and we went into the mess. There was a long table set for sixteen with white linen, crystal wine goblets and blue and white bone china. In the middle of the table, surrounded by heaping bowls of steaming vegetables, was a huge platter with a roast boar. It didn't look much like our mess table in the galley. We sat on either side of Captain Donaldson, who had just entered and shook our hands. Even sitting he was half again as tall as the rest of us with a voice that boomed over the mess. A young steward kept his wine glass filled and when Donaldson spoke he had the total attention of all those gathered.

Without prompting Donaldson told us everything that happened after we left Montego Bay. The wounded man lived almost a day. His brothers demanded justice for his shooting and they had riled things up until the governor in Kingston heard of it.

"Captain Densmore defended his ship as he had a right to do. In fact," he said, "he had a responsibility to protect his ship at all costs. He will be tried and totally cleared. Believe me, there isn't a British court in the world who would find him otherwise."

His officers nodded as Captain Donaldson spoke widely on other subjects. Then, as if remembering what we were interested in, he'd come back to Montego Bay. As the meal progressed, he described how George Cook jumped up and down calling it murder. The stevedores said the man had been shot down for no good reason. The Jamaicans were up in arms and the governor was trying to avert trouble.

"That's why your captain has been charged. They're trying to put a plug in a powder keg. The situation in Jamaica has deteriorated. Every time we drop anchor there, things are worse with Jamaican trouble-makers and outside troublemakers. People like Cook are stirring things up. They should all be hanged. The Jamaicans need to be put in their place. The governor has been altogether far too lenient."

Several officers lifted their glasses in rousing cries of "Hear, hear!"

I never had a hankering to join the navy and in that minute I understood why. Mr. Corbett and I may have looked like country bumpkins but these men were bootlicking lackies under the thumb of this red-faced bully.

Suddenly Captain Donaldson turned to Mr. Corbett, who was overwhelmed by inquiries on commerce and the new confederation of Canada. Mr. Corbett mumbled he didn't know much about commerce or politics, that he was just a simple sailor. Captain Donaldson had no such humility. He didn't believe himself unknowledgeable on any subject. The man had a theory on everything and, as he expounded, his officers continued to nod in agreement. I was captivated by them all. Lieutenants mostly, and I began to count how many times they would nod in unison. Mr. Corbett, preparing for the next question that might be fired without warning, never took his eyes off Captain Donaldson. The captain and his officers were enjoying Mr. Corbett's discomfort.

"Tell me, Captain Corbett, what is your opinion on these new steamships?" Then there were broadsides on trade or politics or the theatre and of course, the American war.

I studied the face of the young steward in a braided mess uniform at the captain's shoulder as he constantly filled Donaldson's wine glass. I wished he would pour the flagon over the great head just to watch the bootlickers piss themselves.

After going on at length about the war, Donaldson returned again to the subject of Jamaica and outlined several recommendations on how he'd handle the situation. His ideas involved a great many hangings, whippings and shootings and of course, the rule of English law. I thought of the wagon drivers from the Maxwell estate. While we had worked side-by-side, one of them who spoke some English told me of his life. Others confirmed what Cook had said. Jamaicans were waiting for the land, their own land. I wondered why Captain Donaldson never mentioned the unkept promise from the British Crown in his talk of British law. I was growing vexed by his bluster. Measured next to Captain Densmore, I found him contemptible and his officers even worse. I was lost in my thoughts, listening to the musical voice of Sadie Muise, when Donaldson suddenly fired a question at me.

"What do you think, young man?"

My father always told me to give a good accounting of myself and face any man with an honest answer to an honest question.

"Well sir, as I understand it, the Jamaicans were promised their own land to farm for themselves but it has never been given to them. That promise by the British Crown has never been kept. Which seems a pity since it was their island to start with."

There was silence. Across the table Mr. Corbett looked as if I'd thrown a dead fish into the captain's lap. The bootlickers froze.

Something in that silence pushed me on, made me continue when I knew I had already said more than enough.

"The promise was made by the Crown and blocked by the governor at the request of the plantation owners. They fear they'll lose their labourers. Plantation owners don't want the locals growing crops in competition with them." I looked Captain Donaldson directly in the eye. "I can understand the frustration of the Jamaicans."

I didn't really know if what I was saying was right or even if I really believed it. But I wanted somebody, anybody, to disagree.

Donaldson abruptly threw his linen serviette on the table, giving me a cold look. "Do you really think," he beat his finger on the table in anger to emphasize his point, "do you really think these people could farm, grow crops and prosper?" His finger kept beating the table. "Do you think?"

Seeing the ashen faces of his officers, he put a lighter touch to it by breaking into a cold smile and putting a hand on my shoulder. "This young man has a lot to learn about the ways of the world," he said.

The bootlickers said, "Hear, hear," and raised their glasses and the meal was over.

Captain Donaldson thanked Mr. Corbett for joining them. He never acknowledged me.

"You made him angry," Mr. Corbett said on our way back to the *Allandale.*

"But he didn't tell me I was wrong, did he? He didn't say they weren't promised land, did he?"

"No, but, I don't know. I don't have the words to stand up to a man like that. It's not that I don't have the courage, Allan. But I don't have the words."

"I know you're not afraid of any man on this earth," I replied. "Maybe I shouldn't have said what I did, but the way his officers kept going with their 'Yes Sir! No Sir! That's right Sir!' like he was God."

"I know," Mr. Corbett said. "I'm just glad he's already written a supporting letter on behalf of Captain Densmore."

I knew what he was saying. I might have hurt Captain Densmore in some way. Except for my father, there wasn't a man alive I admired more than my captain.

At daybreak we sailed for Cape Breton.

Two years later Jamaica erupted into violence with hundreds of people shot, whipped or hanged by order of the British governor. They were all Jamaicans of course. Captain Donaldson would have approved.

We had good winds coming up the Florida Straits and we'd set a northeast course to catch the trades. There soon developed a race to see who could most closely follow Captain Densmore's orders on being gentlemanly, with bowing and scraping to our lady guests. A competition began to catch the favour of Miss Agatha. Big Logan dropped a plate of Beaton's biscuits into the lap of Mrs. Glenford Manning. She didn't scream. Not then. Only when Big, who apparently didn't know there are untouchable places on the female anatomy, tried to pick the hot biscuits off her lap, including the one that had slid between her thighs.

"You'd think them biscuits was alive the way they scurried into that woman's lap," Rector said.

On our tenth day at sea, I was by the wheel when Miss Young came on deck. It was evening and cooler as we moved away from the equator. Mrs. Manning didn't come on deck much since Big fumbled for the biscuits, but Miss Young was flattered by all the attention. She wore a long coat and walked towards me.

"Mr. Graham?"

"Yes ma'am."

"Could you escort me round the deck, please? I need some air and my sister doesn't like the evening chill."

I could feel Marshy's eyes on me and Berry stopped mopping the poop deck to watch.

"Just around the deck, Mr. Graham. Just twice and I'll return to my cabin," she smiled and held out her arm.

Marshy took the wheel. I must have been walking rather stiffly because I recall her asking me if I was embarrassed by her request. When I told her not at all, she chuckled. I decided she was not an unattractive woman and certainly more forward than the farm girls along the shore. Definitely more refined than the hags along the docks. There was a noble bearing in Miss Agatha.

The presence of women changed life on our ship. The men behaved, even though some complained that Miss Agatha got in the way since she was usually on deck.

"It would have made more sense to take on another sailor, rather than two women," said George Berry. Big cuffed him for it.

Mr. Corbett had the responsibility for taking bearings and staying on course. As mate, I worked with the crew and supervised the sails. We were blessed. When the trade winds want to, they can take you all the way home.

Agatha Young spent more and more time close to the crew. Even in rain squalls she would come out on deck to take the air. Often she would stand by me at the wheel and Big would glare at me.

"He's an officer. Striking the mate means lost pay and time in chains," warned Marshy. Big grumbled and went back to mending sail.

Finally the crew devised a signal. A shrill whistle when Miss Young came on deck. The *Allandale* was a small brig and it was difficult to keep away from her. Mr. Corbett had some success when he warned her we would soon be buffeted by high winds. The winds never came but Miss Agatha stayed out of sight the rest of the day. Only Big pouted.

Even her sister would snap at her, "Agatha, get away from that man. He's trying to work."

Mrs. Manning was nothing like her sister. While Agatha was talkative and curious, Mrs. Manning stood back from us with a look of disdain. Marshy said she had the appearance of someone who had swallowed poisoned porridge.

"No wonder her sister spends time up here. How'd you like to be cooped up with the likes of her," he commented.

Aside from Agatha and Mrs. Manning, our talk was of Captain Densmore. We wondered if his family knew of his predicament. Would word have reached DP? Where and when would they hold his trial? Should one of us have stayed behind as a witness?

The third week we were in northern waters. Big pods of whales were off our starboard. The wind had a nip and schools of mackerel provided meals.

In the last week of our voyage, Agatha Young directed her attention almost totally to Big Logan.

"Do you see that woman?" McBurnie asked. "She taking up with Logan now. Look at them."

"Logan had better watch himself," laughed Rector.

Mr. Corbett smiled, "I think the rest of us are free."

Big Logan became a different man. He started washing every morning and warned George McBurnie about foul language. McBurnie was dumbstruck. The sisters weren't even on deck.

"Have you ever seen the like of it?" McBurnie declared. "God Almighty! That Big, the most cursing arsehole alive, telling me not to swear."

Mr. Corbett replied, "Big is as strong as an ox but there never were too many apples on his branches. And what there were, that woman has knocked to the ground."

There was a soft drizzle off Sydney harbour. Mr. Corbett was to take the sisters and their luggage into town and arrange a hotel until they could find transportation to Boston. He would also see about the sale of the salt and docking. He promised every man shore time. I had helped him write a letter to DP. He would visit the British consulate to see if there were messages.

Logan begged Mr. Corbett to let him row the party ashore. The sisters came around and said goodbye and thanked us. Agatha took my hand and looked at me. "Thank you for looking after us," she said.

Standing behind her, Big scowled at me. We watched Big row them into the fog. The last things we saw were the ladies' travel cases packed in the stern.

"Logan will be heartbroken with his sweetie going," said Rector.

We had a full day's work discharging some of our ballast and stowing light sail. I was getting more comfortable being in charge of men who had more sea time than I did. All the way up the coast, I wondered why Captain Densmore had chosen me. That night I stayed on deck during the evening watch with one man keeping the lanterns clear and sounding the bell every half-hour. A wet sea fog was over us, so thick you couldn't see your hand in front of your face.

"My last vessel was hit broadside right here," said George McBurnie. "A fishing schooner coming from Grand Bank and the captain and crew as drunk as skunks, the bunch of them. Lost their ship and twenty thousand pounds of cod. My God! Dead fish were floating all over the harbour. People coming out with dories to get them fish and us pumping and bailing like hell to stay afloat. And do you know, that fishing crew was back out on the water with a new ship before our repairs was started."

By midnight there was still no sign of Mr. Corbett and Big Logan.

"Mr. Corbett is not the kind of man who'd go off on a drinking spree with his ship sitting in the channel," I told Marshy.

"Maybe the sisters couldn't find suitable lodging or maybe Big's taken them dancing."

There was no sign of them by morning and I was getting concerned. It was not likely that two men would have been waylaid by a gang of ruffians, not when one was the size of Big. In early afternoon the fog lifted a bit. Beaton complained about lack of provisions and Victor MacKay and Rector got in a fight. I had to use stern language to stop them. In the late afternoon we saw the long dory coming through the mist. At first there was just a grey form at the oars.

Something was very wrong. Only one man was in the dory.

"What the hell's going on?" McBurnie said. "That's Mr. Corbett. Surely he wouldn't leave Big Logan in there with those women."

"Well that's exactly what he's done. There must be a good reason for it."

We could see a look of consternation on Mr. Corbett's face as he crawled up the rope ladder.

"Where's Big?" I asked as soon as he got on deck.

"Goddamn stupid Big Logan," he said as he shook his head in disbelief.

"What happened?"

We crowded round.

"The simple-minded moron has run off with that woman!"

"Run off?"

"Yes, run off. I hired a carriage and took them to a lodging house and when I turned around, Logan and the woman were gone. I couldn't leave Mrs. Manning there in a frantic state with her sister gone. We waited hours. Then I hired another carriage and went looking myself and finally I reported their disappearance to the police. Mrs. Manning is furious, crying and lashing out at me, saying Logan is my man and she's going to report me to the authorities, the ship's owners and everybody else who will listen. This morning, the police tell her the pair of them left at dawn on a salt bank schooner going to Halifax."

"Halifax?"

"Yes, that's all they could find going out. Goddamn stupid Logan! It will take that woman less than a day to discover he's a half wit."

It took longer than that. As I remember it, about a year. Logan spent the winter with her in Boston, returning home alone in the spring. He stayed alone. I would see him sometimes when passing his father's farm in my horse and wagon. He'd be way up in the fields but I knew it was him. He never went back to sea. After his parents died, Big lived by himself. The old farmhouse is empty now.

I don't know what ever happened to Agatha Young.

Chapter Eight

There are unexplained noises from the sea. Noises at night and in the daylight. The noise from a pod of whales, cormorants and walrus we know. We aren't fooled by the cry of the lonely albatross. After all, we are men of the sea. But there are noises so strange drifting across the rolling water that you grip the wheel more firmly. There are low whimpers, not made by whale or bird. All talk stops as silent mariners search the horizon waiting for the sound again.

There were nights in the lightly rocking seas when voices came from far away. Other sailors say the same. They have heard them too. Out of the vast green world, across the water you hear the sweetest voices, rising above the wind and waves. I have no belief in mermaids but I understand why men go mad. Gaunt and bent from hauling sail, you're standing watch and they sing to you. Go mad or listen. Beautiful, musical voices. They come and go. There is silence for a time and then they start again.

The moon and sea bring visions too. Far off a man walking on the water. You don't tell your mates when the crew is no longer made up of men you trust. As a young sailor I shipped out with kin and cousins and boys whose farms were near ours. As an older man shipping out from foreign shores, I go to sea with strangers, men I do not know or would not confide in. Better to hold your tongue. A long voyage brings tension, fighting and knives.

If you are crazy don't show it. The crazy get picked on or stolen from, making them more deranged until they jump over the side and there are fewer hands all around. Too many visions, too many sounds can't be good. Except for the sweet voices that both frighten you and soothe your soul. When they come we close our eyes, stand by the wheel and let the balm bring us back to who we were before we went to sea.

I am standing in my dark kitchen listening for such sounds. The windows are open wide but all I hear is a fly buzzing through my solitude.

Word has come today that Captain Kerr is dead. Did I not see him at Will Thompson's funeral? Did I not detect his slender frame through my faulty vision? He was one of them standing there. We all exchanged a gruff hello and a few words about the weather.

But Captain Kerr said more to me. Wasn't it him who sidled up to me and cursed under his breath that he hated old age? He was a pious man and his oaths surprised me, but I understood his sentiment. He said he would rather die than spend another day rocking on his porch. "Take a man out of the sea and all you have is an empty shell." I recognised his blurry form moving away and I did not speak to him again. Those were his last words to me.

Dr. Johnson wrote, "When men come to like a sea-life, they are not fit to live on land. Men go to sea before they know the unhappiness of that way of life; and when they come to know it, they cannot escape from it."

"Not fit to live on land." Laura would agree with that. "Go home, Allan, you're not fit to live with."

I got on the train and moved away from her because I hated it there in that flat, dismal place and I wanted to be at the roots of my youth. "Listen, listen. Don't think, just listen." I am only a few hundred feet from the bay and I want to hear the sweet voices just one more time. In forty years at sea I heard them less than a dozen times and once more would satisfy me, but there is only the buzzing of the fly.

Captain Kerr brought his young bride to dinner at my parents' place when I was a boy. He mesmerised John and myself with his stories of the strange sounds of the sea. Later, as a mate I could ask Captain Densmore, who just puffed on his pipe and didn't reply to such foolish questions. Now I realise he thought such explanations would be wasted. Some things have to be experienced.

A couple of years later, coming down the St. Lawrence, just where the river widens into the sea, I was on the back watch. It was an hour past sunrise and the ocean was still, just a light breeze to fill our sheets. Off in the distance I heard a choir of beautiful voices in perfect harmony. They were singing a hymn I had heard in worship, the name of which I did not know. I put my glass to my eye and there was nothing for miles, just water. That was the first time. One hot afternoon, five years later, midway across the Atlantic coming back from England, Marshy and I were on watch and a woman's voice travelled across the ocean. She sounded like she was pleading for her life and crying, "No, no, please, no." The strangest feeling came over me as if I was eavesdropping on a fierce argument. The words were repeated several times and ended with the woman's scream. I looked at Marshy. He had gone pale.

If I keep going to funerals I will be the only one left, the last captain. Perhaps the last man standing who has heard such sounds. Even now, I cannot recognise faces unless the light is just right. But even if I can't see them I know they won't be far. Just off somewhere, the last of those old sea dogs, with their hands around a plug of tobacco waiting to pop it into the mouth. I am getting crazy. But then when he told me about the noises, half a century ago, I thought Captain Kerr was crazy. Not anymore. Now I know better. He was the one who first told me of the sounds of the sea.

I will go to his funeral.

Chapter Nine

Captain Densmore was cleared of murder charges by a British court in Kingston. He resumed command of the *Allandale* seven months later, walking up the gangplank when we were loading softwood deals in Apple River for a charter to New York. He never mentioned a word about his experience and we knew better than to ask.

The Civil War was almost over, Lincoln and the protectionists were in power and DP fretted about trade. We knew by then that what we saw in Charleston was the closing curtain for the Confederate cause. Although the North was certain of victory, much was unsettled. Newspaper editorials in New York were critical of Lincoln and General Grant. People had expected a Northern triumph in months, not years. Boys from the Dominion crossed the border and signed up for a few weeks of excitement. But General Lee won many impressive victories. After Gettysburg the Confederacy never recovered, its army worn away, its ports blocked, its supplies exhausted.

We were in New York when the war ended. Marshy and I hiked up Broadway to hear the bands and watch the parade. Paperboys tried to be heard over the music and noise as they screamed the headlines at the top of their young lungs. Fireworks lit up the Hudson while a dozen bands struck up "Marching Through Georgia," and even "Yankee Doodle."

I looked around at the cheering crowd and remembered what we'd seen a year earlier in New York when rampaging mobs had sacked a Union draft headquarters, smashing windows and setting fires. It wasn't the first riot over the war. They had their reasons, I guess. For three hundred dollars a rich man could buy an exemption and put someone else in his place, a substitute soldier. How many working folk had that kind of money? There had been plenty of dissatisfaction with the war. Nowhere had it simmered and boiled over more often than in New York. We stayed in the streets as Manhattan took on a festive atmosphere. It looked as if all was forgotten and forgiven. Victory is a sweet balm.

DP had told us that when a war ended, trade would drop off and many ships would be tied up waiting for charters. He was right, except for the demand for lumber and coal in the rapidly expanding cities of Boston and New York. If tariffs got high as DP was certain they would, we'd go back to the sugar trade. In 1866 DP landed an unusual charter. We would load bricks, softwood boards, planking and shingles for Charleston. We were going back to the city where we had seen so much death.

Much of Charleston wasn't a city any longer, but only a shell of one. We didn't recognise it. Entire streets were destroyed. The burned-out buildings, scorched walls on the warehouses and rubble told the story. Northern cannon had not spared the grand mansions or tree-lined streets. I made my way to the railway station past partial stone walls and streets filled with debris. Except for some damage to the roof, the station was intact. It was empty and errie. There didn't appear to have been a train in a while. I stood there remembering our mission. I closed my eyes and I could hear the muffled cries. I wondered why I had possibly returned. I stood there a long time reliving the experiences, listening to the voices. I looked at the spot I had last seen her. The tall woman with the scar who had waved at me. I realised how often I thought of her and why I had been peering under the wide brim of every passing hat in Charleston. Why was I so infatuated by a meaningless encounter? Walking through the ruins of Charleston I could see the city's desolation in the eyes of the people.

There were no stevedores in Charleston and no money to pay them so we unloaded the cargo ourselves, meaning hard days of heavy lifting and little time ashore. There wasn't a great deal to do anyway except look at rubble. Marshy and I did go to a little place called the Rosebud Café one evening. By then I had given up looking for her and was laughing at myself for such silliness. But as we were having dinner I saw her across the room. I wasn't certain at first and I wasn't going to jump up and approach her. What would I say? I studied her. It had been three years and in some indefinable way this was, but wasn't, her. She sat with an older couple, perhaps her parents. They were talking earnestly.

"It's her," I said to Marshy, who had to turn around to look. He said he wasn't sure. He didn't remember her well enough.

"But you did, didn't you?"

"It's her," I said. "It is."

"You've already told me that once today."

"I thought it was."

He eyed her carefully as though he was studying some unusual specimen pulled out of the sea. He finally said, "Well, best you go introduce yourself before your eyes pop out of your head."

I was on my feet moving towards her table. A bit unsteadily I realised, as if there was a pitch to the floor and I was walking the deck of a rolling ship.

I could hear that they were discussing some serious matter and my nerve was starting to fail me. This was obviously not the proper time to speak but I was already at her table. They stopped talking and looked up. I thought I saw some glimmer of recognition in her eyes. I just wanted to stand and stare at her, just to catch up for the time we've missed. I knew at that moment why she had haunted me. She was, I was certain then, the most beautiful woman alive.

They were silent, waiting for me to speak.

I stammered, "You probably don't remember me. We met some years ago at the Charleston railway station. My name is Allan Graham. I'm from Nova Scotia. We met one evening when we were unloading the wounded."

She said nothing but nodded slightly.

"We were under the supervision of the Confederate navy. You were looking for your brother. I'm just inquiring, ma'am. How is your brother?"

Her eyes grew wide and a broad smile came over her face. The smile transformed her, giving her the confidence I had seen at the station, the confidence I found so endearing.

"My brother has survived and some would say that's a pity. But then you can't choose your family, can you?"

If she said it to shock me it worked, and my reaction delighted her and displeased the woman sitting next to her who said, "Really Sadie, this is no time for levity."

The man, who had his back to me, rose to greet me. He had deep lines and greying red hair the colour of rust. "You must excuse Miss Muise. She refuses to take life seriously, even the war and its disastrous consequences."

He bore the sad eyes and sallow skin I'd seen often on the streets of Charleston. The face of the defeated Confederacy.

He continued without introducing himself. "Miss Muise unfortunately did lose family in the war, but I think she would agree, not in service to the South as so many families have sacrificed." There was an edge to his voice, an irritation that I thought was aimed at her, although he was talking to me.

I looked down and she was smiling at me with a look of defiance in her eyes. I wanted to say something but I could not speak. It was as if I had walked on the stage during the last act of a dramatic play and was expected to participate without benefit of rehearsal. I could feel a flush in my cheeks. I'd wanted to see her again. I waited for the chance and there I stood, uncertain of what to say to her or her company.

"I'm sorry," I stammered.

"You have nothing to be sorry about," she replied. "I do vaguely remember you at the station and it was kind of you to inquire. Certainly you haven't been in Charleston all this time?"

"No, we escaped the Confederates, ah excuse me, we escaped, fled the harbour at night and made our way to Cuba. My ship is unloading in the harbour now," I replied.

"You're bringing material to rebuild then?" the man asked. "Excellent, excellent."

There was another silence while both women looked at me and I stumbled through an apology for interrupting their conversation and I went back to my table. Marshy took one look at the burn on my face and didn't bother asking.

A trivial meeting, I told myself. Charleston was in desperate condition and out of money. It was unlikely we would be back. Yet I kept rolling her name around in my mind, whispering it over and over, Sadie Muise, Sadie Muise. It had a musical ring, a lightness as if the words could take flight. Her name was the only thing I had really learned about her, except she was brash. I never learned the name of the people with her and they had not invited me to join them. The famous southern hospitality, I guessed, like most of the south had been destroyed.

Months later, through an unusual chain of events we were back in Charleston for urgent ship repairs on our way up from Cuba. Much of the debris was gone or piled in huge mounds. Clearly the city was starting the painful repair. I was walking the East Battery on a Sunday afternoon. It was hot after a week of rain and people were out to take the clean air. You could walk around piles of broken stones and old timbers on the sidewalks. I was enjoying being on land for a few hours when she came directly towards me out of the crowd, so quickly I was startled. Unaccountably I tried to turn away, suddenly afraid of something. To my surprise she called my name.

She was breathless as she took my arm and apologised for being unable to acknowledge me properly in the café. Our arms were linked as we walked together and at that moment, nothing else in the world mattered.

I remember some of what she said but the happiness roving through me was taking priority over my listening. She told me her father was in prison for most of the war and her brother had swindled her out of the family home.

"My father was what you would call an opportunist. We were raised in great wealth one year and near poverty the next. He was always getting involved in schemes. When the war started he became a blockade runner one minute and a smuggler the next, not necessarily for the same side. That couple in the café say my father owes them a great deal of money and they are now destitute. The man was browbeating me for compensation, as though I could do anything for him.

That's why I acted so shamelessly. I was angry. They want me to intervene with my brother when I'm not even speaking to him. I realise how very rude I was not inviting you to join us but believe me, I spared you an uncomfortable experience."

"I understand. I shouldn't have approached you when I saw you were engaged in such an earnest conversation but I wanted to, ah, to say hello."

I had the strange experience of my words not leaving my mouth the way I wanted them to. She seemed to understand her effect on me and lightly touched my arm as if reassuring me. She was candid beyond belief.

"My brother Richard was hanged by a mob in Richmond. Not that that was any great loss. Richard was a scoundrel through and through. He was a cheat, a liar and thief. I hardly knew him anyway. He was gone when I came along. I loved my brother Wilcox. He was my baby brother and he was killed at Pittsburgh Landing. My mother caught the fever just before Charleston fell; the Yankees burned most of the houses on our street except ours because my brother bought them off. So our house stands in the midst of the smouldering ruins, burned barns and slaughtered animals of our neighbours. You can imagine the resentment. People were so enraged they tried to burn down our house. My brother fought them off with thugs and Yankees helping him. I hope he rots in hell."

She was flushed when she finished, as though every thing she told me flashed in front of her while she spoke. This time I squeezed her arm and we continued walking along the Battery, studying the imprints of cannon balls on the walls. After a pause to get her breath she started again with renewed intensity and bitterness.

"I couldn't get a casket for my mother. There was nobody to bury her. Beauregard pulled his troops out and there was nobody to do anything."

I learned her family's difficulties were heightened because they were not sympathetic to the Confederate cause. Sadie had plenty of opinions on the folly of Confederate politicians. She was beautiful but could be most unladylike. There was a hard edge to her, put there by a father who was a con man and brothers who were scoundrels. She was unlike any woman I had ever known.

I bought her a sherbet and we sat under a large canvas umbrella. She explained she was leaving Charleston and my heart pounded when she told me she was going to be resettling in New York.

"So you've spent a great deal of time in New York?" she asked.

"Yes, we are often there."

I told her of the city, its parks and attractions. My cousins in Brooklyn and the picnics we had along the Hudson River. I described the great buildings, the press of people and carriages, the summer wind, the horses and the hot streets. I described the ships tied up at South Street docks, boisterous waterfront saloons, the shops along Canal Street, the restaurants and magnificent hotels.

She was going to be a teacher at the New Holland School for Girls on Park Avenue.

During the next week, we met every day and she showed me the Charleston I'd never seen as a sailor. I rented a carriage and we went past the house her brother had stolen from her. It had a long wooden porch and a portico with wrap-around windows. It was not that she had any emotional attachment to it. Her family had lived in many houses and there was nothing attractive about the property. In fact, the house was ghostly and gaunt, made so by its surroundings. On either side, untouched since the sounds of cannon had ceased, were the walls of the charred ruins of their neighbours houses. On what had been a tree-lined street, not a tree was left standing. Her eyes filled with tears and I was glad when we drove on.

She was contemptuous of Southern aspirations. Her father had predicted, "The fools will lose," but nobody dreamed they would lose so much. No one, not even the smartest people who doubted the South's ability to win, even those not caught up in this stupidity, ever dreamed the war would come to Charleston.

She was changeable, more so than any person I've ever seen. Tears or anger could be replaced with a smile or a laugh instantaneously. I made her happy by taking her to one of the newly reopened restaurants. She ate heartily, digging into her food with relish.

"I am not a lady and don't pretend to be. If I didn't eat fast at home, my brothers would have it devoured."

"Fair enough," I said. "That I understand."

We talked a great deal about New York. There was passion in her voice when she said it was going to be her new start. "You see I am going to the Yankees, sir. Yessiree, going to the Yankees, one two, three."

"You'll stay in New York then?" I asked her.

"If it suits me, I will. But whatever happens, I know I will never come back here. There are too many memories."

She had a way of moving her head ever so slightly to reference things she was talking about. It could be the world around her, a room, a street, a city or a person.

Charleston was both harsh and good to her. When times were good for her family, her father threw wonderful parties. He hosted socials and morning dances. There were hard years too, when there was no father and very little on the table.

"Most of the gentry came home from the war, but many on the poor side, the boys working in the packing houses and farms, the sailors like yourself and the men who work for the rich merchants, they're in graves all over this country."

We were from different worlds and could not always bridge that divide. When she was excited, which was often, she could hardly contain herself. Then sometimes she would sit quietly as if lost. Whatever her mood, I was totally captivated by her, even when she made fun of me. Occasionally she would mimic my manner of speech, giving back to me the rough vowels of the Dominion. She did not have the Southern drawl I heard on the streets of Charleston. Sadie was Sadie. She defied definition.

The night before we sailed, I walked her back to her boarding house, a ramshackle whitewashed building. One of the ground floor windows was cracked and the steps were lopsided. It was temporary, she said, just until she made arrangements. Two old dogs dozed by the door, getting up half-heartedly to sniff at us while we said goodbye. We promised to meet in New York. Then she kissed me, momentarily taking my breath away. I suppose I was embarrassed, unaccustomed to kissing in public, and I tried to pull away as people passed on the street. She pressed me back to her and I could hear my heart pounding. I'm sure she could too.

"When you come to New York, don't forget me," she sighed.

"I promise I will find you."

I began walking away to find my legs were unsteady. What other woman had such an effect on me? Who else could make me slur my words and could weaken my knees as if I were intoxicated. Sadie Muise. God, I have missed her all these years.

I've only ever received two letters from Sadie. The first in her flourishing hand, to inform me she had arrived in New York and was settling in. She was absolutely enthralled with the city. She signed it, 'Sadie', with a swirling tail off the last letter. I read it over and over, seeing something more of her on the paper than her penmanship.

"You're quiet, Allan," Marshy said a few days later.

"Am I?"

"You seeing her in Charleston?" he said.

"How did you know?"

He shrugged. "Going off by yourself. You don't do it anywhere else. Just in Charleston. So I figured you found her. I remember things," he said, pointing to his head and smiling.

"She's gone to New York," I said.

"Ah, New York. You'll be seeing her then. Capt'n says we'll be on the sugar charter soon, Cienfuegos to New York."

Trade changes and three months later we were back in northern waters. We had come down the Minas Basin from Parrsboro, heading for Boston, loaded with coal and lumber. We had a moderate sea, light winds and an uneventful voyage. Without warning, the *Allandale* started listing. It was hardly noticeable at first, just a slight tilt that an inexperienced eye wouldn't notice. We thought we needed more ballast. An hour later, and the pitch of the deck was more pronounced and an hour after that, buckets and mops started sliding towards port. The deck was loaded with lumber; more of a tilt and thousands of board feet would spill over the side, capsizing us.

By four that afternoon the *Allandale* was taking on more water than the pumps could handle. At seven the order came to abandon ship. The brig had been my home for eight years. It was the only ship I had known and I felt a total dejection. I had left our farm after my sisters died and the brig became part of me. It had carried me to tropical islands and introduced me to new customs. It had taken me to cities with wide streets and whiskey-breathed women. It had protected me as a storm tried to lash us onto rocky shoals and I had heard the brig breathe as it lay motionless in a protected cove, waiting out a storm.

We sat in the long dory in the fading evening light and watched the lumber sliding off into the sea. Our brig capsized slowly, gracefully. Its spars touched the water and it disappeared in the dark.

"God bless a fine ship," somebody said.

We were watching an old friend die. There wasn't another word spoken. Men bobbing silently, lost in thoughts of their own and digesting the loss of a ship and of a livelihood.

We were on the water all night, damp and miserable, still knowing it would have been much worse in winter. We were in the sea-lanes with plenty of traffic plying the waves. At first light a fishing boat picked us up and took us to Yarmouth.

A week later I was back on the farm helping my father with the last of the winter's chopping when DP dropped by. He spent some time in the house then came out to the farmyard to have a word with me. He felt as badly as we all did about the loss of a good ship but at least every man was accounted for. There was not a scratch on any man and that was at least some comfort.

"Captain Densmore has a new ship," he said. "He's taking command of the *Dove*. We've been talking about a mate. Mr. Corbett is going on the *Toronto* when it's finished. The captain plans to ask you to be his mate. I have given him my blessing – with one condition."

DP said I should write for my Master's papers. It would take months of studying but I had already learned much of the two aspects that make a master worthy of the name: command and navigation.

Command is the business of running a ship, being the boss over mates and crew. You are the arbitrator of all disputes and you are judge and jury. You make sure the cargo is set properly in the holds, that stores are sufficient, that the ship is seaworthy, her rigging set right. You see to a thousand little things that can keep you and your crew alive. Navigation is reading the stars. Knowing the heavens like the back of your hand. Telling where a star should be even when it's obscured by clouds. Navigation is the business of getting the ship from one point to another, sometimes thousands of miles apart. Raise your anchor in Liverpool, England, and drop it six weeks later in East Advocate, Nova Scotia. That's navigation.

The *Dove* was a hundred tons heavier than the *Allandale*. She was a three-year-old brig owned by DP and his brother Charles. My father had shares in the ship. So did my Uncle Howard and the McBurnies.

Soon after signing on we began making regular runs on the sugar and tobacco charters from Cienfuegos, Cuba, to New York.

So here I was coming into New York and increasingly nervous. She was near. That was all I really needed to know. She was near.

As mate I had responsibilities and couldn't go traipsing off the minute we docked. It was two days before I was finally free enough to draw wages and go ashore.

Filled with anticipation and apprehension, I started off to find the New Holland School for Girls. That was the easy part. I found the school and it was closed for a week's holiday. I left a note with the woman at the door and walked away with a curious sense of disappointment and relief.

On the sugar charters we frequently left New York empty. When the unloading went quickly we would be in and out of New York inside of a few days.

The captain brought a note for me from the British consulate. It was from Sadie. She was boarding with her cousin on Spence Street.

I almost ran. When she opened the door we flew into each other's arms. Her cousin, embarrassed at such a show of affection, turned away. This time I didn't care who was watching when we kissed.

Sadie could make you believe you were the most important person alive. It caused a consternation in me because I knew better, but I wanted so hard to believe. A man is in danger when he ignores his own good judgement and that's what I was doing. I was captured by her wiles and I fought off my practical Scottish nature that told me I knew better. I was younger by more than two years. Younger and wetter behind the ears, from the wilds of Nova Scotia. I was a sailor with small chance for gaining riches.

Sadie wanted riches. Her fineries were gone but she still had the grace of a rich woman and the bearing of a noble princess. I was a novelty to her. Nothing more and I knew it early on.

New York in 1868 was a far cry from war-torn Charleston. The bustle brought colour to her cheeks, the excitement of the city made her talk so fast she almost lost her breath. She wanted me to take her everywhere at once, do everything immediately.

"Please, please, please. Take me dancing."

"I'm not a very good dancer."

"Yes you are. I'll make you good. Please, please!"

She had learned everything about dancing, knew all the new jittery steps that were beyond my clumsy feet. I tried a few times but better dancers swept her away. A young man with flaxen hair and a velvet coat waltzed her round the floor. Then his friend, then flaxen hair again. Next a tall man with spectacles, and on to someone else. She waved as she whirled by. Laughing with her head back, eyes sparkling with pure joy. I drank whiskies and watched.

Sadie was happy. Happy to be there, happy to be escorted home by flaxen hair, his friend and myself. All in her glory at the door, saying goodbye to the three of us.

"Allan, come for tea tomorrow," she said, and lightly hugged me as she had the others.

There was no lover's kiss and I was jealous and peevish, I suppose. The night confirmed what I already knew. Despite my feelings for this woman, I didn't want to spend a lifetime watching her whirl by in somebody else's arms. I didn't go to tea. Four days later we sailed away to Cuba.

Every time we docked in New York I fought with myself, explaining why I delayed seeing her. I was drawn and repelled at the same time. Sadie Muise would never settle for a poor saltwater sailor. It was obvious she could command more than me and I knew there was no future for us.

To put her farther from my mind I started writing to a girl from the shore. Laura Webster and I were reacquainted at a church social soon after the *Allandale* sank. She was a schoolteacher, nine years younger than me. She was not a beauty like Sadie, but attractive, as you'd hear people say, in a sensible sort of way. She had a round face, dark eyes with raven hair. Her biggest contrast to Sadie was her shyness, her quiet demeanour. She did not rise to excitement like a fish to a fly. She didn't laugh easily nor did she pout. Her face was a mask for her feelings. If Sadie was the rushing current, Laura was the channel, deep and mysterious.

It wasn't a romantic relationship at first. Laura was not the type of woman to be swept off her feet, nor was she a woman willing to let you steal a kiss unless the courtship had progressed to that point. Also, we were seldom alone; our meetings involved socials with plenty of chattering so we didn't do a lot of conversing. When we were alone she was quiet shy. When we finally kissed, it was perfunctory. There was no flame or passion causing chain lightning between us.

We made three more trips and I managed New York without Sadie. Then late one summer day I was supervising sail repairs when the sailor on watch told me a woman was at dockside and wanted to see me.

Standing in the midst of the pushcarts, draft horses and dockworkers, Sadie stood out like a ray of sunshine, waving, ignoring all the eyes that fell upon her. She was wearing a pale rose dress that shimmied when she walked, sending off a thousand reflections of rosy silver. She was as beautiful as ever.

Our relationship, without promises to each other and filled with pitfalls for me, resumed more strongly than ever. For months we met like that. Sadie waiting at dockside or sending word of where she was living. She moved often and always had an amazing story as to why. I loved her more with every month but my instinct would not be quieted. Loved her, yes, but more leery of her as well. Our romance would flare and die then flame again as if someone had thrown dry bark on a fire banked for a winter's night.

When the price of sugar dropped, we took the *Dove* back to Nova Scotia and loaded lumber to take to the American states and Great Britain. We were loading from Apple River, Windsor, Hantsport and Parrsboro so I was closer to home more of the time. Closer to Laura. I was surprised she hadn't married, for our letters had all but stopped. But no, my mother said, she had not married and as a matter of fact, she and her mother were coming to tea a week Tuesday.

Laura was more confident by that time and more talkative. In fact, she was quite opinionated in her quiet way. I expect she was getting many of her ideas from magazines that arrived from the American states. Looking back at it now, Laura was, above all, relaxing. Something I could never say about Sadie. Laura would demand less of life, but the things she believed in, she did so strongly. I appreciated that part of her nature.

"You and Laura are becoming quite thick," my brother John offered one day while we were haying.

"I guess so," I replied. Then without really thinking I said, "She's dependable."

John raised his eyebrows. "Dependable? Now that's a good quality." He laughed. "I hope you don't sweet talk her by telling her she's dependable like some draft horse."

"There's more to dependable than meets the eye," I said and turned my back to him. He didn't understand but the words stayed with me and troubled me. Was that all I required?

In contrast, Sadie wasn't dependable at all. She would stand me up one day and be waiting for me the next. I never knew and it frustrated me, at times enraged me and I'd walked the streets of New York swearing I'd never see her again. More than once I sailed away from the East River docks damning her and shaking my fist at the sky. After two years of such frustrations I was certain I didn't love her because her attraction to other men didn't bother me anymore. I would take her down to the oyster house near Fulton's Fish Market. She'd sigh over lobster salad and talk about her life. It was always hectic and always filled with whirling social activities. I listened without saying much. I held no expectations of her. She had become my friend and confidante, telling me of her fellow teachers and students, one of whom she thought she had fallen in love with. Their relationship threatened her position at the school and I advised her to discourage the student but I was never certain she wanted to. I was there to help her through that crisis in her life and escort her places she wanted to go. I kept convincing myself that was all I wanted. I enjoyed her. Who wouldn't?

One day over lunch I felt so settled with her, I told Sadie about Laura. I was dismayed by her reaction. She was hateful! She flew into me, cried and refused to eat. She took a carriage home and I did not see her again for some months.

Then, as we were docking she was waiting. I ignored her, gave my full attention to edging into the jetty. There were no waves from her this time. She just waited, holding her umbrella. Out of the corner of my eye I could detect some change in her, a different stance, her posture, the way she held her head, still proud but a little less so. A thousand men, the roughest stevedores and sailors on the East River, stared at her but she never diverted her attention nor took her eyes off me. It sent a small quiver down my back.

"You best go see that lady before some sailor carries her away and I expect there's plenty of them dogs would like to," Captain Densmore said.

As I walked toward her, she smiled.

"I thought I would never see you again," she said softly. She touched me, oblivious to the eyes around her. "And you know I couldn't stand the thought of that," she said and kissed me. That brought forth a chorus of hoots and catcalls from my crew and others nearby.

"I'll see you as soon as I can," I said.

"I've moved," she said and she placed a crumpled paper in my hand. "My new address."

She had a spacious flat near Canal Street, not only roomy but well furnished with tufted leather chairs, oil paintings and Persian rugs on the floor. I wondered how she afforded such a place on a teacher's wages. There wasn't much talk between us.

We made love in her canopied bed and she gave herself to me in a way she never had before. She gave all, every inch and every ounce of her. We had coupled as man and wife before but in a more off-handed way on her part while I burned with desire.

The months away from her had driven me other places, where a God-fearing man should never go. I had known Blanche, a kind prostitute in New Orleans, then I had fallen into the arms of the beautiful mulatto woman in Port-A-Spain. But that night on Canal Street, Sadie gave me her all. I loved her mercilessly, hard, with a passion even I never knew I possessed. She bit and moaned and cried. Her vibrations were waves of breathless delight.

Finally, worn out by our lovemaking, I fell asleep and dreamed my ship was sailing through rosy clouds with Sadie as my only crew and we glided over all the oceans of the world.

I was horrified and hurt in the morning when she admitted to me that she shared the flat with her husband. I wouldn't believe her. I couldn't comprehend her treachery. But it was no lie. She started to weep as she explained she had been married a month.When I began to realise the truth of her tale, I started shaking. I thought my heart and all other internal organs were going to break loose.

"It has all been such a mistake on my part," she wailed. "I didn't love him. I was alone, and . . . and I lost my teaching job. I was desperate."

"Why didn't you tell me?" I fumed. "Why did you spend the night with me in the bed you shared with your husband?"

I berated her for being a common whore. I threw a vase against the wall and damned her whorish ways again. She cried and crumpled to the floor. I picked her up and kissed her wet eyes and we wept together.

It was late morning when I left her. I was weak and perplexed. Astonished by how much of myself I had given her and how it had all been a sham. For the first time in my life, I understood how a woman was capable of destroying a man.

As I walked along the docks towards the *Dove* another ominous feeling draped itself over my mind. My work. I could see Captain Densmore standing on the poop deck, his pipe clenched tight, the smoke rolling. Disapproval was written all over his face.

"Best we talk, Allan. I have something to say."

I was in for a lecture and I deserved it. Not a man stood near us. A ship is not a place for secrets and the crew knew I was getting a good dressing down. But it wasn't the blistering I expected.

"I expect my mate to be on ship at least some time in a twenty-four hour period unless I have given him permission to disappear. I told you to go see that woman, not to disappear for an entire day." He looked over the landscape of New York. "For the first time since you starting sailing with me, you failed me. I don't want it to happen again."

"Yes, Captain."

"I've heard from DP," he continued, never changing his tone. "I'm taking command of the *Northern Empire* when we get home. DP has a mind to turn the *Dove* over to you if you get your papers. I'll go along with it, if you can keep your mind on the ship and off the skirt."

We sailed north to Nova Scotia and the cool winds were on my face. I tried not to believe the truth but I could not fight it.

Never again would I be as happy as I had been those few hours in the canopied bed on Canal Street.

Chapter Ten

Will Thompson and I discussed many things during our long acquaintance and particularly in his final days when he was able to sit up in bed. We'd talk of fear, pride, stupidity and the stubbornness we had seen in others and I'd seen in myself. He would never admit weaknesses. He was above such nonsense, and I wanted to talk mostly of weakness, my own. That is why I refused to tell him all. I refused to let him know my innermost secrets while he refused to do the same and he is the one dying. It is safe telling the dying your innermost secrets. They have little time to tell others and little inclination. Will Thompson had no deathbed repentance. I was with him to the last and it was evident his time was near. I wanted to confide in him at a time when he should have been confiding in me. He did not fear death and thumbed his nose at it, the way he had thumbed his nose at convention or high-falutin nobility, at false charity or churchly righteousness. I wanted to share something with him, something from the sea but I did not, I could not, tell him everything.

He sneered at me when I confessed a weakness. "Too proper," is how he put it.

"What do you regret?" I asked.

"No regrets," he replied.

Mrs. Marsh said once that Will Thompson's soul dried up and disappeared a long time ago. "You would not want to be in his shoes on the day of judgement."

But when I asked him what he expected to see when he crossed over, he smiled and said, "All the whores I spent time with the last fifty years, and some damn good women too."

Walking home from his house, I often felt he was more fortunate than me. I believed enough to feel the torture of past deeds and thoughts. There is much about Laura and the children that I regret. There is much about my wife that keeps us separated by more than thousands of miles.

I am tortured by the memory of Sadie, although when I've not had the drink I know enough to realise she was not meant to be a sailor's wife. Sadie needed constant attention. She was not a person you could leave alone. She was not above making mischief. Such things amused her. Why would she trifle with a student, risking her position if not for the excitement she thought it promised.

Laura did not need or want excitement. Even the happiness of having a husband at home semed to elude her. My return after a long absence sparked none of the excitement a man might expect. Perhaps she was distant because she had to be, because she knew I'd be going again. There are these things, these bits of guilt, not dealt with, undigested, after all these years and there are other things. Deeper things that bring the sweat to my forehead, that send shivers through me until my legs are shaking under my bedcovers.

When I hold the *Dove*'s log, even after all these years, my hands shake for the fear has never left me. I know that fear must be somewhere in Will Thompson too. Any man with half a century at sea has seen the face of death. All I have to do is remember making my way across the icy deck to the crew's quarters to check on Ruphus. I would go several times a day waiting for him to die. I could never tell by my first look at him. He always looked dead. He had looked that way for days. Everyday he lived brought us closer to the fateful decision. If he was alive I could do nothing for him. If he was dead I could possibly save the others. Repugnant? Yes, but never underestimate a starving man. Could I, as captain, do such a thing? I sat on his bunk and all the weariness of the world descended on my shoulders. I sat there next to him and I cried. The ship's captain crying and not knowing if he was crying because this sailor was still living or because he wasn't dead. My brother was next to him, looking like another corpse; his eyes so sunken, his face so shrivelled he no longer looked like a member of our family. Two breathing corpses side by side. John was still able to get up and walk with my help, if only for a few moments. Ruphus had not moved in two weeks; his breath had the rattle of the dead. I envied him. It was easier just to slip away. The crew was my responsibility. It made me ill to think what I might have to do. My men were at the breaking point. They were starving and I knew the living would do anything to go on living. We were close to being a pack of wolves and the vilest act could be our salvation. That's what I wanted to talk to Will Thompson about. I wanted to borrow his hardness, to wear the armour he had wrapped around himself, even just for a while, so I could pick up the log and read the pages without my hands shaking.

Is that so much to ask for?

Chapter Eleven

Crossing an ocean is the ultimate demonstration of seamanship. As captain I had absolute authority but Sadie Muise would not take orders. She refused to leave the wind and the water.

A person can bury many things but the love a man can have for a woman is beyond burying. All the way across the Atlantic her face was visible in the green water. Her musical voice skipped over the waves and the fragrance of her skin arrived on the north wind.

The brig was deeply loaded with Parrsboro lumber and pushed by the good winds of early summer. We ran full sail, billowing towers plowing around the Yarmouth light and into the open Atlantic.

I had met James Sheridan only days before. We were ready to depart Parrsboro when my mate took a nasty fall. Martin Pettigrew climbed around the rigging of ships all his life without incident but put a sea dog on a wet roof and watch out! His wife sent word he had broken his leg and I had hired another mate. Sheridan was from Windsor. Now why a Windsor man would be looking for work on the Parrsboro Shore when more ships were sailing out of his homeport than any place in the Maritimes I could not understand. The *Dove* was ready to put to sea and Sheridan had his mates papers so, against my better judgement, I signed him on. I soon found out why he had left Windsor. A quarrelsome man, he had the disposition of a mad dog. Belligerent to the crew and worse, argumentative with me. A captain must have command and on this, my first crossing as captain, my first mate confronted me. There is an unwritten law. If a mate questions a command, he does so in private and he does so once. After a good dressing down by me, Sheridan showed he was a good seaman and continued his duties without question. Otherwise, our voyage from Parrsboro to Liverpool, England, was uneventful. In twenty-eight days, we were going up the Irish Sea towards the wide mouth of the Mersey River just below Liverpool.

Upon docking I learned DP had already secured a return charter. DP was always a wonder. The man sat in his office in Economy and had his fingers all over the world, directing his ships to pick up a cargo here, go there on one continent and another time pick up some exotic cargo on the other side of the world.

We would be taking anchors and anchor chains back to the Bay of Fundy and up the Avon River for landing in Windsor. We would be sailing back to Nova Scotia. I was glad we were going anywhere but New York.

By that time I was satisfied with Sheridan's work, but he decided to leave the ship. On good recommendation, I hired a Nova Scotian whose ship had been wrecked a month earlier off the coast of England. His name was William Landry from Arichat and if there is a man on earth to whom I am grateful, it's to him. There would be days full of darkness, when the sun left us and I commanded a ship with tattered sails and a dying crew. Landry's firm hand was my only instrument against the elements – against death itself.

As the heavy chains were boomed over the side and into the *Dove*'s holds it was easy for omens to overwhelm you. The brig groaned and settled farther in the water with each load. When the big anchors were stowed on top of the chains, like iron birds settling into a nest of steel, every plank of the ship uttered a complaint. The *Dove* was riding too low in the water.

I got into an argument with the bulbous agent, a man named Rigglesworth, who strolled up and down the dock declaring the brig was fine. But he wouldn't be in the middle of the ocean with us. Damn agents are mostly scoundrels with hearts of hair. We argued but I held fast to my position that the cargo was too heavy. Three of the big anchors were finally removed, much to Riggleworth's displeasure. I made a note to report to DP what a blackguard this man was.

Papers signed, documents done, provisions stowed, ballast taken and in a light rain at 2 p.m. on Tuesday, September 24th, 1872, we were towed out to Bell Buoy where the Mersey River begins to widen into a bay. The summer had gone and September turned churlish and grey.

At midnight it was blowing a moderate gale. On deck, the wind forced you to keep your head down and press your body into it to walk. The brig was labouring and low waves washed over our gunwales. The crew struggled as they climbed into the yardarms. I can still see them standing on a rope, stowing light sail and looking like marionettes dancing a wild jig. The wind caught an empty bucket off the poop deck and hurled it into the rigging. We manned the pumps without speaking.

Horns Head Light was off to our southwest. There was a grey frothy sea between us. We double reefed our main sail and the brig still laboured. In the darkness that night the lightning was terrifyingly beautiful. Hour after hour it illuminated the rolling mountains of black water with white foaming tops. It rained. It roared. I stood watch and for the first time in days I had no thoughts of Sadie Muise.

At first light the gale intensified. The northwest wind was at war with the sea. If you tried to speak the words were blown out of your mouth. The deck was awash. By noon our sails were in tatters and we were hove to. I gave the order to return to Liverpool.

By the time we docked at New Ferry we'd only been to sea for thirty-six hours. It felt more like thirty-six days. A bad beginning.

It took two weeks to mend the sail and set the rigging. All that time in harbour the rain never stopped. The storm had finally driven Sadie from my mind and for that, at least, I was thankful.

There are times when a sailor, even an ungodly one, has religious experiences. You can see many things in the black waters of a raging ocean. Marshy said the Irish Sea was forbidding us from entering. Mr. Landry replied that the lightning was as near to hell as he cared to be.

Heaven and hell can be close. It was during our repairs that I remember splashing over the cobblestones in Liverpool, following the voice that had called me off the ship. The voice was in my head, yet somehow it wasn't. I tried to resist but finally I followed it and walked the wet streets in search of something. I stopped for some stew and then pushed on. It was late afternoon. The cobblestones glistened. Children on their way from school played in the puddles. An old dog limped out of a doorway to inspect me, but the streets were mostly empty except for an occasional carriage. It was not a fit day for man or beast. Water ran off the brim of my hat. I was cold, tired and wanted to quit. I mumbled to myself about what a fool I was when something made me look up the hill. Above the rooftops I saw a cross. That's all, just the cross. I climbed the hill.

The cross was atop the steeple of a stone church. It resembled a fortress with its granite blocks and large wooden door. A structure made to withstand the centuries, to endure until Christ returns. The giant oak door was unlocked. I stepped inside and waited for my eyes to adjust to the darkness. It was quiet. Even the sound of the rain couldn't penetrate the thick walls.

Behind the altar I saw a stained glass window in shades of blue, gold and green. The colours of the sea and sky. The scene was the Last Supper. Jesus and his disciples breaking bread. They had been men of the sea too, accustomed to storms and the roughness of a sailor's life. I looked at each face. Which had been the fishermen? James, John, Peter? Yes, Peter. Which one was Peter? Peter was the rock. Had he experienced storms like these in the Irish Sea? Why was I here? I knelt and prayed. Prayed for my ship, my crew and for me. Prayed that I would have the courage to face another storm and command my ship across the great ocean. When I lifted my head they were watching me as if they understood the dark waters of fear that can run through a seafaring man.

As a young man I scoffed at much of the misunderstood and unexplained but now in my sixty-fifth year I scoff at nothing. The large world with its vast oceans and complex continents can be understood. But there is a small world within the soul that is beyond explanation. If that were not so, I would not have been in the stone church that day.

I walked back to my ship prepared for the task ahead.

On October sixth we were towed back to sea. For the first time in days it wasn't raining and for a few hours there was renewed hope our voyage would continue safe and sound.

At 4 p.m. we were into high winds and stowing light sail. In early evening we close-reefed the mainsail and stowed the upper top sheets. The gale grew worse. We were in the midst of a hurricane.

The deck was awash again, making it difficult to stand. The *Dove* would plow into the troughs going straight toward the bottom to crash and crumple on the seabed. Then the powerful arms of the angry sea carried it up and the brig would rise: its bow skyward, water streaming off the deck.

My new mate proved himself a worthy sailor, keeping the crew at the pumps and doing shipboard duties with diligence. We went from a hurricane to a gale to a hurricane and then back to a gale again. Through rain and howling wind we went down the Irish Sea into St. George's Channel. Men were hurt when waves took the feet out from under them. If you were unlucky enough to be caught flat-footed by a big breaker, you'd find yourself sprawled on the deck with seawater washing down your neck, setting your teeth chattering. In six days of hard weather we passed Lands End and saw the light of the Scilly Islands, eight miles in the distance. We were coming into the open Atlantic.

The clock in my kitchen has stopped ticking. I know. It was the only sound in the house. I keep forgetting to wind it but yet I miss it when it stops. I pour another dram. This afternoon I've taken Mr. Landry's mate's log from my sea chest to help me through this ordeal. In the open Atlantic is where it really started.

First hail. Ball bearings falling from the sky. Icy and razor-edged, leaving bleeding nicks that burned in the constant wash of saltwater. Sailors curse the goddamn sea and their wretched lives. For an hour the hail pelted us. It stopped as quickly as it started. I remember Marshy with blood spots on his face, yelling into the wind.

"Now, by God we've had everything."

My brother John has just left and he's as good as his word. He has brought me a bottle of rum from Truro. I pour myself an extra dram and promise myself to put the bottle away. Laura always claimed I brooded about things and she was right. It is part of the nature of the dour Scot, but I am not brooding this time. I'm building. Constructing the most accurate reflection I can find. One last glance maybe? Putting things to rest once and for all. The vivid memories and those that are slipping away. Why can't I leave things alone? Will Thompson was right. I torture myself.

My crew on that fateful voyage. God bless them! Jim Wilson, two years younger than me with as much sea time. I made him second mate. He was over six feet, a thin man with the jolly nature of a fat man. He could bend like a willow and climb the rigging faster than any man I've ever known. His young brother, Isaac, stockier and with a more serious demeanour. A competent sailor. Ruphus Smith, strong as an ox and as hard a worker as you'll ever find. Young Jacob Campbell with his long beard that led to tricks being played on him. Jacob was our steward and he could make a flapjack better than any man. And of course, Marshy. Constant Marshy. He refused to write his mate's papers. He didn't want the task of command.

"Leave that to others," he said.

Crossing the Atlantic I needed one more able seaman. There were plenty wanting to sign on, including my brother John.

Mother was adamantly against two sons sailing on the same ship and I made rash promises to her. Promises I couldn't possibly keep. She was relentless in her efforts to stop John from signing on. She tried persuasion. John's feathers got ruffled and he refused to listen. I was in a dilemma. I'd promised him he could sign on before knowing it was going to create such an uproar in our house. John had his heart set on leaving us in Liverpool for a fortnight visit to Scotland as I had done years earlier. He wanted to see the places our father had talked about. His desires and my mother's protests made us a family divided. She would not let the matter rest.

"I've lost too many children already. More than enough, do you understand?"

We did understand and that made it all that much more difficult. But John would not be thwarted by past family tragedies, saying it was unfair to hold him back because our sisters had died. Few ships crossing the Atlantic would sign on a green sailor, but I had promised him and John was steadfast. If I had not kept my word, I wasn't sure he would ever have forgiven me. In truth, I understood his desire. All the eager farm boys from Economy were going off to see the world. Why would my brother want to be left at home?

It is the tin cup that has rattled through my ten thousand nights since then. The protruding handle caused a leap with each rotation, like a sailor with a wooden leg. The tin cup rolled hour after hour and not one of us had the strength to stop it. It became our enemy. A constant reminder that our lives were as empty as it was. We had been days without water and crazy men will drink seawater and become crazier. Whenever the ship pitched the cup scurried, close to a groping sailor then off again. I kicked it once, hoping to send it over the side. My foot touched it but it rattled away laughing at me. Laughing at us all. It started rolling the day I watched Jim digging. His back was to me. He was crouching on his knees, praying I thought at first. Why wouldn't he pray? There had been a lot of praying.

I was so weary myself I wanted to leave him but he had become so frail a good wave would have carried him off. As I walked up to him and saw what he was doing, it stung me. He had gone to the galley and fetched the cup but he hadn't bothered to use it. His blade had gone directly into his mouth. Once, twice, three times. I touched his shoulder but he paid no notice. I pressed on him a bit until he looked up. His face was burned raw by the wind. Blue lips and eyes gone wild. He grimaced as if surprised that I was standing over him, embarrassed but not caring much about embarrassment anymore. My third mate was on his knees digging between the planks of the deck. He was eating it. He twisted his face, his mouth agape with teeth that had turned yellowish green. A trickle was rolling down his face. He was crying. Dehydrated but still a tear. A strapping farm boy turned wild, raw and teary-eyed!

I thought of my brother dying in his bunk. Pale, shivering and speaking less with the passing of each day. I tried to feel my own feet so they could carry me aft. It was time to get them up again, to keep them moving. Jim's brother was badly frostbitten but able to help me lift and steady my own brother on his feet. I had learned from experience that walking keeps the blood moving. Captain Densmore had made every man who took to his bunk with illness come on deck every day. The only escape was dying. We lost the last of our water so many days ago. Thirst made us crazy; our eyes were itchy and sore. My tongue was swollen and turned black like a beaver tail in my mouth, making my talk only a mumble.

Jim kept staring up at me, struggling to understand. I realised I was leaning against him, using his frail shoulders for support.

"Stand up, man," I admonished myself. "Stand up. You're the captain. Be strong!"

"Come on, Jim. Let's go back to your bunk."

"No! I'm so hungry. Just a little more, then I'll go back." He dug his knife into the deck again.

Still I pressed him. "No, Jim. Let's go. You can help me walk John and Isaac."

"No, not yet. Not yet!"

He was going about it madly. Digging, both hands on the knife, thrusting it as far as he could between the planks.

I thought of us as boys, haying in his father's big field in Lower Economy. His mother bringing milk right from the cow. His father was more than sixty then, working his hay fork and us strong strapping boys working hard to keep up with him. He'd look at Jim with a father's pride.

Watching Jim now sent a cold shudder through me. I had brought them to the brink of death. All these lads had been hardworking and healthy when they left home. What I witnessed was so frightening it defied explanation. I left Jim and limped down the deck to attend to the sick. The crew's cabin was damp. My brother was pale. His cheekbones more prominent every day. What would I ever say to her if we lost John?

"Bring him back safely." My mother's words were off there somewhere over the water. She had lost too many. The day never gone from her memory of arriving home from a daughter's funeral to find another daughter dead. It took the soul out of her; she collapsed in my father's arms. Even then it was not over. Beautiful Maria. Her little princess struck down too. My mother had a right to ask for no more sorrow. She had rights and I had refused her.

I refused more than her. I refused help when it was offered and I was left with a dying crew and a dying ship. Two sets of brothers, against the wishes and pleas of their parents. Me responsible. Earning my master's papers at twenty-two and they wanting to follow. And follow they did as we sailed the crooked coast of the American states and the blue-green waters of the Indies. But leaving Liverpool was different. We entered a raging hell unlike any water we had ever seen. Twenty-seven out of thirty-three days without sun. A dark world of furious gales. Like the claws of the devil, ripping pieces off our ship and hurling them into the darkness.

Below deck, they were huddled together, borrowing the warmth from each other, no longer ashamed of getting too close. As a man's needs become more basic, shame is the first human condition to disappear.

Ruphus Smith had fallen from an icy yardarm. His eyes never opened and when I pulled back his lids the eyes were dull and vacant. I thought he was dead and in the days that followed I wished he were dead. He had never uttered a word. The big ox had become a breathing corpse. Next to him, my once stocky brother was wasting away.

"Bring him back safely," she admonished, not caring to hide her bitterness. She transfixed me at the door. Strident, strong and defiant, my mother was challenging me as she had challenged my father over the caustic acid treatment for my lost sisters.

"Take care of yourself, Allan. You're a sailor, he is not. Bring him back safely. Bring him back to me. Do you understand?" What would she have said if she could have looked upon him at that moment?

In the eyes of God, man is frail. In the heart of the ocean, man is nothing. When the sea is enraged, manliness is tested quickly. Mere weeks ago, John was a stout and headstrong man. In a flick of time, he had turned into a shivering ghost. I examined Isaac's hands. If his fingers turned blacker from the frostbite they would have to come off. That would be my job. As captain I was the finger remover, the bonesetter, the flesh stitcher. Captains keep the fingers they remove. Not as sadistic artifacts but to settle arguments on land when the fingerless sailor claims he was unnecessarily butchered. Shrunken digits with dried black skin are the captain's proof he acted wisely and saved the hand or the arm. Or the man.

Isaac knew what his fate might be. He had been trying to move his dying fingers. The frostbite had hold of them but we both hoped for the best.

"I don't want you to take my fingers, Cap."

"I know, Isaac. Neither do I, but it's better than losing your arm."

"I wish we'd gone with the steamer," he coughed. I got up and left him. There is no point in second-guessing a command, even my own.

We could hear the steamer that day and answered it with our bell. It had come through the mist bucking a heavy head sea. Did we want to abandon ship? My crew was ready to take the opportunity. Ready to leave our ship and abandon our charter. They stood in a half circle around me. At that moment the responsibility of command was an anvil on my shoulders. They waited for the word. The wet and weather-beaten faces of John, Ruphus, Isaac, Marshy, Jim, and Jacob. Pale and gaunt. Jim and Isaac with their teeth chattering. Mate Landry at the wheel waited too. All of them. They accepted my decision but their faces could not hide their disappointment, their discouragement, their outrage. The steamer would attempt to rescue in such a sea but would not attempt to send us provisions and I understood the decision. The captain and crew of the steamer had been the first people of the outside world we had seen in near a month. They wished us well and disappeared into the deep mist. We were alone again. Dispirited and silent. Our ship triple-riffed in a grey and rolling sea.

For a land lover, the proper thing was to forfeit the profits, let the ship drift away and save the crew. Or the other possibility – have the steamer put a towline on us and claim salvage. That's the difference between land lovers and mariners. No captain could do either. A sailor has premonitions. He may see storms that have yet to develop and lost ships that are safely in port but a captain's duty is to the day. On that day, and I know it well, November 4th,1872, we were thirty days out. Our ship was battered and broken but still manageable. The tattered sails and bruised crew could still work and no captain could give up. I could not give up. Not for my own premonitions and certainly not for those of my crew.

Ten days and two hurricanes later the *Dove* was breaking up. The low rumble deep within the brig was the ship saying its final prayers.

"We're taking on water," I said.

"We're also developing a slow list," Mr. Landry replied and lit his pipe. Our dory would be smashed to smithereens or overturned by the breakers. "We'd never last in an open boat."

"Better a slim chance than none at all," I replied.

"Aye."

We had lashed ourselves to the wheel as our ship pitched and rolled. Over the hours we pondered our predicament. The brig would not last and seven men in one dory would capsize quickly. But men on a heavy flat raft have been known to transverse a thousand miles of rolling water. If the raft was substantial in breadth and weight it would not capsize, but could the weakened occupants hang on in a raging sea? It was a risk, a last desperate hope. The other question I pondered was this: *Could starving men find the strength to tear apart the deck planking of a well-built ship and lash the planks into a seaworthy raft?* A raft strong enough to hold us and a couple of barrels of pitch to burn to signal a passing ship.

"I've never heard of such a thing," Mr. Landry replied.

"Neither have I but what other chance is there? If we can only pry up the planks."

"Can we?" he asked. "Two men constantly at the pumps, one, sometimes two, at the wheel. Two or three in their bunks unable to work. We can't do it, Captain."

"We'll do it because we have to."

He looked at me and nodded. We had no food or water, just frostbitten fingers and a deck covered in ice. When the next watch came on, Mr. Landry and I held each other up, staggered down the deck to the workshop for lashing rope and crowbars. We would begin, by God. And we would do it.

We worked on our knees with our woolen pants and mittens sticking to the ice until a wave washed over us and then we'd slide down the deck with the pitch of the ship. Hour after hour, day after day we stuck and slipped and cursed and prayed while the brig uttered long moans and listed further.

"It's her death rattle," Marshy said.

"Pry," I responded. "Keep your mind on the job."

He looked at me. We were on our knees facing each other with a maul and crowbar and Marshy got very serious.

"What's going to bother you the most, Allan, if we don't get back?"

It was the first time in my command he hadn't called me Captain.

I thought a second and slowly nodded to the aft cabin. "I promised my mother I'd look after John."

"Ah! I promised my mother I'd look after myself. They may be promises neither of us can keep. What else, though?"

"What else?" I looked at him.

"Yes, what else? I mean, you know, ah, I'm not good with words like you but what else? Hunting, fishing? That girl in New York or other things besides family?"

I wondered if he had been reading my mind. For the first time in days, Sadie had been drifting in and out of my thoughts.

"Why did you mention her?"

"Don't know," he replied.

"And what about you?" I asked.

"Don't know. Maybe I'll miss just being alone in a pine forest in the summer, walking through the trees and listening to them sway in the wind. Or hauling a big trout out of the river. Maybe just living."

We didn't say anything more. Funny how you remember little scraps of information. It hurt to talk and every man was lost in his own memories. Then it hailed and we were saved.

If only an outsider could have witnessed it. Crazy men with wracked bodies and swollen tongues, some in their underwear dancing as if their feet were on a hot stove. So weak we could hardly move yet jumping for joy. Opening our mouths trying to get the hail. Running for buckets to gather the stones. Every pot in the galley was full and we burned the last of our firewood to melt the hail. We drank, coughed and gagged and drank some more. I took a pot of the melted water aft for John and Isaac and I poured some down Ruphus's throat. There was no response. I poured a little more.

The water could barely seep down my own throat because of the size of my tongue. I could feel the first drops slide through me with a strange sensation. For those who could drink they drank too fast and retched. Drunk on water and happy. Oh, so happy! For the first time in days there was the sound of human voices.

The *Dove* did not respond well to our glee. The moans from the aft hold cut through our merriment. The weeping, creaking, groaning deep within our ship startled us momentarily but at the moment it didn't really matter. Nothing mattered. The water from the hail renewed our souls. We were men again. We were alive again. Isaac was on deck the next day trying to work and manned the pumps for an hour. John tried but went back to his bunk.

At the wheel or on my knees with the crowbar, I often fell asleep. On my knees, I would wake and find myself sliding towards the gunwale. That's one of my everlasting dreams. Sliding. Except in my dreams, I don't stop but keep going over the side, into the water and right to the bottom. Into a black hole where I fall forever.

The night of the hail we'd tried to cheer the sick. Feeling fresh water on your face was a blessing. We washed Ruphus's face and wondered if he would ever wake up. We washed our own faces, drank and slept. The hail stopped and the wind grew calm and I awoke to take a reading. There were no stars, but we did have water.

We had four planks up and cut strips from the torn sails for added lashing. The double hitch and sailor's knot and braid around the planks. We kept looking skyward. We hadn't seen the sun, moon or stars in days. Grey, gusty days and dark nights. I couldn't take a bearing. The wind howled from the northeast. We grunted and pried and became numb. During the next gale, two men were needed on the wheel again to keep the brig steady.

Then at midnight on December 10th, after sixty-six days at sea, we saw the LaHave light. We were ten miles off the coast of Nova Scotia but far too weak for jubilation. Just a dim ray of hope came alive deep inside us.

The first light of day turned the nor'easter into a gale and it blew us back out to sea. We had no control. Our sails were gone or in tatters and for forty-one hours we were beaten back into the deep Atlantic. The hurricane howled and we hung on and our spirits died.

I kept them going as best I could but by that time I was prodding dead men. The crowbars weighed three hundred pounds. Pry, pry, pry. A dozen planks up. Fourteen planks. Spiking and lashing twelve footers together. Winds ease. Fifteen planks. Suddenly, we were in the midst of another gale. Jacob Campbell was lashed to the wheel for his watch. He was heavily wrapped in half-inch rope by Mr. Landry, who was suddenly so dizzy from lack of food he lost his balance and stumbled. I thought of getting up and going to help him, but he was a million miles away and my knees were frozen to the deck. Mr. Landry had knotted the rope to the main mizzen line. A mistake we realised only later.

In an hour the ship was labouring in a heavy sea and the rumble and groans gave way to a sharp crack. The winds howled, the deck was awash and the mizzen mast came crashing down. The line lashed to Jacob Campbell pulled taut. Jacob's long whiskers were caught in the half-inch rope and he was lifted into the air. One end of the rope held him to the wheel; the other end flew forward with the broken mizzen, taking Jacob's whiskers with it in an awful tear. The wind howled to the extent we could not hear his cries, even when a wave washed his smarting face with stinging salt water and he wept. We could see his shoulders heaving, his face buried in his hands while he still tried to hang onto the wheel. Then he stopped crying and made no further complaint. Jacob Campbell was a good lad.

I was trying to get some feeling back in my hands. The tips of my fingers were dead. I didn't realise it until Marshy stumbled and dropped his crowbar across my hand. Fatigue overcame me more every hour and I bit my cheek to stay awake. We needed more planks. We were men, encased in cold molasses in a race against time. The sun had abandoned us. So had hope.

By that time we had all tried eating the dirt. Attempting at first to hide what we were doing but after a while as a plank was pried up, we pushed each other away and ran our woolen mittens or our blades along it and put them in our mouths.

We would stumble down to the aft cabin and check John and Ruphus Smith. Give them water and mumble to them and stumble back on deck. John was weaker and Ruphus remained still and white. What if he died? What if he died with men starving? Dirt is dust. Dust to dust. Ashes to ashes. I secretly knew I wanted him to die. Each man had gone through the galley searching for anything. A forgotten crumb, a dried apple peel. Hunger and exhaustion held us in their grip and I began hearing voices. They came cascading from somewhere out there in the water. Sometimes the voices shouted at us, then they were calming. Voices I did not recognise. Sometimes they were kind, then profane. Hurling insults and laughing at my danger. My danger was failing my crew by failing myself. Hours later I plunged the knife into my arm.

"Stay awake in the name of dear God! Stay awake!"

The pumps couldn't keep up. The ship listed more to the starboard. Jim had fallen asleep, bent over the pump handle. The deck was a steep slope. The raft would have to do. We tethered a rope to the raft and tried to slide it over the lower starboard gunwale. Every move felt like sleepwalking. The list of the deck was severe but the raft would not slide. We needed all hands.

"Keep it going, lads. Keep it going!"

Keep yourself going, Captain.

The tin cup had slid to the starboard gunwale and stuck. There were new gullies where we had pulled away the planks. I made a decision that everyone but Ruphus was going to help. Best get my brother on his feet, best have him up no matter how uncertain his step. "Take good care of him," my mother had said. And I had promised her.

We were the walking dead. Gaunt men moving the raft a hairbreadth at a time. Jim was delirious. He talked to himself and would laugh like a hyena. John was on the other side of the raft. He was crying silently. Mr. Landry and I kept them going. There would be a problem with the pitch. We would need a big enough flame to light it. Our signal. The last act.

As I pushed next to Isaac and Marshy, the knife wound burned but the sight of my blood gave me a reassurance. I was still alive, still feeling, still a man and a captain. I had responsibilities. We tied down the wheel for every hand was needed at the raft.

Myself, John and Marshy, Jim, Isaac, Mr. Landry and Jacob.

"Push, boys, push!"

We grunted and strained though our strength was gone. We would stop, resigned to failure and I rallied them with Mr. Landry's help.

"Push, push, push!"

Over a number of hours we dragged the heavy raft to the gunwale, raised it over and slowly slid it into the water. We held the raft close with the tether and rolled one barrel of pitch on. We could only get one aboard. We knew we were done. When it was over we sat and breathed hard and didn't speak. When we tried to get up, our trousers had frozen again to the deck. There was consternation and profanity.

Shredded pieces of sail slapped the air as if applauding us. There we sat, our asses frozen to the deck. Jim thought the devil had hold of him and he started to scream. I had to slap him hard.

Sixteen hours later when I saw a ship I wasn't certain that it was real. My eyes had been playing tricks. Through the glass I had seen a city off our starboard. Green fields and white castles. But when I looked again they were gone.

A second look and the ship was still there but how could I be sure? I bit into my cheek to get my senses. A steamer all right, only three miles off. It would soon be dusk. I called Mr. Landry and he groped his way down the sloping deck. It had been days since a ship had been near enough to see us. It was the best we could hope for. We hauled in the raft, lit the pitch and prayed.

We were saved by the *Olaf Tayvejeson* sailing from New York to Dublin. Captain John Killand slapped me on my back because he thought I was choking. I felt blood in my mouth. I felt nothing more and slumped to the deck. They had just revived me, the men picking me up and holding both my arms when someone cried out. They were pointing and exclaiming excitedly in a language I didn't understand. With difficulty I looked in the direction they indicated.

The *Dove* was half rolling, half sliding into the sea. Her masts were at a forty-five degree angle with the surface of the water. Bits of tattered sail looked like a hundred flags, white remnants finally surrendering. There came a great screech, the tearing of timbers and what sounded like a scream as the brig uttered one last curse and its deck disappeared beneath the surface. We watched mesmerised as the masts moved sideways, lower and lower, like three pencil-shaped bathers taking the tide at Coney Island and stepping down into deeper water. The tops of the spars disappeared together, dipping below the waves with only a few seconds of foam and bubbles. Then there was nothing, like our ship had never existed and our voyage had been a hellish dream.

Still held up by the strong hands of men on either side of me, I slipped into unconsciousness again. Just for an instant, I saw the stained glass window in the church in Liverpool. I knew which one was Peter.

Chapter Twelve

There are some days that stand out in my life with such vivid images I can still feel the tremor as if I was living the circumstances again. The last days of the *Dove* are like that and I remember everything about the day of the bells. I can close my eyes and taste the fear, that feeling of dread as I raced up and down the street and I can still feel those little swirls of dust leap up to brush against my face.

I remember the dog. A little dog, black and white. He wouldn't stop. He grabbed my pant leg and tried to hang on. I ran and kicked, lifting him off the ground. He finally let go and ran beside me, barking. It was only a game to him. We were near the church before he stopped his chase. He was sniffing other people by the time I took the church steps two at a time and pushed the gape-toothed lad from the rope.

One church then another, the dog, and the surprised people and then the sullen quiet of a hot, dry morning.

There is no other village in the world that leaves me with quite the same impression as that of Great Village on that Sunday morning when the church bells went silent. Walking the road back to our house I had never felt so far from the sea – or so alone. When I was near the front door I stopped and looked up at the window in the second floor bedroom, just in case the doctor came to the window to give me a sign. I had taken a tremendous gamble, risked my child, and risked the love of my wife. If I was wrong, if things failed I would never be able to repair the damage. I waited for a sign, a sign from the window, some signal that things were right. There was nothing.

I walked inside. The house was quiet and there was queerness to it, as though it had not been lived in for a long time. I looked at the rooms, the furniture still in the same place as I'd left it only minutes earlier, but it was somehow different. As though the floor hadn't been walked on for a decade and a door hadn't been opened. It was our house, the place my family spent their winters, yet it felt abandoned. As though magically changed and the life there had withered and died. The stairs creaked under my weight and I walked lightly to take my seat outside the bedroom door. I was the sentry again, guarding against intrusion as nimble fingers cut flesh, snipped tendons, moved muscle and worked against blood and bone. I was guarding my hopes too. I realised at that moment how very, very frightened I was. What if I was wrong?

I waited another hour then quietly got up and went outside again to draw some deep breaths into my lungs. People were coming home from church and no one came close, for I'm sure the rumour was that I was either drunk or filled with madness. A man and woman I did not know crossed the street to avoid me. They then thought better of being that close and turned in the opposite direction.

"I am not mad," I wanted to yell after them, but I did not. I could not make a sound.

I heard the squawking of a seagull, defying the order of silence I had placed on the village. I looked up and saw a lone gull gliding across a sky. His white wings spread like full sails. He was a sleek ship at top speed, in a beautiful ocean of blue. Suddenly I felt reassured. I was all right again.

Chapter Thirteen

After our rescue the *Olaf Tayvejeson* brought us to Halifax where we received medical attention. We were a group of ghost-like men, frail and wild eyed. Those of us who were conscious had the startled expression of surprise that we had survived. I returned home in early January of 1873 and remember little of the next few weeks. I know John was bedridden for a long time. How many crews faced such deprivation and lived to tell about it – except we didn't tell. We had been as close to death as humanly possible and neither John nor I nor the rest of the crew ever talked much about our ordeal. Not in those days and not now. Maybe that's my problem, too much bottled up. But what could we do? To talk was to relive it. How could we expect our family and friends to understand?

I forced myself to sit down with DP. It was his ship and I had an obligation to recount the story, but I gave him the only barest outline and he didn't pry any further. He was more understanding and considerate than I expected, for the truth was I had refused help when I should have accepted it but he didn't see it that way.

"No," he said flatly. "You made a decision. You tried to save the charter. You did what I paid you to do and you couldn't foresee the future. That charter was your responsibility. A captain has to do everything he can to bring the charter to port."

He walked to his window and looked across the sloping fields covered with snow. Often when he was deep in thought, he'd stand at his window and he could look down the meadow to the bay. In the spring, he would build a new ship. Men and horses were already in the woods cutting and hauling out the first logs for a schooner. He planned to call it the *OK*.

He'd lost ships and he worried about trade. "Our friends in the United States have been very preoccupied but the Republicans are Protectionists." His brig *Toronto* and barque *Harmony* were running charters and he was trying to keep them busy at all times. The nine-hundred-fifty ton *Northern Empire* under Captain Densmore had made money some years and less other years. Trade was always unpredictable. But returning sons to their mothers and fathers was never a question of uncertainty.

"You saved the men. Imagine what a relief that is to us," he sighed and turned to me. "It's always been risky business. Go home, Allan. Get your strength back. The insurance will cover the *Dove* and I've got other ships to worry about."

He didn't offer me anything and I didn't ask. In the following days I felt a great sense of failure come over me.

I remember the inordinate kindness of my parents during those days. My mother told me she had prayed as hard for John and me and our crew as when the girls died. We were so long overdue she feared we were lost forever. But in the ordeal, she found her faith again.

"When the Lord took my third child all those years ago, I felt He deserted me. Your safe arrival has given me back everything I thought I had lost."

"There's nothing like farm work to make a man feel good," my father said half in jest, trying to pull up my spirits. We were in the wagon going over Economy Mountain to Five Islands.

"You're taking it hard, but you're not the first man to lose his ship and I can assure you right now that you won't be the last."

"Father, two ships have gone from under me."

"What of it? You were the skipper on one and mate of the other. Many captains lost a greater number and died contented old men in their beds."

"You don't understand, Father. It was my first command, my first crossing. It's a bad omen. I had a chance for assistance and turned it down. I made a bad mistake that every man on that ship paid for."

"Hogwash! Every bit of it is nonsense! Every man on that ship respects you for saving his life. You tried to save the charter. That's what you were supposed to do. You made no mistake."

People said my father and I had our grandfather's characteristics. Tall and slender build with ruffled brown hair and high cheek bones. He had understood my desire to go off to sea although he had never put it in words. On that day in the wagon, he said quietly, "If any good has come of it, John is cured of the sea and your mother is relieved. Now, if she could only convince you to stay on land, her life would be complete." He paused. "The farm would be yours, you know, Allan. You're the eldest."

He looked away. We were on top of the mountain looking down on the farms on the valley floor. Ahead of us, the coast ran off towards Parrsboro in the morning mist. The incoming tide caught the sun and we were quiet for a while, watching the silvery waters. Then he spoke.

"I know it must have been awful out there. I can see it in John's eyes. The first day you were home, him so weak and pale, telling his mother he would never go to sea again. Will you?"

"Yes," I replied and we didn't talk anymore.

My father wanted our farm to continue yet neither John nor I had the inclination or desire to farm. I was for the sea and John made more money not being a farmer.

John kept his word. He became a carpenter in the shipyard, saved his money and bought shares in the vessels he worked on. Those vessels made more money and he bought more shares. He married Addie, who had to be the craziest woman on the shore, and built a house at the other end of the farmyard, just behind the orchard.

"You're missin' the sea, brother, is that it? You want to go back. What happened out there isn't going to stop you?" John asked.

I didn't answer. I needed work and maybe needed the sea. For the good and bad of it, the sea was me and I was the sea.

I sat on our front steps sipping tea as big snowflakes fell on me. Darkness would come while I was ambling along the shore. At night, I'd read Boswell's *Life of Johnson* and Macaulay's *Essays* and at dawn I'd look over the water.

I saw Laura only a few times that year. She was teaching in Bass River and our paths had gone in different directions. She and her mother came to tea one afternoon. I don't know how that was arranged but I suspect my mother wanted to take my mind off matters that kept me brooding. I remained restless and fidgety. A sailor without a ship.

A month after Laura had come for tea I wrote her a note. Perhaps I wrote it out of boredom. Perhaps I felt something was left unsaid, although I had no idea what. The note turned into a rambling epistle that I could not send. I tried again a few days later with similar results. I didn't know what I wanted to say. I wanted to know her better, to probe beneath those dark mysterious eyes. I waited and did nothing. She would be home in the spring and I would make it a point to see her.

It wasn't to be.

In late April, Josiah Soley drove two prancing horses down the winding shore road to our farm and had tea with us. Josiah was DP's brother and like DP he was a farmer and lumberman who invested in ships and trade. He was building a three-hundred-thirty ton brig in Great Village called the *Busy Bee*. He was looking for a captain.

"Captain Densmore has bought shares in my vessel. Both the captain and DP recommend you as master."

I did not hesitate, not for a moment. My mother, father and John were astonished when I jumped from my chair. "If you're offering me the command, I'll take it."

Josiah raised his eyebrows and smiled, "You're not what I would call a hard bargainer."

I was back in New York unloading lumber when Laura came home for the summer. I then sailed into the heat of the equator bound for Brazil. Our paths wouldn't cross that year.

My return to sea was what I needed. I regained my confidence and felt at peace again. It was only on a return voyage to the Irish Sea that it bothered me. We were two hundred miles below the Mersey where the sea funnels into the wide river, taking you up to Liverpool. It started to rain and a chill ran down me. I experienced an unnatural worry about my ship and crew. It was fear. I knew the taste, the sour bile it leaves in your mouth. We had run charters to New England, Britain and the West Indies and South America but only in the Irish Sea did I feel the pungent taste and feel the beat quicken in my chest. I had seen the face of death, heard the haunting cries of men turned to animals. I knew fear but only on the chop of the Irish Sea did it imprison me.

A year later arriving with rum and sugar in New York, there was a letter waiting for me at the consulate. It was from Josiah and he had big news. His scrawling hand gave me the address of the company wanting a charter to China.

The St. James Trading Company was on Factory Road near the East River. A huge plaque on the brick building announced its name and beginnings – "Est. 1827." Men with warm hands and big stomachs said they were expecting me. They had already made the deal with Josiah, pending the readiness of my ship.

The *Busy Bee* was to take Virginian tobacco up the Canton River above Hong Kong. They were arranging a return charter of Chinese spices and rice to New York. The company president, a man named Lang, told me they had an agent in China who looked after their affairs. He would arrange the unloading of the tobacco, the loading of the spices and any demurrage charges would be their responsibility.

The voyage was my biggest navigational challenge. I had to purchase charts for oceans I had never sailed, plot courses I had never plotted. My first mate was a man named Benjamin and we poured over the charts, setting a course that took us to the other side of the world. We would re-supply at Cape Town on the point of Africa, a port accustomed to refitting whalers. From there we would go up the Indian Ocean and sail into the Sunda Strait between Java and Sumatra then into the China Sea.

With more water and provisions than we'd ever carried and our holds full of sweet smelling tobacco, we left South Street on a windy Tuesday morning with representatives of the St. James Trading Company waving farewell from the dock. We sailed south to catch the trade winds to Africa and crossed the Atlantic, coming in below the Tropic of Capricorn and down the coast to Capetown. For several days running, we saw great pods of whales. The crew was telling each other if the ship had been a whaler we'd be rich. Then, as suddenly as they came, the whales disappeared.

We had weeks of good weather and two mid-Atlantic gales, one so vicious we lay to under the lower topsail. Sanford, our second mate, was swept overboard but by all the power of God in Heaven he was saved. We made the Cape of Good Hope in forty-two days.

All I remember of Cape Town is dusty streets and hard-headed Dutch merchants. They were tough bargainers and tried to squeeze the last shilling out of you. When I tried to get a better price they pretended they didn't understand, but they spoke English as well as anyone. As Mr. Benjamin said, "There's nowhere else for a thousand miles, so they've got you."

In the Indian Ocean we were moving towards the equator again and the water was warm and blue. We saw plenty of American whalers, but no whales. There were large schools of small, colourful fish that often travelled in front of us, jumping out of the water like silver raindrops in the sun. There were strange fishing boats with brown men who waved and chanted a foreign language. It got hotter, then cooler but our winds remained steady and at daybreak of our ninety-seventh day from New York, we sailed into the mass of shipping in Hong Kong harbour.

There were hundreds of brigs, full-rigged ships and thousands of small sampans with one ribbed sail. Even at dawn there was chanting and excitement on the water. It was unlike any port I'd ever seen.

Hong Kong is an island. The town itself is called Victoria. It looked more English than Liverpool. Behind the town is a great sloping mountain, steeper than Economy Mountain but just as empty. A little steamboat pulled us next to a British full-rigged ship. The captain told me he made regular charters carrying opium from India.

"It's a fine run with a guaranteed market," he informed me.

After dropping anchor we rowed through the sampans to the customs house where I declared my cargo. Getting around China was not as perplexing as I expected. Many of the merchants along the waterfront spoke English.

Donald C. Dutsworth or Duts, as everyone called him, had worked for the St. James Trading Company for seventeen years. His parents had been missionaries and he was born in China. He took me around Victoria in a covered two-wheel carriage pulled by a skinny little man who could run at an incredible speed and ferry us through very crowded streets while Duts explained the local landmarks. He said entire families spent their lives on the harbour sampans, without ever having a home on land.

My crew was certainly ready for some dry land. They wanted to go ashore but Duts warned them to stay away from the opium dens and the brothels. What might be safe for Chinese would not necessarily be safe for foreigners.

He explained there had been tension in China for the past thirty years, ever since the Opium War. China had tried to restrict British ships from bringing in opium. It was a profitable business and Westminster refused. The dispute led to a war which the British won. In doing so they demanded even more Chinese ports be open to them, with the absolute right to sell opium to the masses.

"They are forbidden by law from selling it to their own people, so they sell it to the Chinese. It is a curse to this country," Duts said with bitterness.

I did accounts and gave each man a draw of his wages, keeping two watches on ship. The crew's initial enthusiasm was gone after a couple of days and so was their money.

Two days later a longboat manned by a dozen men poled us up the river. The farther from Hong Kong, the more mysterious the country. At one point we passed a cemetery that stretched thirty miles. Duts said it held a hundred generations of Chinese families. Cemeteries and the rivers were the reasons China had no railways. People refused to disturb ancestors, and fear that trains would replace the livelihood of the thousands who live and work on the river systems, led the Chinese to refuse to lay tracks.

We tied up below Canton and Duts took me to the island of Shameen, across the river from the city. The huge mansions were owned by British and Germans. The Chinese were not permitted on the exclusive island unless they were domestics working there.

Opulence was everywhere. The large branches of banyan trees formed a canopy over the roads past the splendid houses. The wide driveways permitting two carriages to pass led to grand courtyards and wide verandas.

We spent the night at the home of Duts's friend, Robert Norwood, formerly of Boston. The Norwoods loved news from home and as I spent considerable time in Boston, I could tell them items of interest from their city. Their home was large and comfortable with Chinese servants on every floor. When I went to bed that night there was a flower on my pillow.

In the morning we crossed the long bridge to Canton. I remember that day because there was an event that burned into my mind, over-shadowing everything else that happened during my voyage to the Orient.

China was different but little did I understand how different. The contrast between Shameen and Canton was striking. The city itself was a noisy ribbon of criss-crossing, crowded streets filled with half-naked vendors and dark alleys. Chickens and small creatures in wooden cages contributed to the constant bedlam of the merchants calling to custom-ers and to the coolies.

It was in the afternoon that we came upon the gruesome site that I have never forgotten. One of those things decades never dim.

Duts was taking us along the part of the city next to the river. Sever-al men were kneeling on the ground as we happened by and Duts order the little man pulling our rickshaw to stop. This was the weekly execu-tion. The kneeling men had their hands tied behind their backs. Fifty or sixty people were standing around, including a dozen guards with rifles. They wore tan uniforms with peaked hats and there was an element of cordiality between the soldiers and onlookers. It was almost a festive mood and I thought it was a theatrical event for the delight of the on-lookers. Duts spoke Chinese to some of the soldiers who told us these men were pirates. Before he had finished giving me the details of their crime, a stout Chinese man in a bright silk kimono stepped out of the crowd flashing a huge sword. Before I could catch my breath, his blade flashed in a mighty arc as with one swipe he severed the first man's head.

It was so fast and stupefying I was sickened. Many of the onlookers kept talking as the severed head rolled on the ground. Swooshing through the air again, the blade came down on the second neck and dis-connected the head from the body. The blade was never smeared with blood and the sun reflected on the shiny steel with every swoop in the air. It was a dance. A dance of death. A flicker in the sun, a rolling head, a step to the next man. Again the flicker, the sun, the severed head. Never did the stocky executioner need a second blow. It was a precision dance and the condemned died without protest. There were no plain-tive wails, no requests for mercy. The heads just rolled, mouths open, dim eyes staring skyward. Up went the blade and down again. One, two, three. I lost count, looked away: ten, eleven, twelve, thirteen. Thirteen heads. It had taken no time at all. No prayers, no ceremony.

Thirteen bodies pumping blood and the onlookers still talking.

When the horror was over, a little man ran to the front and set up his box camera. The laughing guards had their photograph taken behind the headless bodies. The little man then gestured for us to have our photographs taken. I shook my head.

Duts turned to me. "Welcome to China, Captain Graham."

"Yes," I replied, "I certainly know it isn't home."

On my ship that evening, I told Duts such barbarity should never happen in a Christian country.

"You're not in a Christian country. You're in China. Never forget that."

I never did and that event has stayed with me to this day.

I learned that night from Duts that the Chinese are people of extremes. They can be the most courteous, kindest people on earth. They can also be the cruelest. The main thing he wanted me to know was that they were different and the fact was, foreigners can't see the world as Chinese do.

"I love this country," I remember him saying. "It is my country and I suppose to you it seems very strange, but I have never known any other place."

One thing was certain – little in China was done in secret. Opium and executions all in the open. Chinese officials could be bribed openly, and I learned policemen could be bought on the street when you needed them.

I learned that just a few days later, when two of my crew had to be rescued from the clutches of a pleasure palace by Duts and myself. Duts hired two policemen on the spot.

An able seaman named Smith ran breathless back to the *Busy Bee* at midday to report that two of the crew were being beaten and robbed in some shameful place they had stumbled into. Dutsworth happened to be on board going over our manifest and he knew what to do. Once we got into Canton, Duts hired one, then another policeman as we followed Smith down narrow, crowded streets. He lost his way twice, but finally found the alley he'd run out of. At the end of the alley was a painted door. The policemen rushed in, yelling at the top of their lungs.

A dozen women and undressed patrons scurried off in different directions like hermit crabs under a rock. There was more yelling by the policemen as they rushed upstairs and began a great commotion in the hall. Balding men, Chinese and English, were rushing around, putting pieces of their clothes on as the yelling policemen beat on the bamboo doors then flung them open. My sailors were in the back of the building on the ground, intoxicated and bloody but not badly hurt. I tried to make them pay Duts back for what he had given the policemen but their wages were gone. I paid Duts and took it out of future wages. Then I confined the two idiots to the ship. They didn't go ashore again.

The next day my cook got into a fight on the docks over a misunderstanding. He was glassy-eyed and dumbfounded when Benjamin hauled him aboard.

"It's that damned opium that's making them that way," he said.

Duts said such problems were common on ships except that most captains, unless they really needed a man, wouldn't bother rescuing one of their men in trouble. If a sailor was in jail or failed to report on time, he was left behind. Many sailors remained stranded thousands of miles from home, without any money or the ability to speak the language.

I had met sailors stranded in foreign ports. Cursed with drink as their ship raises anchor, they awake penniless. A man can starve to death in the middle of a city if he doesn't know the language. Try to steal and it's off with your hand or your head.

I never left a man unless he wanted to be.

I met a Chinese man years ago in Baltimore. His skin was like aged parchment and the backs of his hands had the spots of a long life. He told me the story of a captain who had stranded him. He didn't know the captain's name or the name of the ship because he neither spoke nor read English at that time. The man said it had happened in 1859. He and two shipmates were in Shanghai and were offered pay and passage to the United States and papers if they signed on. But there was no pay or papers. They were left on the docks of Baltimore. He spent months escaping authorities, finding relatives, getting false papers. He worked day and night as a dishwasher in a place where he was often beaten and most times not paid. He learned to cook and worked sixteen hours a day, seven days a week. He finally saved enough to marry and his wife worked with him. Years later they bought the little café we were sitting in.

He was proud now, he said. He and his wife were official citizens of the United States. But he never forgot. He told me he set up his business near the waterfront so he might have a chance of seeing that captain again. He always planned to kill him. But by then he doubted he would. He had children, grandchildren and a house. Maybe he would just cripple the man, breaking his arms and legs. Yes, he thought that would be fine. It was mid afternoon and his place was empty. My ship was in repair and I had plenty of time to listen to his story as he poured tea and rum for both of us. Finally, I asked him to describe the captain who had stranded him. He knew every whisker of the man, every detail, including the jagged scar above the eye, a deep tearing cut intended to kill.

When Captain Thompson was dying, I told him the Chinese man's story to see if there would be some flicker in his eyes, any sign of recognition.

"His place in Baltimore was called the Blue Moon Café. You ever been there? It's right on the waterfront."

Cagey old fox. He studied my face and was saved by his cough. The harder he coughed the more his face turned rosy, except for that jagged scar above his right eye that stayed absolutely white.

My men all left China with me. It was a year before the *Busy Bee* sailed into Parrsboro. We had crossed most of the oceans of the world and were making money. I was a successful master mariner and it was time to have my own home and someone to come home to. Sadie no longer haunted me. I was finally free.

I had received two letters from my mother in the seventeen months I'd been away and she had not written anything about Laura Webster. If there had been a marriage, or even an engagement, she would have included the news, I was certain.

There was much I admired in Laura. She was stable, dependable, not given to the flights of fancy. Three days after arriving home I put on my best suit and called on her.

"Laura will be happy to see you, Allan," her mother smiled, uncertain of what to say next. Laura was out with Billy Lewis. "They've gone for a picnic with the Elliotts on the Five Islands beach."

"I will call again."

When I went back a few days later she was out with Billy Lewis again. This time I was invited in for tea.

"May I ask a question?" I inquired, putting down my teacup. "She and Billy, are they, well, is Billy her beau?"

The question made Mrs. Webster's eyes flutter and she hesitated. "I'm not exactly sure. You know how secretive Laura can be. She really doesn't tell me and I don't pry. They have been seeing each other a lot lately, but I'm uncertain if they are serious. I can't decide if Laura is serious."

"Oh?" I replied, hoping for more.

"I just don't know. But Captain Graham, perhaps you should call again. Thursday. I will ensure she is here Thursday."

"Maybe you can tell Laura I'll drop by Thursday around two."

"Yes, I will. I'm sorry you came all this way again."

"It's not far. Thank you, Mrs. Webster."

I got in my wagon and started back around the shore. Across the cove I could see Lower Economy and the red bluffs below my father's farm, although the farm was hidden in the trees. The summer breeze swirled light clouds of dust from the dry road. Out in the bay gulls glided over the water. I stopped and took off my jacket and tie, convinced I was too late. I had waited too long. A raven screeched from the dark woods on the mountain. I looked across the bay to the place where I would like to build a house below my father's in the glen. I wondered why I had never written Laura. The raven continued to screech.

The next Thursday, Laura was waiting on her front steps. Her hair was pulled back in what they would call the Gibson Girl look. She wore a soft yellow, cotton dress that gave a contrast to her dark eyes and black hair. She looked prettier than I had ever seen her.

"Allan." She held out her hand as if she knew I felt the need to touch her.

She led me down the path to the beach. It had been a long time since we'd been alone and we were a little awkward in each other's company. Out of nervousness, I suppose, I started talking. Usually I'm a quiet man like my father, a man who keeps his counsel to himself, but I felt the need to discover Laura and to let her discover me. I related how we'd had a prosperous year on the *Busy Bee* and she told me about teaching and how she loved it. Then I told her about China, about Hong Kong and Canton and the millions of people on the streets and on the water. She listened attentively. She became embarrassed when I moved onto the *Dove* but I wanted her to know, maybe not everything, but enough. I told her things I hadn't shared with my parents, things I had not shared with DP. I realised I was talking too much and, as quickly as I started, I stopped. The silence was less strained. We walked and listened to the sounds of the shore. Hundreds of little sand birds were scurrying just ahead of us, almost under our feet. Then they would rush away in a group, peck in the sand and wait for us to catch up with them.

"And you?" I finally asked. "What is your life like?"

She told me more about her school and her students. At some point I probably cut her off because I interjected, "What about Billy?"

She did not blush but smiled and said, "Billy is a friend."

"But more perhaps?" I asked.

"Yes, he would like to be more, but I am not certain."

"Why, if I may be so bold?"

She looked at me. "Billy expects me to defer to him in all matters. As a wife I would expect to be deferential to my husband in many aspects of married life but certainly not all. If I defer to him on everything, I will not be his wife as much as his servant. It also means I will have to defer to his mother as well."

"You and Billy have done much talking about this?"

"Yes. Too much talking. He knows how I feel but he persists and so I hesitate." She paused for a minute, uncertain if she should say more. "Then there is you," she said softly.

I felt of surge of warmth rush through my veins. "Me?" I asked.

"Yes, you. I was never certain of your intentions, Allan."

"My intentions have not always been clear to me," I replied. "Not until recently anyway. However, now I have a better understanding of where my heart belongs." We stopped at that point and I put my arms around her. We stayed in that embrace until the first tiny waves of the incoming tide lapped around our feet. Sea gulls shrieked far overhead as though approving of our embrace and I knew that I loved Laura Webster.

Laura's mother did not hide her enthusiasm or her surprise. She opened her arms to Laura and both women wept. Then Mrs. Webster embraced me. Her daughter would marry me. Being deferential in all things was not an issue. A captain's wife can not be deferential. She is often alone for months or even years. Decisions can't pile up like unused firewood, waiting for the man of the house to arrive. I was the skipper on water, but on land, decisions about the home and family belonged to the captain's wife. Laura was well qualified.

It would be a year before we were married. I had made my choice and, having done so, I breathed easier. I had been at the crossroads and I was finally free.

Laura and I would have a home built in the glen, sheltered by the side of the hill, below my father's house. We would build two stories, large enough for children and a parlour with windows big enough to let in the sun.

After the planning it was back to sea. The *Busy Bee* took a charter of lumber to Boston. But trade with the American states was changing. DP worried about high tariffs on lumber as the protectionists in Washington were bringing their policies to bear. He got us charters in the south and we sailed empty to Cuba and brought back sugar and rum to New York.

It was a hot, sunny morning when we sailed up the East River and I saw Sadie Muise waiting on the dock.

As the pilot boat nosed the *Busy Bee* into the jetty I didn't allow myself to look at her. We were nudging up against a big Norwegian whaler and its massive grapples were catching our rigging; I was dispatching sailors to untangle the lines before damage was done. I knew she was watching me. I could feel her eyes on the back of my neck. I felt naked and vulnerable in her stare. I can see her yet, so out of place amid the commodities of the marine trade, push carts, barrels of whale oil, stacks of rope, sea chains. Longshoremen in sweat-soaked shirts, winking at each other, showing tobacco stained teeth with their knowing smiles. Never for long did they take their eyes off the tall, picturesque beauty in a dress that came alive in the breeze. She took two steps towards my ship and her garment reflected the thousand different shades of silvery blue that shimmered in the light.

She waited, indifferent to her surroundings. I took my time. When I finally approached her, she smiled at me and I was unduly courteous, wanting to keep her at a distance. Time had etched little lines on her face, the faint suggestions of years lived. Strangely they did not distract from her beauty, but somehow only intensified it. Sadie defied time.

We had lunch the next day near her new flat on Fifth Avenue. I asked how she had known I was coming into port.

"It wasn't difficult," she said. "I have a friend who knows someone in the harbour master's office. And you know they have lists of all ships berthing, where they're from and the name of the captain. When ship's agents reserve berths they have to supply that information, so it wasn't difficult. I didn't know the name of your ship but they found your name and they expected you on the 24th, so here I am."

"But we were two days late," I interrupted.

"Yes. Well, I came those days."

She played with her salad, running her fork over the bits of lobster and lettuce as I had seen her do so many times.

"And waited?" I asked.

"Yes, for some time," she paused, " I waited."

"You must have really wanted to see me," I replied and was sorry because it gave her an opening.

"I always want to see you Allan," she said softly.

"I'm getting married," I cut it in quickly, unwilling to let her carry me away.

"Congratulations."

She said it quietly, offhandedly, as if the news was unimportant. She took another nibble and turned her eyes on me. "So let me ask you the two important questions. First, are you happy?"

"Yes," I replied without hesitation. I had to cut her down, keep her under control. I had to contain her at all times. I felt my heart racing as if I was in some contest with this woman. A contest I was always in danger of losing.

We continued our conversation. She had left her husband and been employed as a nanny to take care of the children of a prominent New York doctor. I did not press her on their relationship but he had loaned her the money to buy half interest in a Fifth Avenue dress shop. She was making it a success and was in her glory. It made her happy that she was one of the few women business proprietors in a growing and bustling New York. When Sadie was happy, Sadie was even more desirable.

"Now the second question regarding your coming nuptials." She raised her head with one eyebrow arched just enough. "Do you love her?"

There was a silence. A deadly second when my defenses missed a beat but it was enough. I said yes too loudly and with too much strength. Victory was hers.

"By the way. What is your married name? I never really knew," I said, trying to regain my position, to take that look of triumph out of her eyes. It was too late and she ignored me.

"You don't. Do you? You don't love her. It's written on your face."

"You're wrong. I love her deeply," I replied, trying to sound calm.

"I don't believe you, you're not telling me the truth. You don't!"

"I do."

"No. No, you don't. I know when you're being truthful."

"You don't."

"Oh, yes. I have seen you in truth." She was thinking of the canopied bed. "I have seen you in absolute truth, my dearest Captain." She touched my arm. I was defenseless.

She had done what she could always do, cut through my deceit and unmask me. I was more determined not to bend, not to twist to her, to keep her at a distance.

In the following days, amid ship business and arranging charters, we had innocent encounters as old friends and nothing more. But if I ignored her she would come to the ship to fetch me, although I preferred she stayed away.

She had a small flat above her dress shop. It was not the grand place she had shared with her husband and the canopied bed was gone. Things had a way of coming and going in Sadie's life. I wondered why I was the exception. As the days went by I could feel my desire growing just touch her, to feel her breath on my cheek. She was winning and we both knew it.

I was confused beyond belief. I could not live with such a contradiction boiling inside me. Laura was too fine a woman to be deceived. I loved Laura, I was certain. But was love going to be enough? She had a right to expect all of me and I was no longer confident she could have it all. Sadie seemed to possess just enough to make me an unworthy husband.

I wrote a long letter to Laura, trying in my inept manner, to explain things as best I could. I couldn't explain them to myself, let alone to someone I loved. The attempts were messy and convoluted. Unfinished letter after letter, the words not coming in any satisfactory order. The wastebasket in my cabin held the crumpled paper that I'd end up throwing overboard late at night.

I went back to Sadie's flat the evening before we sailed. My limbs felt numb and disconnected, carrying a heavy body that didn't belong to me. Walking, but not of my own free will. Twice, I was almost struck by charging carriages, the hot vapours of the horses breath on my face and hack drivers hectoring me with warnings to be careful. Sadie opened the door and we fell into each other's arms. Before daylight I kissed her lightly on the cheek as she lay sleeping. "This is goodbye, dear one. This is goodbye for good and may life be kind to you." She stirred slightly and I left her sleeping.

All the way down the coast to Cuba, into the sweltering winds of the West Indies I was wretched. I could never have foreseen that such turmoil would embroil me. I would tell Laura. Tell her everything, that there had been another woman I did not have the courage to stay away from. When I said this out loud, actually spoke the words, they sounded trifling and silly. One woman in one port that I could not resist. How ridiculous it sounded.

It was months before I returned home but Laura had read between the lines of my stilted letters.

"You are very quiet, Allan," she said politely.

"Yes, I know. There is much on my mind right now."

"The wedding is planned, the stone has been delivered and our cellar is dug. They will start framing soon. My sister and I are making our dresses, with Mother's help. If you have worries, I hope they are not connected with our wedding plans," she said and kissed me on the cheek.

"I love you, Laura," I said suddenly, grabbing her in such a strong embrace I startled her and she pulled away.

"Oh my, Allan." She coughed, trying to catch her breath. "My darling," she whispered as she settled into my arms. "It won't be long and you will have me completely as I will have you."

I buried my face in her hair while a great wave of guilt and shame washed over me. I was, as Will Thompson told me many times, too prone to such feelings.

There were times when Laura felt my silence, or something else surging through me, was cause for greater concern. She had been reading reports in the paper of Susan B. Anthony and her supporters, who were encouraging woman to press for the vote. Even being arrested didn't stop them as they called for women to be more forthright and independent.

"I will release you from your promise, Allan," she repeated again one evening, impressing upon me her seriousness. "It is not shameful now for either of us to be released from this pledge. I can teach. I will not be disgraced."

At home along the Economy Shore, hundreds of miles from New York, Sadie Muise was but a dream. At such a distance I had control of her. She was less wily, less difficult. I had her bottled up. I swore and cursed and prayed to myself that I would keep her that way.

New York reflected Sadie. With its bustling traffic and commerce, its crowded streets and cafés, the city was noise and chaos. It wasn't growing as much as galloping like a wild horse. There were new pinnacles in the skyline with every docking. The Irish and the Italians had sections of the city they called their own. Newcomers were flooding into the harbour every day. Brooklyn had open fields that were turned into streets overnight, surrounded by shanties, homes and hotels, porters and policemen. Huge markets sprang up with fruit stalls and fishmongers. New parts turned grimy overnight and looked old. New York was teeming. Its momentum and movement, unlike any other city, set my nerves on edge. New York suited Sadie. Her flightiness and need for change matched the city. She fit the place. But I felt like a foreigner within myself, trying to identify this man I didn't know.

While New York was frantic, the soft sea breezes of Nova Scotia soothed me. The festering burn of my conscience dissipated in the swaying pine trees dotting the side of Economy Mountain. Laura and I took long walks through the fields and along the shore. Every time I came home it was as if I was met by a changed fiancée. It was still Laura, still the woman I loved, just more certain of herself as I was less certain of me. When we were together I tried to understand the subtle changes my months away had made. I watched her as she walked, studying her manners and movements. I liked the way she swept back a strand of hair or bent the branches of a white pine to pass by, the way she stooped to pick wild asters in the meadows. She was everything Sadie was not. Laura had opinions while Sadie had preferences. Laura saw a person's duty as important. Sadie saw only her own needs as important. Laura opposed children working in the mines, Sadie never thought about miners, "with all that filth." Values mattered to Laura. Fashion mattered to Sadie. Laura never wavered while Sadie wavered constantly. There was no choice. How could there be?

Trade had slacked off but DP never stopped looking. We had a charter to load Springhill coal in Parrsboro for the Boston market and then we'd go to New York to re-supply with food and water and then on to Cuba. Sailing down the coast away from Laura, I felt renewed. Every sunset I repeated my resolve. We were going to New York but not for long, and I would not see Sadie.

Two weeks before the wedding I was surprised to receive the letter from Sadie. It had been months since I'd seen her, yet she sounded as if we had been together only days before, as if time hadn't moved from the morning I'd kissed her goodbye in her flat on Fifth Avenue. She begged me to come to New York and take her away. I walked through the snow to the bluff in front of my father's farm. The tide was full and I intended to read her letter once and tear it up and throw the pieces into the sea. But I read her message several times, feeling my heart pounding in my chest. I spent a long time looking out into the bay, the letter still in my hand. Then I folded it and slipped it into my pocket.

Laura and I were married on January 8th, 1876 at the Presbyterian Church in Five Islands. It was a sunny, cold day with wind swirling the snow on the ground. Brother John stood with me and Laura's sisters were her bridesmaids. I had chosen. Chosen again really, and I was happy. We built our house and kept the trees that lined our driveway. From the front door I could see the roof of my father's house, farther up the hill. At the end of the driveway I could see the bay.

A year later, James Bertrand was born. I held my son, a twisting, squirming, pink infant who grabbed at my finger with his little hand and I knew I had won my battle.

I sailed away a happy and contented man. My struggle was behind me. My resolve and vows had given me freedom.

While I was at the wheel on a moonlit night off the coast of Maine, there appeared a reflection on the water that reminded me of the burning ship outside Charleston Harbour. For an instant I saw Sadie's smiling face on the silvery waves and a searing pain tore through me.

Chapter Fourteen

When I pass the church in Five Islands I look the other way, avert my eyes and study the houses and fields on the other side of the road. There are too many memories connected with the church. That little white building had played a major part in my life. Each chapter has been touched by its timbers and there is one more for it to play. A final chapter, "Into thy hands, dear Father...."

I remember the day of my wedding, so blustery and windy with snow cascading and swirling in the winter sun. I waited at the altar at the front of the church, standing next to my brother, the best man. The pews were full, the slow organ music filled the air around us. Every time I entered that church I crossed the threshold with my eyes closed for a second or two, just to postpone the haunting memory of the funerals of my sisters. Even on my wedding day with the music, the musty odour of antiquation, the pews – there was nowhere to look and not feel that heartbreaking wariness of a family ripped asunder. I half turned for a moment and studied the congregation. I know I saw my family sitting where we always sat and my sisters had come back for my special occasion. Mary, Martha and Maria, sitting right between Father and Mother, smiling at me.

That little church was essential to our family life – and death. It was our core. Every Sunday we hitched the wagon and came over the mountain. We prayed there, asked God to give us good crops and protect us from evil. We went to weddings, funerals of friends and neighbours. We witnessed the baptisms of babies whose parents farmed next to us. As youngsters we tried to be fetching or coy at church socials to catch the eye of a certain person. We pitched horseshoes, had three-legged races and ate ice cream at Sunday school picnics. It was just outside the church that two boys beat themselves silly one day for the right to take my sister home. She was pouting by the side of my parents and already over Economy Mountain. It was also in that very church the young preacher had told such outrageous lies about Will Thompson that the congregation prayed for the preacher.

As a bridegroom on that winter day I stood at the front of that church and remembered everything about my thirteenth year.

"Pray for the Graham girls who have been stricken with diphtheria." and "Rock of Ages, cleft for me … "

There I stood in new shoes, waiting for my bride and remembering the grief of my father at their funerals, so stricken by the time Maria had died he could hardly stand and I loved him more at that moment than any time in my life. He recovered enough during the winter to stand straight again and walk without being bowed. The grief never left him, but I did. In the spring I went to sea. He didn't blame me. He let me know that by hugging me hard when I left, my sea bag on my back and my father clinging to me. It was the only time he ever hugged me, but it was the most important time. He didn't blame me, even if I blamed myself.

I wanted to divert my attention to something happier, so as a groom I would have a less grim countenance. I remember looking toward the ceiling and wondering how many hymns, how many notes had risen heavenward, how many sermons had echoed off the walls, and then Laura was coming down the aisle. My marriage, my parents funerals, my sisters, church socials. So much of me oozing out of one small church. I turn my head. I don't need to look. I know.

Chapter Fifteen

I've been up in the attic again going through old junk without any idea of what I'm looking for. You can't imagine what a man collects in his lifetime. Dusty knickknacks that were once in our parlour. Things that Laura would remove while I was at sea, like the spears from the African coast and wood vases from China. My sea chest still contains woolens from the Hebrides, a mother-of-pearl lamp that burns whale oil from someplace and a piece of Graham tartan. I feel the rough fabric of "The Graham of Montrose."

As a young man I'd had such a burning desire to see Scotland. My father had filled us with vivid images of the villages and hills he'd left behind. John and I would sit by the stove and listen to the stories about our ancestors. Father wasn't much of a talker until he got on to William Wallace, Robert the Bruce and the great Scottish battles. The Reivers, including the clan Graham, who were those border raiders that brought centuries of instability to the borderlands between England and Scotland, was another favourite story.

I signed off in Liverpool and took the train north, watching the rolling hills instead of the rolling waves. I spent two months tramping through the heather of Scotland, down the Great Glen to Fort William, back to Glencoe where the MacDonalds were massacred, then on to the great shipyards of Glasgow. The eerie moor of Culloden was cold even in the summer sun. I touched the stone where Wallace fought and lost at Falkirk. I met my cousins near Dumfries and strolled to the Globe tavern where Robbie Burns wrote and drank.

I crossed the border back into England and heard Mr. Charles Dickens do a reading in Carlyle. Dickens had a long pointed beard and amid much applause he started reading in a very low voice that made the audience strain to hear his words. As the story moved on, almost imperceptibly his voice grew stronger. He read several passages from a number of his finest books. He would hold the book in his left hand and often gesture with his right to emphasise a particular point. As he spoke the words of Mr. Fagan in *Oliver Twist*, I remember his slender fingers stabbing the air, his voice rising to a new height and rolling every syllable off his tongue. The audience was spellbound. I lost track of time so engrossed I became. Many stayed behind to shake his hand, including myself. Up close the great man looked weary and tired. Within a year he was dead but on the stage, Mr. Charles Dickens held an immense power.

When I returned to Liverpool I sought to sign on a ship. The agent told me there was one vessel that was leaving for Canada and looking for a crew. That was the schooner *Mildred Bell*.

"There must be something else," I replied. "Anything."

Touring Scotland I had used up all my wages and the *Mildred Bell* needed a mate. I knew the ship and considered trying Southampton or London but that would mean an added expense.

"Nobody's looking right now, Mr. Graham. Only the *Bell*."

Will Thompson was leaning against the gunwale as if he had been expecting me. He knew where I'd been and what I'd been doing.

"So you've been tripping around with the highland lasses, eh? They're not nearly as accommodating as the whores in Marseilles," he said as he spit his tobacco over the side. "Now you're ready to go back to work?"

Within minutes he launched into an awful harangue about Captain Densmore, whom he disliked intensely. Then he offered me the mate's position. As I would come to learn, the *Mildred Bell* needed more than a mate. His previous crew had walked off, complaining about conditions.

"What they were really complaining about was me," he smiled. "I drive them too hard, the lazy bastards. We make sail on my ship, Mr. Graham, and we make profit. You better understand that before you sign on."

I signed on to show him I was not to be intimidated. It was our only crossing together, although for the next fifty years we had a connection on some plane that I was never able to explain.

Will Thompson confounded me yet he saved me. When I was distraught or needed help he suddenly turned up, a guardian angel with rum on his breath and a whore on his arm. What could I make of such a man who could repel and horrify with one hand while lifting you out of the water with the other?

He was insulting of my sea-going ability one minute and taking me to meet the ship's agents the next. We visited chandlers along the Liverpool docks as he bargained for rope and sailcloth.

I made up my mind I wouldn't be cowed by this man.

"You seem to have lost a lot of sail," I remarked, trying to needle him as we walked along the cobblestones. "Captain Densmore always said, making sail is only helpful if it moves you," I declared.

He didn't answer but he took me to supper in a noisy waterfront saloon and lectured me on making winds east to west and what he expected of his mate. During the following days he hired his crew, a few good sailors plus some scraps and misfits paid off by other vessels. I got the ship ready for sea.

The Franklin D. Miller Company had a mixed charter for Saint John including gin, sheets of Sheffield steel, wool and barrels of British beef.

Our last order of business in Liverpool was to provision the ship. Captain Thompson took great care he got the most of everything for the least amount of money. In many cases his decision was unsatisfactory and I told him so. We disagreed. He became snarly and I only became more adamant.

"If we're out longer than thirty days, we'll have no meat at all," I complained.

"We'll make do," he answered, looking at me harshly. "I suppose Densmore's ships carry more."

"Enough for the men to at least have decent food."

Will Thompson could ridicule. Without saying a word he could rile a man to such depths of anger, the enraged party would throw a fist into his face. He'd been in many fights and had been stabbed twice. The jagged, ripping scar over his eye was the result of a lunge by a stevedore. He carried another wound on his back. He was a bulldog of a man, with a barrel chest, huge hands and a head just a little too large for his body.

There were many stories about him along the shore, whispers of horrid things he had done, firsthand reports brought back by sailors. They said his crew had mutinied once and he held them at gunpoint. There were rumours that men jumped overboard, cursing his name as they disappeared into the black sea. He was supposed to have one family in England and another one in New York. His poor wife and son, they said. How dreadful! He was hateful to many people, but at certain times he could show great kindness. He particularly enjoyed helping people who were trying to avoid a rule or get out from under a regulation. If you wanted help breaking the law, Will Thompson was your man.

My father said Will Thompson was a bad man but a good sailor. He could take a ship anywhere and I learned some reasonable things from him. But I could never be like him. He enjoyed none of the natural respect accorded Captain Densmore. I told him this after signing off in Saint John and he scoffed.

"I taught you more in one voyage than you'll learn from Densmore in five years."

I walked down the gangplank into the Saint John fog with my sea bag over my shoulder, knowing that in some respects he was right. He had shown me the other side of running a ship: dealing with agents and shippers, bargaining for charters and how to get the best price. Captain Densmore had never done that but Captain Densmore had DP behind him and when it came to finding charters, DP was the best.

Will Thompson also taught me how to cheat, how to get more and how to take advantage. He demonstrated to me that you could sit in an office and tell the most incredible barefaced lie and be convincing. He did so with the Franklin D. Miller Company during our meetings in Liverpool.

Miller was the owner, puffy and prosperous behind his oak desk, his oily assistant sitting at his side with the open ledger. Thompson startling them by saying he couldn't take all their cargo, since one hold of his ship would soon be loaded with a charter he'd committed himself to previously. Straight-faced, he said one hold was committed for flour to Halifax. He knew they were urgently pressed to move their charter and he played his hand. He told Miller taking all their charter would cause him great inconvenience in time and money. It was, of course, subterfuge first and last but they were desperate. You could see the sweat on Miller's massive forehead, his Adam's apple moving up and down. I was watching Will Thompson play a gigantic fish. He did it without effort. Miller would pay a higher price for the captain's inconvenience. Will Thompson had a vulture's sense of sight and smell. He could read desperation as if reading a sea chart.

He was worse with stevedores. He made promises of rum and extra shillings if we were loaded in record time. Had the stevedores not stopped the pilot boat as it was ready to push us off the dock, had they not threatened to throw him and his cargo overboard, he would have gotten away with it. There was a real row and the harbour watch was called. Captain Thompson ordered the angry stevedores away from his ship, vehemently denying he owed them anything. The stevedores, as rough a lot as you were ever likely to see, were furious. Knives were drawn and heads were clubbed by the harbour watch. We left the jetty in a storm of curses and shaking fists. Rocks and belaying pins hurled past our heads.

In the open Atlantic I asked him if he wasn't worried about going back to Liverpool.

"Not a bit," he declared. "I'd go back tomorrow if I had to. In a year from now those stevedores will be working other docks or they'll be dead or swindled by bigger crooks than me! I'll deny any accusation they make."

He cut a plug of tobacco and then jabbed me in the ribs with his finger.

"I'll tell you this. If I want to load my ship fast I'll promise them again and you know something? They'll believe me. Why? Because they want to believe me. They're men who work with their backs, not their heads. They want to believe. Who knows, maybe they need to believe. People who need to believe are always suckers. People who need anything are always easy to cheat."

"But don't we all have needs?" I asked.

"Need and greed aren't the same things. I need a ship, grub, a warm woman once in a while, that's all. The rest is greed and because I know that, I can't be easily cheated. I get things because I know I can. I take chances because I like to and because I'm greedy. People talk of need when they really mean greed. Once you understand that you have a leg up."

He didn't believe in right or wrong. When he did something kind, loaned a hand to a down-and-out soul, it wasn't out of benevolence. There was something else that made him do it. Will Thompson was a pirate at heart who thought I could benefit from his experiences.

On his deathbed he told me, "I was a bastard, but unlike most bastards, I knew it."

Bastard and exceptional sailor. We'd been at sea a week on the *Mildred Bell* when he passed me the sextant.

"Look at the North Star," he said.

There seemed nothing unusual in its position, but Thompson told me of the anomaly of the star if you were sailing sou'westerly in the North Atlantic. He adjusted a two degree variance for an accurate compass reading. He corrected minor mistakes in my readings and told me I was poorly trained in navigation.

"You'd have us twenty miles south of Saint John. I'll have us dockside."

I had taken bearings by then across vast oceans and knew my ability, but when I walked off the *Mildred Bell* thirty-four days later I knew I was a better sailor.

I also knew I would never sail with him again.

It didn't matter much, he always took credit for my training anyway. He was fond of telling people that Densmore had taught me the basics but I'd come to him for the more advanced study.

Most of my life I hated to acknowledge how he could slice through subterfuge. I admit everything now, including how much I hated his truthfulness. I admit now he was a good man to have at your side when facing trouble. It was uncanny the way he had of showing up just when I needed him.

Once in New York when I was master of the *Busy Bee,* my young steward, a man named Murphy, got in a fight with a sailor from the Greek steamer tied up next to us. The Greek captain tried to break up the scuffle and Murphy, enraged over some injustice, punched him. The Greeks rallied around their captain and threw Murphy in chains. I was anxious to get underway but the Greeks refused to let him go and I was damned if I was leaving him in New York, a prisoner on a Greek ship.

The answer was to pay but it wasn't a cost I was prepared to justify to DP. I was squabbling with the Greek captain. He pretended to speak very little English and his mood was made far worse by the blue swelling under his eye. As we were bickering on the dock, Will Thompson appeared out of nowhere. He just came strolling along, smoking a big cigar and smelling of liquor. A woman half his age and rather unsteady on her feet was hanging on his arm. He listened to my problem and immediately boarded the Greek steamer. He gave them an ultimatum: release the steward or he'd be back in fifteen minutes with his entire crew and there wouldn't be enough left of their vessel to use for firewood. It was bluster, of course. His crew had quit on him and his ship had been seized for debts. Even when he didn't have the things he said he needed it didn't seem to bother him.

As we were being towed away from the dock at South Street with Murphy safely on board, I remember Thompson standing on the dock, grinning at me, looking like he owned the world. I can still see him standing there, his face flushed and beaming with that big cigar. His lady friend got caught up in our departure. She waved wildly, calling to us in a Cockney twang to have a safe voyage. Will Thompson smiled and patted her shoulder. I kept watching them for a long time. The dock, the ships, the woman, the waterfront: they all got smaller as we moved down the East River. Only Will Thompson loomed large on the horizon.

There were other kindnesses over the years and I kept telling myself that's why I visited him every day when he was dying. I never really believed it and neither did he.

Of course he always went too far. In New Orleans there had been a shooting on the docks and I'd been called as a witness. I didn't really see much, two drunken men struggling as I walked by. A gun went off and one man slumped to the dock. My ship was loaded and we were ready to put to sea. Will Thompson had just arrived and had yet to unload and find another charter. He would be in New Orleans a few weeks making arrangements.

We went to dinner that night in the big dining room of the Brecken Hotel and I told him my predicament. The trial business was keeping me at dockside when my ship was ready for sea.

"Write out what you saw and I'll go in your place."

"You'll what?" I demanded.

"I'll be you. They won't know and won't care either."

So I took him by the ship where the shooting happened and told him exactly what I had seen. The tall, thin tattooed man and the short stocky man struggling and the tall man getting the upper hand when the stocky one brings out a gun. They struggle, the gun goes off and the stocky sailor grabs his stomach, takes an unsteady step and falls. I walked him through it, just exactly how it looked to me. An accident, I said. The dead man drew the gun. Thompson nodded.

At first light the next morning I sailed away with an uneasy feeling. Fifteen months later we met in Barcelona and he told me he'd been a star witness.

"Did the tattooed man go free?" I asked.

"No, they hanged him the next morning behind the jail. As a matter of fact, I went to have a look."

"But ... but how?" I gasped. "He was innocent!"

"Not the way I saw it," he grinned and gulped a large drink of rum.

My trips to his bedside these last few months were a search. I know that now. It was a search for some sign of repentance or at least an understanding of something in both of us. Why was his repentance important? Why did it matter to me? Was it because his repentance is somehow linked to mine? Maybe I wanted to see if a man close to the end veers his course closer to the Almighty. It was not out of mercy I kept going to face his insults or, worse, his truth. Was I sympathetic to him? There were few who cared how long he lay there spitting up blood, watching his life flow into his handkerchief.

I cared but I cared because of myself, not because of him. Ah, I'm becoming as truthful with myself as he was with all of us.

There are things mixed up in me, things that demand clarification. Little bits of evil float across my dim eyes. Was it his evil or my evil? On one of my last visits, I finally found the courage to confront him with the vilest stories.

"Did you? I want to know. Did you at times throw black men off your ship? Africans you brought on board to work crossing the Atlantic, and close to port when you didn't need them – " I paused trying to find the words. "Well, ah, there are stories that rather than give them wages you threw them overboard."

It had taken strength to ask the question and I felt breathless and fatigued by it.

He looked at me without an expression. His bloodshot eyes were two watery globes. He put the handkerchief to his face, coughed and wheezed.

"What's done is done," he said. His thoughts had gone somewhere else, lost in a thousand voyages on the green waters of the world.

His words remained. I said them silently as his coffin dipped and disappeared.

"What's done is done."

Why was he not driven by the demons that drive me? Why was he not driven, not asking for mercy from the tattooed beanpole in New Orleans he left twitching at the end of the rope? Maybe a man cannot leave the sea with his soul intact. He can withstand the vileness of waterfront women, the skullduggery of agents, the dark loneliness of ocean nights, the lashing of storms, the years of howling winds, the separation. He can withstand one or two but maybe not them all. Can any man remain untouched?

My sea chest was always locked. Even Laura never had a key. Had I died at sea, someone would have hacked it open, I suppose, and gone through my things and given away my pea jacket. The new owner might have felt something in the lining and slit it open to find Sadie's letter. It would have meant little by then, just a long lost letter from a long lost lady to her lover, a sad and desperate call for help. The reader might have wondered at the outcome. Did the man go to her? Did he rescue her from her pain?

"What's done is done."

I'm climbing down the rickety stairs out of the attic with the letter in my hand. Over the years when I was alone in the house I would unlock the chest to verify it was still there under the lining like a prized possession. I'd just slip my hand in to feel the outline of the envelope. Once, in a fit of loneliness, I slit the lining, touched and smelled the paper to see if her scent was still there, if the paper still held her vapours. There was nothing. She was gone.

What's done is done. Or is it?

Here I am again, sixty-five years of age, half blind and trying to read an old letter. I need to see the message in case there is something I might have missed many years ago.

My hand is shaking. The letter is very close to my face. Her looping letters strike my eyes anew.

God in heaven! I have always loved two women and ended up with neither one of them. I left Sadie waiting in New York and left Laura wretched in Alberta.

"Go home if you want to," Laura had said, "but I'm staying here. Near our grandchildren and our daughters."

She was also staying near James Bernard. Twice since his funeral we'd gone to his grave in Red Deer. He had died quickly, they said. The horseless carriage had upset, throwing him onto the road and the blow broke his neck.

Our daughters were living there. James Bernard was lying there and Laura was staying there. Only I was going, leaving them all behind.

I did her a favour. She was past putting up with my misery and bad temper. A weaker woman would have meekly packed and come home with me. I respected her for not doing that. She was strong enough to refuse.

I bluffed out a story at first for the folks along the shore. Told John and George that Laura would be coming later. There were some I couldn't fool. George's wife Rosa was one of them. She told me without speaking that she could see the deception. It was just in the way she nodded and touched my shoulder, letting me know it was okay.

Captain Densmore knew as well. We had been through shipwrecks, cannon fire and storms from hell. It's hard to hide things from someone who has shared so much with you.

There had been other things Captain Densmore and I never mentioned to our families. Once we took shelter in a little cove on the rocky cliffs of Ireland. We found the dashed ribs of a Spanish barque and the decaying bodies of an entire crew. The barque was pounded to pieces on the rocks while the strong waves had carried the bodies to the beach. Rigging and pieces of their ship danced around them with each wave. Eye bolts on jagged wood, deck planking and lengths of rope, pots from the galley and clothing washed up, over and away from bloated sailors who looked like they were only resting. Occasionally a big wave would roll one of them onto his back or turn a body around so the head pointed south instead of north.

It took a full day to bury them all. We carried them away from the cove to higher ground where the waves would not uncover our work. Birds like pelicans perched overhead, screaming as we dug. Side by side the captain and I shovelled. We became gravediggers as well as shipmates. We gave each man a Christian burial and prayed over him. We had been through much together and there was nothing much I could hide from him.

And yet bonds break. I had loved him like a father. Was I not the one who clasped his hand when he returned from his trial in Kingston? Was it not he who first put the sextant in my hands, who gave me my first command? Yet without a hurtful word between us, the bond has been broken.

The bond between Laura and I wore away through years of separation.

"Go home if you want to," she said.

That was all. She walked out of the room and I packed my bags and went to the train. That's how we ended thirty-five years of marriage. For better or worse. The better for her was to be near her children, the living and the dead.

"For better or worse."

Better for me was away from the dry, barren prairie.

I have been home three months. George and Rosa hired Mrs. Marsh to come in each day to cook and clean. I would rather be dirty and hungry. The woman is a nuisance who keeps moving things so I'll trip over them. I've had a year of Mrs. Marsh. Months of drinking more and seeing less, trying to understand everything.

I truly wish Laura would come home.

Yet it is not Laura's letter I hold in my hand. I am snapped out of my reverie. It suddenly strikes me – Sadie might be dead! Of course it's possible. It's been thirty-six years. She could have been dead for a long, long time.

The lines of the paper are deeply creased, yet they fail to cover the flamboyance of Sadie Muise.

New York
November 4th, 1875
My darling,
I have been waiting. Everyday I hope I will be in your arms and everyday I do not hear from you, I think the worst. Away from me you have not the courage to press forward. Is the decision that difficult, dearest? If you do not act, your mistake will only grow. It is best to use a sharp knife and cut the engagement cleanly. I am not being cruel. She will not be the first woman jilted. She will get over it. As for us, Allan, if you do not act we will never get over it. Never. Do not leave me in a state of perpetual unhappiness. Bring the bliss to me please – please!

Mr. Tremblay says he will interview you as soon as you arrive and may have a position for you if, as he says, you are suitable. I told him you were more than suitable for any position he might offer and that I know you would climb in the company to a senior position.

Please, please write to me. Come to me. If you decide you can't do this, I will accept it but I will always be broken-hearted.

I wait in anticipation of good news from you. I cherish you, my darling. Please come to me.

Forever,
Sadie.

She was right – I lacked the courage. Months later from Lisbon, I wrote her. I gave the letter to a skipper bound for New York. Did she even get it? Did it matter by then? Sadie would not long be broken-hearted. She would feel the sting, for rejection was something she seldom experienced, but men fell at her feet and she soon would find another.

"As for us, Allan, if you do not act we will never get over it. Never."

Thirty-six years later I know she was right. I am now able to confess the truth. Is this what Will Thompson has taught me?

Chapter Sixteen

The word was around the shore that Will Thompson was dying. "Another mate for the devil," they said. I didn't speak against him. There were enough people doing that. I simply said nothing and went to visit him. Some days I would find him alone in the house, propped up in bed, the way a relative had left him after "cleaning up." There would often be a far away look in his eyes. I knew he was reliving the crashing and dashing of his life. The ships, the women, the great gales. I knew what he was going through. Was I not doing the same? Was I not at his bedside for that very reason? He was the other part of my puzzle. The opposite end.

When I asked him if he had regrets he shrugged and coughed. The next minute a trickle of blood oozed from his handkerchief.

He wheezed.

"There was a countess in France. A real beauty. I always wanted to bed her but she got away from me. Oh yes, and that dance hall singer in Liverpool, what was her name?"

"You know what I'm talking about."

"I'm not the kind of man who has regret." He coughed again. "That's your category."

"What do you mean by that?" I asked.

"You're the worrier. The one who counts the right from the wrong."

He coughed and shook while I looked out the window so as not to watch him. I thought of that time in New York on the dock in the rain when I was low and he was there with the carriage.

"You've always been there to help me," I said.

"Then you carry the regrets for both of us," he said and closed his eyes.

He was dead within a day and I feel the obligation.

Chapter Seventeen

I wind the clock in my kitchen everyday. Its ticking keeps me company and I am less likely to dip back into unpleasant memories. It is late afternoon now and the house is silent except for a light wind moving the curtains. The clock has stopped again. I am sure I wound it this morning. I'm sitting at the table studying the scar on my left arm. A broken, egg-like blotch on my skin. Uneven and milky-white. It throbs when I drift back to the *Dove*. I find myself rubbing it, not realising I'm reliving my blackest moment. I have other scars but this is my only self-inflicted wound. I had plunged the blade deep as a tonic to fight sleep. There was little pain. Too numb by the perishing cold and the terrible thirst, that by then made me tremble. The blade sent a thousand pinpricks through my blood. It was enough. Kept me going another hour. Time enough to get the raft into the water.

So many wrecks and none the same. Like women, Will Thompson said. Some gentle, just a slight list, taking on water, going quietly. Silently slipping away like the *Allandale*. Others are full of fury. Violently gnashing hulls and ranting fabric, like the *Dove*. DP's brig *Harmony* was rammed off the coast of France. A steamer split and ripped her. She rolled on her port side, bubbled and sank. We all mourned her loss.

John and I had shares in the *Harmony*. How quickly fortunes rise and fall. John's have mostly risen. Mine have mostly fallen. Losses come in clusters and so do wrecks.

We were on the *Busy Bee* bringing "the sweet charter" up from Cuba. An uneventful trip. We found the trades off the Florida Straits and our sails were full and steady with the aroma of sugar and molasses permeating our planking. South of Boston the sky got hazy and pieces of fluff started floating by. Just small tufts at first, sweeping through our rigging like sugary puffs of frosting. The fluff turned into a veil of mist, wet as rain on your face. The mist deepened into a blanket of fog and the blanket turned into a bank so thick you couldn't see your hand. I sent men into the rigging to double reef by feel. Any sailor will tell you it's eerie up there in the fog, your feet on nothing but a rope, grappling with lines and sail, unable to see the man groaning next to you. Yet you feel. Feel more! The power, the sway of the ship, is intensified. In the fog you are hurtling through a great sheet of nothingness.

I posted a double watch with all ears and eyes ordered port and starboard so another ship didn't cut us in two. We sounded the bell every fifteen minutes.

Fog banks are not uncommon. We often work in them but this one was different, so dense our ship was invisible. I could feel the curved wood of the wheel but I could not see it. Boston Downey, my mate, stood next to me. I could hear him breathing but I couldn't see him. The hours rolled by. We whispered and listened.

More hours in the hushed damp fog and then a violent lurch. Every man was sent sprawling on the deck. My right knee buckled into the wheel. Mr. Downey was face down, the wind knocked out of him. The cook, taking a pot of coffee up to the watch, had been thrown onto the hot stove. Dishes were breaking in the galley. Men were cursing and getting to their feet. The cook was shrieking.

I sent the mate to attend to the cook while several sailors and myself rushed forward to assess the damage. We couldn't see anything but knew our bowsprit was gone. We called to the vessel that had struck us.

"Ahoy, Ahoy!"

There was no answer. Had they sunk so fast? I've heard of ships going down in seconds but considered such tales far fetched. The only sound was a soft gurgling coming from our forward hold. We were taking on water. We had been struck with such an impact our brig was jolted and driven backward. At three-hundred and thirty ton, our holds loaded with heavy molasses in crockery casks and wooden barrels of sugar, we had been shaken like a twig.

"Give me a lantern! I'm going below."

The cook was crying pitifully.

"Cold water and grease him," I heard the mate yell. "Grease him good!"

Water was pouring into the hold in torrents on either side of our keel. The bow was bashed and there was a strange, pungent odour of rawhide mixed with smashed crocks of molasses.

We worked like madmen in the cold water and molasses, trying to contain the damage. Straining, sticky and grunting we tried to patch, cut and fit new planking. Passing buckets of hot pitch but we still couldn't stop the water. We were up to our waists in molasses and sea-water and some substance from the ship that struck us. The *Busy Bee* was becoming perpendicular, buckets sliding along the deck. We could hear men trying to keep their footing as we clambered out of the hold. There had been no word from the other ship.

"What the hell is all over me?" MacBernie said.

"Molasses," I replied.

"Doesn't smell like molasses," he said.

"Cap, what hit us?" a sailor asked.

"I don't know," I said. "But they couldn't sink that fast. We were there in seconds."

"It's probably just yards away there, struggling like we are."

"Why don't they answer?" someone asked.

"We can't help them now," I said. "Prepare to abandon ship."

The *Busy Bee* kept dipping at the bow, bringing her stern out of the water, getting higher, the deck steeper. Two hours after the collision we abandoned ship.

There was no clamour or confusion. We packed our duffels with the quiet resignation of men preparing to spend hours in an open boat. It was late September. The North Atlantic was earning its winter nip. As we lowered the dories there was a sudden roar in the forward hold. The timbers had given way.

"She's broken through!"

"Jesus," someone said softly, not so much an oath as a prayer. There wasn't much else to say. We fumbled with cold fingers in the foggy darkness, putting our dories over the side. The cook was put in the long dory and I held the lantern close to him. A welt the size of a fist was protruding from his forehead. His left eye was swollen shut. He'd also scalded his hand.

We rowed a little way off and waited. We could hear the roaring water and the crashing of cargo.

Suddenly it was over. Quiet! Just blackness and nothing. Then off in the distance there came the mournful cry of a whale. That was all.

Huddled in our dories we smoked and coughed as we drew the thick fog deeply into our lungs.

At dawn the wind came up and the fog lifted. At first all we could see was the dawn, a thin strip of gold in the mist. It lifted slowly, not revealing too much too soon. Hour after hour the veils of mist pulled back, first showing the outline of our ship, just a silhouette in a silver frame. She was incredible. The *Busy Bee* was standing at attention. Straight up as if saluting, her stern high in the air, her bow into the brine. The ship was equalized.

"She might not sink," a young sailor said.

"No matter. She will never sail again."

"She'll sink," I said. "Just slower now."

"Aye," added Downey. "She'll sink. But where is the ship that hit us? Where the hell did it go?"

The *Busy Bee* was a thousand yards in front of us, standing like a tower, straight and still in the midst of an oily plume that formed a shiny circle on the water. It was more than molasses. The same odour we'd smelled all night, rancid, pungent. Like wet rawhide and cattle guts.

"I want to have a look."

"Cap'n, she could go down any minute. Too close and you'll be caught in her pull."

"She won't go for a while," I said. "Row me in."

We were at the edge of the circle when I dipped my hand in the water. It was reddish brown and that smell– that odour of wildness.

"It's blood!"

"My God!" whispered McBurnie.

We rowed back to the other dory and waited. Late in the afternoon, without any warning the *Busy Bee* went straight down. Silently, majestically. Her stern the last bit of her to plunge into the deep. A soft gurgle, a few ripples and she was gone.

"God bless our ship," I said.

"Amen," said Boston Downey. No one else spoke.

We rowed and drifted and rowed for two days. Sometimes in the day we could see a black, uneven mass floating a mile or so in front of us. At night we heard the whale cry.

"That's a big cow in distress," Boston said. In both dories we drifted and listened.

DP didn't want me talking about whales. He walked around his cluttered office munching his cigar, both hands behind his back and his fingers locked. Occasionally he'd untangle them to stroke his bushy moustache.

"They won't pay if they hear such a story, I know them. Best thing is to sink in a collision where it's the other vessel's fault. Storms are all right. They'll do but whales are, well, fish. They don't like stories about fish. Besides," he turned to me like a prosecutor in a trial, "you don't really know what hit you. I mean, you didn't actually see it, did you?"

"There was blood."

"Yes, but whose blood? Where did it come from? You don't know. It may have washed up from some place."

"There wasn't a gale. We had fog but no gale. There was a lot of blood. We hit something big and we hit it hard and it bled."

"But you never did see anything, did you?"

"No, nothing really."

"Well then, let's not say whale."

We didn't say whale. But I refused to report the ship was lost in a gale and it put a strain between us. A month later we tried again, walking through my father's orchard. DP was in his Sunday suit and fine hat. He was a dapper man who had reason to worry. He had lost two ships in a year. He wanted an insurance settlement. He wanted a report from me. I should say, he wanted a different report from the one I'd submitted.

"I can't say the ship just sank! They'll blame the construction," he said and continued. "The *Allandale* just sank! You know what that means? Two sinking and they'll say we're not building good ships, when they just keep sinking for no reason."

"But not a gale," I said. "There wasn't any gale."

"Understand this, Allan, I am not trying to cheat the ir company. I pay a lot of insurance. There are lots of settlements and a iot of disputes. Ships hit whales but they don't sink. If I report a whale sunk my ship there will be no end of it. Give me something else."

"There is no other answer."

DP went away shaking his head, "You hit a rock, shoal, something."

A year later he told me the insurance had settled the *Harmony's* sinking but not the *Busy Bee's*. Not mine.

"Fish, Allan. They don't like fish stories."

"Whales are mammals," I replied.

He got up from his desk and looked out to sea.

"Fish," he said softly and went on to other subjects.

Economy Mountain blocks part of the afternoon sun so there are just long golden fingers slanting across my yard into Laura's garden. The garden shows neglect, the loving hands are gone. Queen Anne's Lace and clover are competing with the primrose and asters she loved. Late afternoons bring a hazy stillness, interrupted only by insects buzzing at the window and a fish hawk crying out in the bay. They are sounds but not disturbances. Quiet overrules everything.

Little Percy brings my mail and tells me he is going in the army when he's old enough. Today there is a letter from Laura. It takes me a long time, steadying the magnifying glass to read it. Her letters are usually perfunctory, void of emotion, a shopping list of the children's comings and goings. This time there are a few signs of feelings. She talks of returning, testing the idea on me. I can have Rosa write a letter for me but it is unnatural to talk to your wife through someone else. I will try myself. Laura knows my limitations. I read her letter twice, trying to hear her voice, holding the glass close to the paper.

John comes down and we talk a while. He is feeling poorly but looks fit. They are having stew for supper and I walk up with him, risking the wrath of Addie who is usually in a stew herself over something. John and Addie have no children, which I say, with full respect for motherhood, is a good thing. Meals would be quiet except for Addie's nattering.

Next door George and Rosa's brood numbers seven, or is it eight? Suppers there are filled with noisy laugher, bickering and teasing. It reminds me of my own brothers and sisters before the bad autumn. In her last years, my mother lived with George and Rosa. She has been dead five years but I'm still disappointed she isn't sitting in her rocking chair, the pipe clenched tightly between her teeth. Her hands are busy. Always busying, knitting needles dancing with a twitch and a bob in a life of their own. When she was very old, Percy and Jack would tease her, asking why she was knitting on Sunday. She would hurl the knitting basket and needles across the room in horror that she had broken the Sabbath and they would run away shouting that it was only Thursday.

Addie and Rosa aren't speaking again. Addie has been shooting at Percy and Jack with that damn revolver. Bullets whistling through the apple trees, splintered limbs flying in all directions. She's going to kill someone. John hid the revolver but she found it. He can't do anything about her and might get shot himself. He walks me home and we drop into George's for a minute. I suspect he wants to soothe the friction between the families and I am his backstop.

George has also been reading the papers. He keeps up with things even more than John. He and John talk about politics. I pay scant attention for the ghosts have already reached me, taking me back fifty years. Whenever I'm with my brothers I hear the happy laughter of the past. My mother, Mary and Martha, little Maria. I breathe deeply, trying to inhale the sweet aroma of hot fudge on the stove. George asks me if I think war is likely. I am the oldest brother and maybe my opinion still matters. I hope not, because I don't have one. Why should I? Someone, somewhere is always getting ready for war. As they talk on without me, I move my tongue to the corner of my mouth to the space where I lost the tooth in my own war. By the time a man is sixty-five his body is his diary. A scar here, a bump there, a broken nose from a swinging spar, a missing tooth from Marseilles. The body becomes a scrapbook of small wars, neither won nor lost.

I don't know why I remember that day in Marseilles but I do. It was a fine spring morning. The fishing fleet was leaving, for sardines I think. They was a great clatter on the waterfront. Despite the noise I knew his voice, like the high-pitched call of a crow, filled with the edgy rattling of wretched syllables refusing a sensible order.

Captain Nutting Wadman never overcame his stutter. As a boy, everything had been tried on him from great heaps of shame to elocution lessons, to more shame and punishment. He grew up in an unfriendly world burdened by not one, but two disabilities: a stutter that would not be controlled and a large birthmark, a pink spatter on his face. Such a child can expect the worst. They used to call him flower face and he fought them, in shame and rage. They ganged up on him sometimes, knocking him into a snowbank and he fought them anyway, mercilessly. The last time, he was sixteen and it happened behind Sydney Smith's barn. He refused to give in. His knuckles were bleeding, scraped and cut from teeth he'd extracted and noses he'd bloodied.

Parents complained about the beating he'd given their sons but they were quieted when they learned it had been four to one. The dull flame of humiliation burned behind the fathers' faces when they were told he had bested their boys. The bullies had been beaten and some were marched to the woodshed for the shame they had brought on their families. The birch rod was not spared and no one ever touched Nutting Wadman again.

He married Sarah Doyle, who became not only his wife, but also his companion and translator. With Sarah he gained a new respectability. He learned navigation and convinced people he could be a master mariner. He had succeeded and spent his life on the sea.

Our paths had not crossed in years. He was a friend of my father and I had much admired him. His prowess as a navigator was legendary and he had risen above the obstacles of life.

I was leaving the waterfront on my way to the consulate in the heart of Marseilles for mail that morning. While making my way through the crowd that had come to cheer the fishing fleet, I heard his jabber and then the crystal clear call of Sarah.

"Captain Graham!"

They had docked the week previous and were unloading spices from the African coast. "Have you heard from home?" Sarah asked over tea. "We have not been home in a year."

She craved news and read me a recent letter from her sister. William Fielding had become premier of Nova Scotia. Two boys, brothers, had drowned along the shore. A most terrible tragedy, she reported. They were stranded by the tide. Their parents could hear their cries but couldn't reach them. I thought of my own children who played along the same shore and I was never there to protect them or warn them of the dangers of a creeping, silent tide. Sarah went on, the Albert Hills were building a new house in Economy and a new, fully rigged ship had recently launched in Bass River.

Captain Nut, as the world knew him, nodded as she read. He was perfectly in tune with her news, a sympathetic slow rising and falling of the head to the tragedies of one family and a swifter celebratory nod to the happiness of another.

There was a peacefulness between Captain Nut and his Sarah. How fortunate a man is to have a wife who loves the sea. Laura had tried; once to Boston on the *Busy Bee* and once up the St. Lawrence when James Bernard was small. She was seasick and unhappy. When the girls were born it became impractical. After that, my long absences caused a rift to begin between us. We had tried to stop the drift and had succeeded at times, but it is difficult to close the years apart and return to where we started.

Captain Nut and Sarah had been inseparable. They never had children. There was a strong and simple attachment based on love and need. I envied them.

The morning I met Nutting and Sarah in Marseilles my ship had tied up only a few hours before. The crew was waiting for pay to go ashore and I had messages to get and provisions to look after. I thanked Sarah for the tea and got up to leave. Captain Nut made several short noises to his wife who nodded slowly and smiled.

"The captain would like you to join him for dinner at the Marble Hen."

I knew she would not be coming, not to that sailor's den, famous for steaming bowls of chicken stew cooked in wine and tankards of strong ale. Canvasses of famous birds lined its walls. Strutting roosters, regal swans but mostly fighting cocks of different colours. The Hen was a noisy, rowdy place of fancy men and sport but safe enough for even the reserved, who occasionally ventured into its smoky sanctum.

I knew the challenge ahead of me. It was difficult to understand Captain Nut in quiet surroundings, but in the Hen it would be impossible. Above the boisterous chatter, wagering and watching the fighting cocks, he would jabber and I would nod. He was an intelligent man so he knew it was impossible to understand him. Maybe it didn't matter.

He enjoyed lively surroundings, enjoyed the fights and his stutter went unnoticed.

Sarah was eyeing me cautiously as I hesitated. She was entrusting me with her most valuable possession. I accepted the captain's invitation.

I don't remember much about our dinner except one drunkard wandered up to our table and tried to decipher the birthmark on Captain Nut's face, apparently thinking it was a map. Captain Nut simply nodded at him and kept on talking to me.

I would switch topics. Starting on a new track gave me a chance to contribute to at least one subject. Sometimes, when he was trying to make a particular point, he would write it down but that was seldom. We watched the cocks for a fight or two. The second contest filled the large room with incredible noise as the losing bird spouted blood over its white feathers and gave out a bellicose squawk that sent the sailors and painted ladies into a frenzy of yelling and cheering.

As we walked back to our ships Captain Nut was talking away about his experiences in Africa. In the open air I could understand much of what he said. He had some narrow escapes in Africa but he could purchase spices at rock bottom prices and he learned the waters. Sarah knew the port officials by name.

It was dark and we had stayed too long at the Hen. In some places that wouldn't have been a problem, but not in Marseilles. It was a rough port. Barrel-chested thugs roamed the waterfront and thievery, even murder, was common. In the company of three or four sailors you had nothing to fear but two men on a dark night could be considered prey. You learned quickly to watch your back in Marseilles.

The shops along the waterfront were closed. Behind them was a maze of narrow unlit lanes. A group of street urchins stopped their rowdy chatter and watched us as we passed. Cold-eyed boys, sneering, unfriendly and wanting so much to be threatening. Hungry dogs smelled the wheels of empty wagons in front of tall, dark ships and silent warehouses. We passed a night watchman making his rounds. Two women were ahead of us. Fallen doves, we figured, for no respectable woman would be so far off course. They stopped and waited; as we passed I caught the fragrance of rosewater. We kept walking. As we turned the corner, the street ahead was empty. Shoulder to shoulder we walked, brothers of the sea, brothers of the shore.

Around another corner we encountered men lounging against a darkened door. Stevedores or sailors maybe who watched us as we passed and then we heard their footsteps on the cobblestones behind us. Step by step they paced us. More footsteps joined them.

We got very quiet. Captain Nut lightly touched my arm and I sensed something. I cannot explain it, just a change in his presence. He seemed to get bigger, like a balloon expanding. His walk became more calculated, every step chosen, his backbone solid and straight.

The chandlers shops were locked up tight, we were on the docks and the ships seemed deserted. A big square-rigger tied up nearby without a sign of a sailor.

"Where in God's name are the night watchmen?" I said in a whisper.

Suddenly the footsteps behind us quickened. They were running. I assessed our pursuers. Five, some with belaying pins. Fear moved our feet and they couldn't gain on us. A belaying pin flew over my shoulder and clattered on the cobblestones. Another pin whistled through the air and caught Captain Nut behind the head. He fell with a groan and every instinct in my body told me to run. I cursed myself as I turned to face them. The man in the lead tried to kick Captain Nut, but the captain had grabbed the attacker's leg. I plowed into them swinging. Once, twice, three times. Captain Nut got to his feet still holding the man's leg. Using him like a battering ram he drove the man backward until he fell, taking another man with him. A third attacker tripped trying to get to the captain who still held the first attacker's leg. He was deadly quiet.

Pain ripped through my shoulders when one of them slammed a pin into me. The captain was banging two heads together, making a sickening thud. I finally wrestled the pin away from my assailant and one of the other attackers backed away. I was cursing, punching, kicking, my free hand still holding the pin. The two with sore heads were on the ground unconscious. I struggled, swinging and grabbing. I hit the man across the top of the head but still he hung on, grabbing my wrist. Captain Nut suddenly picked up his opponent and threw him in the air. The man came down hard on the cobblestones with a groan. The man backing away now moved farther down the street. Captain Nut grunted something, grabbed my assailant from behind and lifted him up over his head. An incredible feat considering the man dangling in the air was of a burly build and he certainly weighed more than the wiry captain. This is what I remember most. Captain Nut spun the man around and as he did, he roared at the top of his lungs: "You'll pay for the mud flats, Smitty. You'll pay!"

Even in the pain and confusion, his voice was so strong I knew his meaning. Smitty was one of his tormentors. The one who had pushed his face into the wet mud yelling, "Better brown than pink," referring to his birthmark. The others had laughed. It had taken him a year or two to grow and work and get stronger but he got even.

Without a stammer or stutter, his voice carrying along the docks, Captain Nut threw the man into a stack of barrels with such force they scattered like kindling, rolling off in different directions. The two attackers who were still conscious hobbled away. We were suddenly alone, too winded to run or even walk. We sank on the cobblestones, breathing hard. A quarter of an hour later the harbour watch found us, hobbling along, not a hundred feet from the scene of the attack. Again we sat on the cobblestones, relieved to be found. They gave us some wine from a flask and proceeded to kick the two men, still unconscious on the ground.

In the quiet of my kitchen I can still hear him. That violent voice, naming his persecutor so distinctly and concisely th'at his name cut the night like the piercing cry of a wounded animal. During the next thirty years I never again heard Captain Nut utter another clear word.

Chapter Eighteen

No good ever came from the South Street docks. I remember walking between the brick warehouses while a fierce cold gripped my lungs. My weakened condition made me even more alert. There have been great gangs roving the streets, stealing what they wanted. The owners had given their night watchmen bigger whistles and longer lectures on why we were getting paid. More than one of my colleagues has had his head bashed in. One poor chap from just down the way left behind a wife and seven children, none of them old enough to earn a living.

Poor Jacob Campbell had done this job. He was a night watchman too and beaten within an inch of his life. After almost dying on the *Dove,* Jacob wanted a safer life and came to New York. He traded his sea legs for a night watchman's lamp. A gentle soul, he was a man who might hesitate before using his club. Thugs could see, could smell a greenhorn. Thugs schooled on the street smell vulnerability in a man's stride like wolves can taste fresh blood in the air. Grown up hard on the Lower East Side, without benefits of loving home or school, they were men who took what they wanted. Jacob tried to stop them. I wondered what I would do. Blow my whistle and run like hell or face up to them. I was a fraud. What defense, aside from my whistle, could I provide? I was sixty then, too old to run and too weak to face them. I was poor protection but I did not steal. Some watchmen need watching themselves, as did some of the harbour force. New York was not a safe harbour and an honest man was a rarity.

While Jacob and I watched warehouses and walked the cold nights along the East River, my brother John slept at home in Lower Economy. That was a safe harbour. Many a night I wished I were home. A man has to be grateful for his blessings. I always tried to be thankful. I was better off, I told myself, than some of the poor lads who sailed with me. How could I complain compared to them? Jim Wilson, a living skeleton when taken off the *Dove,* could never be nursed back to his former health. He remained unsteady on his legs up to a year later and soon drowned in the St Lawrence. Isaac too. He could not escape, swallowed up by the Atlantic and my good mate Landry lost somewhere in the south. Ruphus remains alive but he too has never been the same, an old man at twenty-five. The *Dove* forever etched in his eyes.

I was wet and cold with a chest full of congestion but alive, earning a living protecting warehouses full of groceries. That was only three years ago during the winter of 1907. It was at that time the blurring started but I paid no heed to it. I could see enough and I could hear more. Whenever there were footsteps I would put the whistle to my mouth and think of Jacob Campbell. I'd raise my club and wait to see if it was danger or just another noise in the night.

Chapter Nineteen

There are many reasons a man and wife are pulled apart. In 1886 Laura and I were put to a test of wills. When a child is involved, both parents can demonstrate their best and worst qualities.

There was great dismay in Laura's letters. Little Blanche had always been a frail child, never as robust as her brother and sister. She always walked with a limp and would cry at nights because of the pain in her hip. It was getting worse, she walked only with great difficulty. By the time she was four she was bedridden. That's how I found her upon my return from sea. In bed sobbing, her big eyes looking up at me, pleading for my help.

"The child's hip is dislocated. I don't know why, exactly," Dr. MacPherson told me. "There's something wrong, like rough cartilage grinding against something. It's mysterious. She needs an expert and there aren't any here."

"Where are there experts then?" I asked.

"Boston. New York." He threw up his hands. "It is mysterious," he said again. "She was probably born with this affliction. As she grows and gets taller, it becomes worse. She has grown a great deal this past year."

He sighed in desperation, "There are things rubbing together that should be separated by tissue. It is complicated."

"There is no one here who can help her? Can you not read up on it?"

"I have been reading up on it, but there is little information. There is a procedure. It is little known and rarely tried. I'm afraid the movement would be too painful if you could take her to New York. Blanche does not have a strong heart. She could not tolerate the travel."

"This procedure, who does it?" I asked. "Where are they, these doctors? Where?"

He looked at me, suddenly afraid of what he saw. I have been told my eyes can glow with stark intensity. Years later when he was able to talk about it, John told me that on the *Dove* a fierceness came over me. It showed through my eyes and made them keep going. Keep pushing the raft, the final task when they had nothing left.

Dr. MacPherson cleared his throat.

"The nearest man is in Boston. He has had some success, but there is no guarantee and the trip would be too taxing for your little girl, even by rail."

He looked away and sighed. He had a wise, kindly face. The ultimate voice of healing along our shore. His word was the gospel of curing.

I had not been much of a father. At sea for birthdays and Christmas, I'd return to find my children transformed, altered by a year. New teeth, new faces, new people. I would marvel at the changes and what I had missed. I had missed too much.

There was silence in the doctor's office. He sat at his desk and looked at his hands, letting me digest the news that my daughter was condemned to a life of discomfort. He would administer medication when the pain got too bad but that was all.

But it was not all, I would not let it be all. "What about bringing him here?"

"Bringing him here?"

"Yes. Bringing him here."

"From Boston?" He raised his white eyebrows. "Why, you can't just get a doctor, a surgeon no less, a lecturer, to drop his work and come way up here. It would be out of the question."

"What's his name?"

His look of shock did not dissipate and he shook his head more vigorously. "His name is Archibald, Dr. George Duncan Archibald. He lectures at Harvard and .... "

"And he has done this procedure that Blanche needs? He has done it successfully?"

"Yes, but you can't get him here and even if you did, there is no guarantee in your daughter's case. Every situation is different."

"You could prepare something for me. Information I could take to him on her condition."

"He won't come, Captain. A man like that has great responsibilities. He can't drop his work and just leave."

"Will you write the information I need? What you have found?"

I left Five Islands without waiting for his reply. I galloped to Economy, not letting old Eddy slow down on Economy Mountain. Vapours were coming off the horse when we got to DP's house. He was sitting in a pile of papers looking particularly thin and tired. Ledger books were open and askew on his desk. He was doing his accounts. Debits and gains. Trade had slowed. His new ship the *Treasurer* was not making money. It stung him more because many had criticised his decision to build a square-rigger. He had persisted, gone stubbornly ahead. A beautiful burden, DP called it. The *Treasurer* consumed him as no other ship had.

I had known him all my life and we had been associated in business for over twenty years. He entrusted me with his ships and I sailed them around the world. We were even kin through marriage. Next to my brothers and maybe Captain Densmore and Marshy, I knew him better than any man alive. I was not above asking him for help.

"I need a charter to Boston, as soon as possible."

He raised his eyebrows. "We don't have a charter."

"I'll take her empty and find one there."

Maybe he read something in my eyes as I told him about Blanche. He didn't argue.

"Have you contacted this doctor in Boston?"

"Not yet, I've just come from Five Islands. I want to get the ship ready and leave right away."

"You contact him. Go to Truro and send a wire. See about getting him here."

He wrote a note for me to send to Charles Huntley in Boston. As a lumberman and long time associate, DP asked Huntley to meet with Dr. Archibald and explain why I was coming. DP would get a ship crewed and ready.

I didn't have an address for Dr. Archibald and neither did old Doctor MacPherson.

"Send it to the Harvard Medical School," he suggested.

I borrowed a horse from John and rode to Truro, going over the message in my mind. Mine would get to him first, even before Huntley.

"It's by the word, you know," the telegraph operator told me. "This will cost you a fortune."

He helped me shorten it, but not by much. I wanted Dr. Archibald to know this was a matter of great importance. I repeated the sentence again.

"I am bringing my ship to Boston to bring you to Nova Scotia."

Three days later we put the small brig *Toronto* to sea. It was empty and sparsely crewed. Marshy left his family to come as did George Berry and Victor MacKay. They were our crew. Just the four of us, but all men with sea time who knew a ship and knew the wind. As we left Parrsboro, the first rays of the morning sun were coming over McLaughlans Head at Greenhill. If ever a man prayed upon leaving port, I did that day. I prayed for good weather, I prayed my trip would not be in vain. I prayed and prayed and felt the warm sun on my face.

I stayed at the wheel, going over and over how I could persuade this busy doctor I didn't know to come with me.

In Boston it took me half a day just to find him. They hunted all over Harvard Medical School before sending me to his office in Beacon Hill. But he wasn't there either. At the city hospital, they said. I was nearly frantic when I finally found him. He was a towering man, standing in the hospital's main hall conferring with a colleague. He watched me come down the hall. He stopped talking and turned to me. I was in my captain's uniform, my best brass buttons. He told me later he would have known anyway by the grim determination written all over me. As I reached him he held out his hand.

"I've been expecting you, Captain."

Gordon Duncan Archibald was a red-haired Scot, balding, with a rosy complexion and broad shoulders. He was a friendly, gregarious man who told me immediately that no one had ever travelled so far to meet him. I followed him on his rounds as he inspected a variety of patients of all ages and shapes. He was telling me, showing me the scope of his work, the number who depended on him.

His approach to me was calculated, measured, gentle. There was no way he could go. It was out of the question. He was too busy and he had too many responsibilities. I showed him the letter from Doctor MacPherson. I told him how Blanche was suffering, the pain she had just turning over in bed. I told him about her heart, why I could not bring her. He nodded patiently. I pleaded and he shook his head but not as firmly. I mustered my arguments again. I promised I would pay all costs. Just come, please come.

There was just one item left in my leather pouch that had held Dr. MacPherson's papers and a letter of introduction from DP. It was a photograph of little Blanche.

He explained again why it was impossible for him to make the trip and how, even if he did, there was a possibility an operation could not help my daughter. I was weary and had used up every argument, every avenue of reason I could muster. A surge of hopelessness came over me but I would not give in. No, I would not let Blanche suffer. I slid the photograph in front of him. He stopped in mid sentence and picked it up. He studied it for several seconds.

"She is my baby," I said quietly. "I have missed so much of my children."

He nodded slowly.

"It is unfair of you, Captain, to try and appeal to my humanity. She is a beautiful child but...." he looked me straight in the eye, "I see beautiful children every day."

"Do you see children crying, trying to get out of bed, trying to walk?"

"Yes," he replied. "Do you know how many children suffer every day in front of me?"

"But you have helped many."

"Some I have helped, yes."

"But there is no one else," I pleaded. "No one near her. There may be others here in Boston, other doctors to help children. There is no one near my daughter. You are the closest."

He put the photograph down and rubbed his forehead vigorously.

"How long?" he asked.

"What?"

"How long to get there?"

"A week. With good winds, less."

"I will need to take Mrs. Archibald." Still rubbing his forehead he smiled. "My good wife complains how little she sees me. Wait until I tell her we're going on a sea voyage."

"Bring her. My ship is ready. We can sail in the morning."

"No, no, Captain. I'll need a few days."

It was miles from the hospital back to my ship but I walked. It was evening and the leaves were out on the trees that lined the boulevard on Commonwealth Avenue. I was suddenly invigorated. On my way back to the waterfront I thanked God over and over again I had brought Blanche's photograph.

We arrived in Bass River twelve days later, after being lashed by a gale off New Bedford and another in the Gulf of Maine. It had not been a comfortable voyage but the doctor's wife made it better than it otherwise might have been.

I liked Mrs. Archibald immediately. She seemed to understand my determination to get back to Nova Scotia with all due haste. She was a plump woman, half the height of her husband. She was easy to laugh and even seasickness did not dissipate her good spirits.

"I will appreciate my home even more, Captain. I do not believe any experience is without some benefit."

We did not have a steward on board and Mrs. Archibald declared she was not above preparing food. Working in a galley is no easy feat for someone unaccustomed to the pitch and roll of a ship and she did quite well until the nor'easter in the Gulf of Maine caught us broadside, giving the ship a good knock. I had just passed the wheel over to Marshy when we were hit. There was a great clatter in the galley and all free hands rushed to the hatchway, to see Mrs. Archibald on the floor. She was covered with flour from head to foot. She didn't move, just looked up at us and spit. A fountain of flour spewed from her mouth.

"It's my damn sea legs. Apparently I left them in Beacon Hill."

Something let go in me like a dam bursting. I couldn't stop myself. I laughed until I cried. Real gentlemen would have rushed to the good lady to give her assistance, to help her to her feet, but we all stood by the galley hatchway bent over in hysterical laughter. Mrs. Archibald herself was laughing so hard her eyes were wet. That made her look even funnier, watery holes in a floury face. Marshy couldn't leave the wheel but our merriment was contagious. He started laughing too.

In Great Village, Dr. Archibald spent a long time with Blanche. He pushed and probed and measured and finally, against her will, he made her walk, first by herself then with his hand firmly on her hip. He listened to her heart and made notes.

Later we gathered to hear his report.

"Your child has a type of, well, call it grit in her hipbone. It's not grit really; they are small nodules of muscle that should not be there."

He was standing in our living room, his wife next to him. Laura and I were sitting there trying to absorb the details of our daughter's condition.

"I will tell you, Captain and Mrs. Graham," he finally said, "a medical procedure is somewhat risky. Your daughter's heart has a small irregularity. An operation will be a strain."

"Do you think her heart could stand it?" I asked.

"Yes, yes I believe so, but there is, of course no guarantee," he replied.

"She can't go on like this," I said. "What kind of life would she have, constantly tormented by pain?"

Laura was silent, uncertain. Maybe the shock of my seeing Blanche had sent me to Boston too quickly. But here was a doctor who could help.

"What if the procedure kills her?" she asked.

"Well, there is that risk," replied the doctor. "But the longer you wait the larger the nodules will grow."

The next morning I told Dr. Archibald I wanted him to operate. He sighed heavily, "Yes, and your wife agrees?"

"She is uncertain."

"I see."

He would talk to Laura and he told me what needed to be done. He would do the procedure in the quietest room in the house. One of the upstairs bedrooms, maybe the middle room at the centre of the house.

"We would need to thoroughly wash down the room, remove all the furniture and curtains, wash the floor, the walls, the ceiling."

Laura remained distant. There was an unspoken struggle between us. I had gone ahead, bull-headed, she would say. Gone on my own and found a doctor who was ready to cut open our daughter.

I told Blanche as much as I could and when I did, a voice deep within told me this was the right thing to do. I prayed the voice was right. If not, we would lose our daughter and Laura would never forgive me.

"Daddy, is that doctor coming back today? He keeps hurting me."

"I know, dearest, but he is trying to make you well. I want the doctor to fix you, so you will be strong and walk."

"Will it hurt like yesterday?"

"Yes, only for a little while. The doctor will make you well."

"Can I go outside and play with James and Mary then?"

"Yes, Blanche, you can."

A despondency settled over Laura. Finally, out of frustration, Dr. Archibald challenged her. Then she became more forthright and stood up to him. She said I had brought him to our home without her approval and now he was here, the feeling seemed to be that the procedure must go ahead as quickly as possible.

Dr. Archibald took her hand and sat her next to him so quickly Laura didn't have time to resist.

"No, Mrs. Graham," he said gently, "you are wrong. I am here because your husband has great intensity in his persuasion. I have stayed because I believe I can help your daughter."

"But you can't assure me, Doctor." Laura replied. "You can't guarantee you'll be successful. Can you tell me her heart will stand the strain? You know she is weak. She has always been a delicate child. So, Doctor, give me peace of mind before you cut her open."

"There is no guarantee, Mrs. Graham. I say again, there is no guarantee in anything. I can only tell you I believe I'll be successful."

Mrs. Archibald stood by the window listening while I remained seated, watching. "No guarantee," Laura whispered.

"No guarantee," the doctor repeated softly.

"Doctor," I broke in, "I want you to operate as soon as possible."

"I think it is important, Captain, that Mrs. Graham gives me her blessing. She is the mother of this child," he said to me rather reproachfully.

Laura looked up suddenly, as though startled. First at the doctor and then at me. She arose from her chair and left the room. Mrs. Archibald followed her.

For the next few days Laura and Mrs. Archibald spent much time together. On Friday I asked Laura again for her blessing on the procedure. "No, Allan, I cannot. The risk is too great. Blanche may not survive."

"You underestimate her," I said. "Blanche has a great will to live, to run on the beach, to play with James Bernard and Mary."

"She will never run on the beach if the procedure is unsuccessful," she answered.

"Have faith," I urged.

"I have faith. Faith she will grow out of this affliction without the operation, or at least she may grow stronger first. Then we shall see."

"No," I said. "We cannot wait. I will not wait. The procedure is going ahead, with or without your blessing."

"Then it is on your hands," she said and I lost my temper.

"Is that what this is about, whose responsibility it is? All right, it is mine. It is all mine!"

I was yelling to an empty room. She had left but my words flew all over the house and Blanche called to me and cried because her mummy and daddy were arguing and it was over her and she was sorry. I held her and kissed her and, for the first time, felt my own doubts.

Saturday we prepared the middle bedroom. The doctor and I carried out the furniture. Mrs. Archibald and Laura washed the walls while Mary and James Bernard helped. Blanche watched and said she saw the shapes of animals on the wet walls.

I helped the doctor acquire several items he needed. Sheets and towels were boiled in linseed oil. Iodine and large needles were borrowed or bought and catgut had to be scraped thin with a sharp knife. He had alcohol and ether.

He would operate the next morning.

"Normally I don't work on the Lord's day but it is when the village will be the most quiet. I have patients waiting for me in Boston and students without the benefit of my wisdom at Harvard," he laughed. "The patients can survive, maybe not the students. I trust the Lord will bless us for we are doing good work on the Sabbath."

"This is the Lord's work," said Mrs. Archibald and smiled.

At ten o'clock Sunday morning I carried Blanche into the stark room. It was empty except for the kitchen table covered with a sheet where the doctor would operate and where I gently placed little Blanche.

"Mrs. Archibald will attend me. It's best for you and Mrs. Graham to wait outside. Please do not let anyone into the house and keep things as quiet as possible. I require complete concentration. This is very fine work. Do you understand?"

"Yes, doctor."

I kissed Blanche on the cheek and forehead. She smiled weakly. When Laura hugged her, Blanche said, "Don't cry, Mummy. Daddy tells me to be brave. You be brave too."

"Oh, my little darling," Laura sobbed. "You are brave. You are the bravest little girl in the world."

I put two chairs outside the bedroom door for Laura and myself. A final look into the room at my daughter. She was so small and frail on the big table. Dr. Archibald began to administer the ether.

"God bless you, my darling," I whispered. Mrs. Archibald nodded, smiled and slowly shut the door.

Laura did not stay with me as I had hoped. She went downstairs without a word. I sat in the hall, suddenly feeling very alone. Then I trembled, thinking of the faith I had placed in this doctor. I put my hands to my face and prayed fervently as a father does when struck by grief and doubt. I was lost in despair. My hands were wet and salty. The sea was rising up, coming out of me, offering eternal support. For a long time I prayed, staying very still and listening to the soft murmurs of a summer morning: a bee buzzing at the hall window, a bird chirping somewhere and a gentle breeze rustling the new leaves on the poplar trees.

Then, all at once, an explosion of noise. The gong of a church bell!

"Stop it," called Dr Archibald sharply. "Stop it."

I tore down the stairs and out the door. Down the village I raced toward the Presbyterian Church. Faster, faster as the bell rang again and again. A lady watched at her window as her lazy dog aroused from his sleep on the steps, barked at me once. Then behind me, the dull first gong of the Baptist bell. They were both ringing.

"Stop it, just stop it!" I shouted, contributing to the noise I was trying so hard to prevent.

The Presbyterians had the highest steeple, the biggest congregation and the oldest bell ringer. Church janitor Caulfield Geddes was a white-haired septuagenarian. When he walked into the service, people prayed he would not sit next to them so they could avoid the rancid smell of horse barn and castor oil. He gave me a bewildered look as I rushed into the vestry and literally pushed him away from the rope.

"No! No bell, Caulfield. No bell today. They're operating on my doctor."

I didn't stop to correct myself. There was another bell to silence. I was out the door and back down the street toward the Baptist Church. As I passed the dog that had barked, he gave chase, his owner yelling after him.

"Sam, Sam. Come here boy, come here." But Sam was trying to gnaw my ankle and I was trying to kick him away and run at the same time.

"Get, get!"

The Bernard Smiths were beginning their leisurely stroll to the church when I rushed by, still kicking at the dog.

"Get away, damn you!"

Way down the street, the dog's owner was still calling but in a more forceful and formal manner.

"Sam, Samuel, you get home!"

The command partly worked. Samuel stopped the chase to give the Bernard Smiths a smell.

Up the hill I ran to the Baptist church. Up the hill and up the steps. I was gasping, my heart racing.

I didn't know the young Baptist bell ringer. He was a blotchy-faced, strapping boy with broad shoulders and a wide gap between his front teeth. I burst through the door holding up my hand.

"Stop." I tried to make it a command but the authority of a captain had left me. All I possessed with a hollow breathy whisper.

"What?" the youth replied and I grabbed the rope out of his hands.

"They're operating on my daughter. The doctor needs silence."

He stared at me dumbfounded. Then I heard the peel of the Presbyterian bell again. This time I found my voice.

"Damn you, Caulfield," I roared, and the small Baptist vestry vibrated with my anger. I shook my fist at the blotchy boy and threatened him if he so much as touched the rope. The first worshippers were arriving. The Marley Andersons had been coming up the steps when they heard my ranting. Was it safe to enter the House of God? Oaths and blaspheming on a Sunday morning?

"What's going on?" they asked Mrs. Lester McCully and her daughter Julia. They all waited for the Bernard Smiths who were still being pestered by a bothersome dog.

I raced down the steps, apologising to them all. How could I be so stupid? Caulfield Geddes had been deaf for years.

As I was rushing back towards the Presbyterian Church, the bell suddenly stopped. There was nothing. I stood there, rumpled and exhausted in the dusty street, my chest heaving. Slowly I walked back towards my house and wondered and worried about my little Blanche.

A buggy was coming up the road. The dog that chased me was hesitant now, perhaps sensing danger. He barked once and turned for home. A small child was crying somewhere but the bells had stopped. On that spring morning in 1886 Great Village was, again, mostly quiet.

At two-fifteen in the afternoon Dr. Archibald stepped out. His face was beet red. He simply nodded.

"I think it's good."

That was all he said. He went downstairs for tea.

Dr. Archibald and his wife took the train back to Boston. His trip cost me two-hundred pounds, more money than I had. I didn't care. The next Sunday when the church bells rang I opened every window in the house and stood in the sun and breathed in the sound. And thanked God.

There was much more that summer. Blanche got her wish. She could play with her brother and sister on the beach, not run exactly, but walk without pain. Her limp was far less noticeable.

It was the happiest time in my life. I was home for the first summer since I was fourteen. We moved back to Lower Economy and I spent every day with my children. We did all the things I had always wanted to do with them. Picnics under the trees, walks in the meadow. We fed George's pigs and chickens and made sand castles on the beach. Some nights George and Rosa would come down with their daughters. Even John and Addie showed up and we roasted chickens outdoors in the glowing hardwood.

My brother George, we didn't call him Georgie any more, had married and taken over our father's farm. I thought him a most unlikely farmer. He would rather have his face in a book. His daughters, Jessie and Sadie Belle loved my children and I often had all five, four of them romping along and Blanche holding my hand, walking and smiling up at me.

Laura could hardly stop hugging Blanche. Toward me there was a tenderness that had been missing for a long time. We were young again, in love again. Our daughter was walking again. Laura took my free hand and held it tightly one night coming down from George's with Blanche asleep in my arms. A silvery moon lay on the water. Way out in the bay, a brig waited for the tide. I looked at little Blanche and then at Laura and knew I would soon have to go. I would wait for the sea to call. I knew it would and I knew I'd have to answer.

In late August DP drove into our yard with a beautiful pair of white horses. They pranced down my long driveway as if delivering a Roman emperor. He tied them up and refused the glass of lemonade Laura had offered.

"Walk with me, Allan. Let's talk a bit."

There was good reason that DP Soley was an admired man. He had the gift of business. He could smell the winds of change. He sat in his office in Economy, Nova Scotia, miles away from city lights or centres of commerce and he smelled a shift in world fortunes.

"Your daughter seems so well. It has been a good recovery."

"Yes," I replied and touched him on the shoulder. "I know I've said this before but its bears repeating. Thank you for the ship and the crew. I haven't been much help to you this season."

"You've been busy with other things." He stopped and looked at me. "Frankly, I want you to take over the *Treasurer*. I've got my pick of captains. To be blunt, Captain Densmore was my first choice and why wouldn't he be? He has been with me longer than anyone else has, but he doesn't want to leave the *Northern Empire*. That ship is making money, so I'm happy to keep him there."

We walked up the hill to George's house then through the orchard past John's to the open meadow.

"You've never commanded a square-rigger."

"No, but I can. I want to."

"I thought you might. Make us some profit, Allan. That's what we want. Some profit."

She was often called *The Parrsboro Treasurer*. That wasn't her real name but that's how it was printed in the newspapers. Maybe people in

Parrsboro just wanted to adopt her as their own. Almost everyone agreed the *Treasurer* was one of the most beautiful ships ever built. She came together lovingly under the careful eye of DP's brother, Josiah. One thousand, three hundred and twenty-nine tons. Big, bold and beautiful. As with many full-rigged ships, the *Treasurer* was cut to the European design. Four masts: the fore, main and mizzen carrying square-rigged sails and the jigger or aftermast with a fore and aft set. When she was in the wind with everything running, she was a billowing city of white gliding magically on the surface of the sea. It was a different job, a bigger ship, more cargo and crew but a sailing ship is a sailing ship. I put her into the wind as we left Parrsboro on October 12th. The rigging hummed in the breeze coming off McLaughlans Head and I knew that seagoing would never be better than this. Yet at no time in my life did I ever so much regret leaving home.

Chapter Twenty

The end of sail was not yet apparent along the Parrsboro shore. George Cochrane's beautiful schooner *Scotia Queen* had just eased down the slip in Fox River. Plans for the Tern *Willena Gertrude* were being drawn up in Parrsboro and the ribs on the tern *Ronald* could be seen in Port Greville. In the inner harbour of Parrsboro and along the coal wharf, a dozen brigs and schooners were at anchor. The only steam hissed from the lumber mills. But the signs were there. Full-masted ships were built with steel hulls and more and more the talk was of steam. Those knowing enough or smart enough to understand such things, already knew.

Old men, no longer fit for sea, stand on the docks and slip a wad of tobacco into their mouths and study the derelicts they once sailed on. Soon the hulls of these ships will be as gnarled as an old salt's hands. When a stooped sailor studies the dry bones of a derelict he has known, he's in a place where there is only room for him and his ship.

I have come to Parrsboro with my brother John. He thinks I want to see the ships, those working and those recently retired. Although it is only a few miles from Lower Economy, it has been a while since I have been in this port. Not so many years ago I sailed the *Treasurer* out of here. Before we got to West Bay, we had every piece of canvas catching the wind. The most beautiful ship afloat and I was at the wheel. Captain. A self-made man.

I'm glad none of my ships are here rotting on the beach. I nod to one or two men I may have known once, before they were bent by time. We are all part of a world that is slipping away. Not totally apparent in Parrsboro. Not yet.

I tell John I want to go. I have seen enough. Even the tobacco has lost it flavour.

Chapter Twenty-one

I admit it now while I am able to admit all things. I liked the prestige of the *Treasurer*. A ship like that increases a man's rank in society. I was invited to social occasions by the upper crust. In New York and Boston I'd find myself twirling around fancy ballrooms with ladies in long gowns who smelled of lavender. They forgave my bad dancing.

I was master of a ship that could carry a great deal of cargo. I was hobnobbing with the rich. A new man at teas. A captain from the Dominion, chatting with the likes of Mrs. Henry Astor in Beacon Hill, who made me accompany her for carriage rides around the Boston Common. The Vance Chattenbergs of Virginia held a dinner in my honour where Vance took me aside to tell me he hoped the Dominion would become part of the United States.

"It is not likely now," I replied.

"Pity," he said.

In Connecticut I met a man who would go on to be president of the United States. William Howard Taft was a judge in New London and had a hardy laugh that fitted his comfortable girth. There was a subdued power about him that gave you the idea there was grit underneath his considerable charm.

I don't remember much of what we talked about, except he told me he had never been as far north as Nova Scotia. He believed it to be very cold and icy. Our American cousins, the lot of them, think we live in igloos and eat raw fish. I simply nodded and didn't remind him the Connecticut winter had work parties chopping ice to free the ships in New London harbour.

He went on to become the twenty-seventh president and I kept the newspaper of his victory. It's in my sea chest.

It was a phase, I guess, all that gaiety in the early nineties. Some of the women reminded me of Sadie and maybe that's why I stopped. I realised I wasn't quite over everything I thought I was over. There were long afternoons in New York when I would walk up one street and down another, hoping she would suddenly appear.

There was another reason I stopped accepting invitations. Her name was Mrs. Robert Malcolm. She was a tall, vivacious woman who was even more forward than Sadie Muise. We met at dinner one evening at the home of Jason Downey, a well-to-do shipping magnate. Mrs. Malcolm didn't believe in wasted words. She suggested a drive in the country the following day. She arranged for a carriage and we drove along the Hudson River.

"I am an adventurous woman, Captain. And you? How much adventure do you have? Plenty at sea, I'm sure, but what about on dry land? Do you flap about like a fish out of water?"

She was married, rich and bored and although we were friends for a year and lovers for longer than that, she never held my heart the way Sadie Muise did.

There is an interruption to my daydreaming now. George and Rosa are on their way to Parrsboro. It is no good asking them to bring back rum. They're abstainers, temperance people like Mrs. Marsh who has left a grocery list for them. Items I apparently need but wasn't consulted about.

John will get me a bottle. He is less strong in his temperance. George has more of our mother's influence. Our mother would not be pleased with me. I am not pleased with me.

Rosa says she will write a letter for me to Laura when she comes back on Thursday. Then they leave and I'm alone again.

I can no longer remember what Mrs. Malcolm looked like. Her name was Emma. I have not thought of her in a long time. We used to go out to Coney Island and swim in the surf. We had dinner on the promenade or in the big hotel by the beach. It was always crowded and I asked her if she ever worried that someone would recognise her. She had a husband some place. She was fearless and told me once that Mr. Malcolm knew of our liaison.

"Really?" I said, rather shocked.

"Really," she replied.

The nineties started with such promise. There was excitement in the air, news of many marvelous inventions. Men of the sea coming together from different corners of the world bringing news of what they'd seen. Things we could hardly believe. Horseless carriages we knew about, but talking machines and moving pictures and electric lamps lighting up London?

By the time I sailed up the Thames, many restaurants and all the theatres had replaced their oil lamps. Electric lights changed everything. More people on the streets at night. More people in the pubs. It changed the way women looked. Their heavy rouge was far too revealing in the brightness of the foyers in the great theatres. As their rouge changed, their dress and fashion followed.

Yet for me, I realise now, the nineties were when it all started to go to pot. Even with the prestige of a fine ship, I could feel a restlessness building in me. A feeling the sea was releasing its lifelong grip on me. Mrs. Malcolm was getting bored with me and I with her. But it was more than just her. I was becoming disconnected in some strange way from my life's work. I began the drift that haunts me today. The feeling so strong that life has missed me or I missed it. There were days I couldn't close my eyes and picture the faces of my children.

Jules Bergen articulated what I felt. He was the youthful head of Bergen & Company, Ships Agents on Regent Street, London. He inherited the firm from his father but Jules' ideas were very much his own.

"It's a different world, Captain Graham, but I wish I could say a better one."

He liked to wax eloquent while waving his cigar, despairing about the world around him. He felt a higher standard of living had cheapened the working class.

"Popular pastimes of people are ruining the national fabric of British life," he would say, exhaling smoke. I had difficulty following his reasoning. He was too young to be so dour and too wealthy to be so forlorn. The working class, the poor, world order. I just wanted to load my ship and go. For me in those days, going was preferable to staying, in London or anywhere else.

I particularly didn't want to go with Jules Bergen. He was too full of conviction. He saw spiritual desolation everywhere and wanted to share his experiences with me. I begged off on several occasions but I finally relented just to shut him up.

He took me through a section of London called Whitechapel where a few years earlier Jack the Ripper had done his heinous deeds. The squalor was worse than I imagined, worse than I'd seen in New York. Hollow-eyed children in rags, unconscious drunkards covered in vomit and piss with people stepping over them totally unconcerned. Tenements were encased with grime and dark alleys smelled rancid to the nostrils.

Whitechapel's streets were filled with prostitutes, some of them very young. They had a haunted look. The eyes of a zombie and none of them could sound cheery, even when they first noticed Bergen and myself.

We were so out of place. He with his stovepipe hat, velvet vest and gold watch chain and me in the brass buttons of my Captain's uniform. There were many eyes on us, some curious and some cruel yet it was not unusual for Bergen to hand out money. A coin for a crippled boy, a bob for a girl with rickets. More hands held out from the alleys. People living in the dead vapours and putrefaction.

We went to Lambeth next and saw only more dark streets and hungry children, then on to Seven Dials in the East End where we saw women with their faces eaten away. Bergen lamented over it all and I thought of my own children.

We argued that night. I saw nothing of pastimes or pleasure, just degradation and I accused him of wanting to keep the working classes in chains.

"Not chains, Captain, but horse racing, fancy cockfights and billiards. They all lead to where we were today. Do you not see the connection? It is all moral degradation."

"It is not that simple." I replied. " Are you saying those children are immoral? I say they're just unlucky."

I was getting irritated with this young man and did a good deal of talking that night to keep him quiet. Eventually we were able to get back to our business at hand, to fill the empty holds of the *Treasurer*. In a few days I realised I may have stopped his talking but I hadn't changed his opinion. It was easy to see he had another calling that had nothing to do with ships, charters, cargoes and crews.

His passion, he said, was society. He wanted to help. He showed me General Booth's *In Darkest London and The Way Out*. He wanted to debate Booth's thoughts with me, to test them on an outsider and see how they sounded. I left London just before Bergen was to meet Booth face to face and debate with him. I've always wondered how they got along.

Circumstances being what they were, I never returned to find out. In 1897 the *Treasurer* was rammed as we were entering the crowded East River in New York. A drunken captain on a Portuguese brig was to blame. He was taken away in chains but The *Treasurer* had a hole in her port bow, broken timbers above the water line. We were in no danger of sinking but repairs would require several weeks. I paid off the crew and started arrangements with the shipyard in Brooklyn.

When I wired DP with the cost of repairs, he cabled back, telling me not to proceed. He wanted the ship towed to Baltimore where I was to hand it over to the superintendent of the Rolland Shipyard.

He continued, "I am not prepared to commence repairs at this time. After you have delivered the ship to Baltimore, you are released."

He was discharging me and laying up the most beautiful ship on the East Coast. It was a strange turn of events after months of wrestling with the conflict within myself. I knew I would never again have a ship such as the *Treasurer*. I was angry and alarmed that the best of seagoing time was behind me.

It is late at night now and there is just a little rum in the bottle, the last I have. It burns going down. I did cut it with a little water, didn't I? I'm no longer sure. I wonder if the Taft newspaper is in the trunk. What difference can it make? An old newspaper about an old president. I put a little water in the empty bottle and swirl it around and pour it in the glass.

I nursed a bottle throughout the night on the train from Baltimore. Mad as hell at DP. The train swayed in the darkness, crossing fields and bridges and the branches of big hardwoods trying to touch our windows. Small towns and whistle stops and changing landscapes and my wounded ship farther and farther from me.

When I left the *Treasurer* I stopped and kissed the main mast. I was saying goodbye to more than the ship. I was saying goodbye to a life I had loved.

Homeward bound from New York, the talk on the train was all about gold in the Klondike. People were caught up in it. Excited young men declared they were ready to quit their positions, leave their families and go off to God knows where. Mile after mile the train clicked and clattered while the idea grew inside me. Why not? Why not go myself? A short stay at home and off to the Klondike. Two hard years giving it all I've got. Then home for good.

"Home for good."

I suppose deep down I knew it was a foolish dream.

I was stiff-legged when I stepped on to the station platform in Truro. A porter was waiting for me. There was a telegram from DP.

> *"Return to Baltimore immediately-stop-Important-stop-Treasurer undergoing repairs-stop-Charter from San Francisco to prospecting fields in Klondike Ivans & Company-stop-Ship ready in four weeks-stop-Funds for crewing from First Capital Bank, Baltimore see Mr. Franklin-stop"*

It had been raining. As I tore up the telegram, bits of it stuck to the wet boards on the station platform and other bits were carried away on people's feet, going off in all directions.

That night I lay awake listening to voices in a Truro hotel. A woman's laughter drifted down the hallway, there was music somewhere and later raised voices, an argument. It rained again and I got up and watched the rain drops splash on the empty street.

The next morning I took the stagecoach to Great Village. Laura was expecting me. DP had been down. I told her my plans but she was not impressed. "It's a gamble and you are not of the right age to go gallivanting off to the Klondike."

"Better to spend two years looking for gold than spending another ten on ships looking for a charter. Besides, I have no ship."

"You can find another," she exclaimed.

"No, I won't find another. You don't understand. There is no sail, not like there used to be. Steam is coming and I have no papers for steam. Besides, there are too many sea dogs looking for a ship. I want to look for something else."

Three days later DP was standing at the door when I tied up my mare.

"I sent a message to Truro."

"I got it."

He nodded and I followed him inside. "I was hoping you could get back to the *Treasurer*. This came up rather quickly. Our agent in Halifax came all the way down here himself. They're looking for ships for the Klondike."

"I spent a week arranging the tow, a week on the tow and another week on the train," I told him. "I'm unhappy with the way things are. I may go out myself and try my hand at the gold."

"I see," he said. We went into his parlour.

"You took the ship away from me. I could have had the repairs well underway by now. The planking replaced. Everything done! You took the command away from me. Business wasn't that bad, we were getting charters."

"We weren't making money." He was agitated. "The *Treasurer* has never lived up to our expectations. If I could have found a regular charter, something guaranteed."

He went to the window and looked down the sloping hill to Faulkners Cove. The tide was coming in, forcing clam diggers to retreat.

"When we can load her with lumber that's fine. But when we're away from Nova Scotia, it's hard to come by enough good trade these days to fill the holds. We've got eighteen men on her. Three times the crew of a brig."

He shuffled away from the window.

"We've got a chance now. Plenty of people on the move from San Francisco to Cook Inlet. We can fill the holds and carry people too."

I was tired. Tired of it all. Tired of his frugality, tired of waiting in ports, tired of the storms and yes, maybe tired of the sea itself. I'd come home to find my children and my wife were strangers. James was grown and gone. Mary and Blanche were off living their own lives. A few years and even my youngest, little Sadie would also be gone. Time had etched thin lines at the corner of Laura's mouth and eyes, her hair had turned grey. A slight stoop in her walk. She was growing old without me.

That thirty minutes in DP's parlour was another indication of the slow unravelling of a life's work.

I took one of his cigars. We never mentioned Baltimore or the *Treasurer* again. We talked about the world, the government, the crops. I think he understood, maybe because he also had had enough. Over the years we remained cordial, but I never sailed for him again nor smoked another one of his fine cigars.

Chapter Twenty-two

The Klondike was not so much a place as a condition and I learned quickly that gold wasn't everywhere. I did stake a claim and even found a little gold but not much. Pick and shovel is for younger men. The old and broken men are not working sluiceways but in the saloons, disillusioned and sitting trying to read their whiskeys.

They needed men with sailing papers more than they needed prospectors. Eventually, I got a job as master of a small supply ship. I carried cargo up the coast from Seattle and Vancouver. Business was brisk until the gold ran out. The fever, which carried such excitement, faded as quickly as it started. The ship was mothballed and I headed home.

Sometimes we set our hopes in a strange way. We will deny the truth, refuse to let it enter our thoughts, yet in the depths of our souls we know we can never regain what we have lost. There was a need in me to find my family as it was fifteen years ago. Maybe I dreaded the alternative. It was uncomfortable. Laura was unaccustomed to living with a husband and me trying to regain a position that had disappeared.

Laura was there, yet she wasn't. She was pleasant but distant and always busy. A house to run, a church group to see to, preserves to prepare. I chopped the winter wood and helped George with the last of the hay and picked apples. I sharpened the axes and spent time in the yard like the hired man. I bought rum and Laura disapproved.

Only little Sadie saved me. My daughter was still young enough to be delighted at having her father home. She flew into my arms. We walked along the shore and up Economy Mountain through the autumn woods.

James was working in the west, in the town of Red Deer. Mary was married in Saskatchewan. Blanche was in Teachers College. I had missed so much of them. I would not miss my little Sadie.

Or so I thought, but even an eleven-year-old can quickly get too much of her father. I was walking her to school but after a week of such excursions, she told me she wanted to walk with her friends. I watched her go down the road and I was flooded with a thousand things I couldn't put in words.

I remembered my heart pounding when Laura wrote me saying we had a new daughter and she wanted to name her Sadie. I was dumbstruck, knowing that child would be part of my life forever. Every time I picked her up, held her in my arms or looked into her eyes, I might think of another. My daughter might ask me a question and I might look at her and be a thousand miles away. How could a man be happy that his daughter carried the name of his lover? Sadie, Sadie. Would I have an excuse for rolling her name over and over in my mind? What strange things we think! I was elated yet awestruck and a little afraid of having a daughter named Sadie.

I was relieved when I saw she had the raven hair and round features of her mother. A beautiful child, who truly made me realise how fortunate I was. As I watched her walk away from me that day on her way to school, my daughter turned and waved, much as Sadie Muise had done in the Charleston station. While I was sad to see her walk away from me, this lovely, bright daughter would be coming back.

My brother George named his second daughter Sadie Bell. I was surrounded by Sadies. Brothers, next door to each other with daughters named Sadie, and of course the other Sadie. My secret Sadie who I could call upon at any time and she would appear in a dress that captured all the colours of the sky. The roses and soft pinks, the light blues, the greens and golds, sparkled and swirled around her as if she was the centre of a dazzling flower that could only be admired but never touched.

"You need a job," Laura said. She was making a pie and when Laura did something it held her full attention. She talked without looking at me. That was the way she was. Making a pie, cutting the dough, rounding it on the plate. Her eyes were on her work but her words were on me.

"Go see DP," she said.

"No, I'll find something else."

"Are you too proud to go see him? He's going to build another ship. Go."

"No."

"We need money."

"We have money."

"Not enough for all winter and next year with Blanche in Teachers College and clothes for Sadie. Go see him."

"I won't go see him! I want to stay home for a while, I've missed so much of my children."

She put the pie in the oven and shut the oven door with deliberate force. It was trivial of me to want the life of luxury, to spend time with my youngest daughter, to become reacquainted with my wife. How unimportant in Laura's eyes, compared to a man's work and responsibility.

I went to New York in 1900. The hiss of steam boilers along the East River docks sounded like small boys trading secrets.

"A sailing captain, accustomed to yardarms and topsails and reading the wind, is lucky if he can get a job shovelling coal on a steamer these days," was the way a shipping agent, a friend of mine, put it. I had plenty of acquaintances in those days and I made the rounds of them all.

I was hired finally as third mate on a steamer making regular runs between Havana and New York. The captain was a man named Eastman whose first question to me was, "Are you a man of God, sir?"

He said he refused to let a life at sea harden him and I wondered if that was possible. He said grace before each meal and since he ate with the crew, we all did likewise.

As third mate, I worked with the sailors on deck. It was different. More than once when the wind changed, I would look aloft, ready for the captain to order up a change of sail. But instead of billowing sail, what I saw was billowing smoke. Wind no longer mattered.

Our ship was the *Gertrude Madison* and we plowed through heavy seas facing a good nor'easter or gales from the sou'west. Battered by foam-tossed seas, the steam engines hummed, the stacks smoked and a sailor never went aloft.

Laura wrote that DP was proceeding with a new ship to be called the *Ladysmith*. They were laying the keel in Faulkners Cove. The same slip where the others had been built. Where the keels had been laid for The *Allandale*, the *Harmony*, the *Treasurer*, the *Northern Empire* and the *Dove*. These ships had all rolled into the same bay. DP was building another one and I wondered why.

I stood by the rail of the *Gertrude Madison* and thought about the sea. They were right, all of them. Those old captains with weather-beaten faces and long memories who had been saying it for so long. Their predictions were true. All I had to do was stand on the deck and look up. The stacks, the smoke. The dependability. You could set your clock on our sea time. Winds didn't matter any more. They were right, all of them.

The age of sail was over.

Chapter Twenty-three

If I go completely blind, which I suspect will happen soon, I know what I will miss the most. It will be the twilight, that hand-me-down light of day. On land or sea twilight is a magical time. Twilight transports me. I am here in Lower Economy and in Cienfuego, half a century away on a warm Cuban evening when a little girl died and on the Russian docks, fifteen years ago, where my best friend vanished. I am here and I am in those places too.

Twilight begins to linger now. The sun is ever so slowly sinking over the mountains. The bats are in the field, swooping and diving. The sky glows golden, the flame of a Cuban fire. I think of Maria Mendoza. When conditions are right, little Maria with her dark, curly ringlets, comes bouncing into my dreams. I have never forgotten her. She was joy. Her large eyes sparkled with laughter. Running timidly, she stops and runs again, encouraged by her brothers.

We had been sitting on her father's wide veranda with tall glasses of Cuban rum. He was one of the few Cubans who clawed his way up from poverty. We carried his wares to New York and that night we are his dinner guests. His chest was so full of pride he could not hide his satisfaction at his large ranch, his beautiful children, and his wife, languid with the graceful motion of captured liquid. Senior Mendoza had it all and more than anything else, he loved Maria.

That little girl so many years ago and a continent away, trying to jump the fire as her brothers had done; leaping just as a gust brings the embers to life. Her long dress is suddenly ablaze and the evening and Senior Mendoza are shattered forever. I can still hear her screams, startling the parrots who fly squawking from the trees.

By that time I already knew pain, but that night in the flickering of the twilight I learned a lesson reinforced by the sea. On ships as on land, only the sea is permanent. A sailor can be working the deck next to you and suddenly be gone over the side, never to be seen again.

The fading sun in Cienfuego turned Senior Mendoza's tears to streams of ice, flickering in the light. The twilight could not mask the dignity of a mother's pain as she saw the raw flesh of her child's arms and legs as the small, still breathing body was placed on the dark wooden floor. Twilight.

Oh yes, there was my dear friend Marshy. My companion all those years. He disappeared at twilight. Down the gangplank just before dusk and into the crowded jetty on his way to the fig market at Samarkand. Where are you Marshy? What happened?

How wretched I felt that twilight in Canton after witnessing the fate of the pirates. The sword catching the sun like the great silver fish jumping in the Indian Ocean.

I've gone outside, standing in front of my house just to watch while I can. A bat swoops by, I hear the whirl of its wings. Twilight is the bridge between night and day, a time of peace for me. There are other things I will miss. The dawn of a new day as the sun fills the meadows on the mountain and pokes its fingers down into the deep ravines. I will miss the beauty of a ship in full sail and the soaring grace of the majestic hawk aloft from its mountain perch. I will miss the flowers in Laura's garden, and yes, I will even miss the look of disapproval on the flat face of Mrs. Marsh.

But I will miss twilight most of all.

Chapter Twenty-four

The next year the *Gertrude Madison* burned while we were tied at the jetty in the East River. Captain Eastman and I watched the flames lick out of the galley, envelop the deck and the aft cabin until the ship was lost in a black cloud. Cooks are usually to blame for fires and, despite the captain's pious ways, the cook was known to take a nip or two.

Even the loss of his ship could not put Captain Eastman in poor spirits. He would retire and move to Concord, New Hampshire. Just as well, he said, all things considered. The Boer War had ended more quickly than expected and many ships were without charters.

Eastman was a good sailor and work on a steamer was less rigorous than sail. I was beginning to have trouble with my eyes. If I'd been working on a sailing ship the top of the masts would have been a blur.

I had other afflictions as well. My knees and knuckles pained and Captain Eastman and I were often comparing our aches and pains. He suffered from a ringing in his ears that would not stop.

"Too many storms, too much water going over us, too many rough seas. We're not young men anymore."

He took me to the Plaza Hotel for fish chowder and advised me to follow the Lord. He also told me to get my eyes looked after. We shook hands and he left me on Broadway outside the hotel.

Once again I was walking the streets of New York looking for work. Blurry people passed me in the cool afternoons. The leaves were starting to fall. I'd walk up Seventh Avenue deliberately, as though I had a purpose or a place to go. Then over to Fifth and Park. Crossing the streets was more of a challenge and I strained to see the approaching carriages.

I checked into the Seamen's Mission on State Street. Some days I'd make my way along Canal Street just to pass the building where Sadie used to live. Some days I'd walk to the Battery and during the long empty afternoons I'd wander down to Hell's Kitchen, past the bars and meat shops with sawdust floors and well-fed dogs. I'd sit with other old men I didn't know.

Most of the time I looked for work. Lots of sailors were doing the same. We'd meet each other day after day coming out of agents' offices or shipping companies. Some were captains I knew well and we'd stop to compare stories. I'd see men I sailed with lounging along the docks on the East River and try to remember which ship they sailed on.

One way to pass the day was to wander uptown and watch the rising of the Flatiron Building. It was causing a sensation in the papers.

"Three hundred and seven feet high with an edge as sharp as a ship," was the way *The New York Tribune* described it. There was always a crowd standing around. Men watching other men work. You could feel the restlessness in the onlookers, the desire to be up there, off the ground earning wages.

In the hot, sultry autumn days swirls of dry horse dung would still be swept up by breezes gusting down State Street. Gentlemen with bowlers turned their brims into the wind to shield their faces from the cloud of dung particles.

New York had opened its first subway. You could go from the Brooklyn Bridge to Grand Central Station, on to Times Square and up to 145th Street. When I wrote Laura about it, telling her I'd given it a try, she replied that only in New York would people try to imitate ants. It had not been a happy letter. She reminded me I had not sent money recently and things required attending to. The next week she wrote that word had come the *Treasurer* had sunk in the River Platte on a charter from Boston to Buenos Aires, all hands saved.

I sat in a small café near The Seamen's Mission with a glass of rum and remembered my ship. With a good wind, I could stand under the main mast of the *Treasurer* and stare straight up. It was a city of living canvas, white billowing hills before the breeze. So much sail and rigging the sky came to you only in small patches of blue. It was the most magnificent sight I'd ever witnessed in my forty years at sea. I had another glass of rum and remembered that morning in Truro when I tore up DP's telegram and people carried it away on the wet soles of their shoes.

The next day I swallowed my pride and applied for a job as a night watchman. It was a comedown, but it was honest work. My nights were spent patrolling three warehouses on the docks of old South Street. There was always a lot of thievery around ships, and the company of McKibbin and Cayley had unreliable watchmen. Men who didn't patrol and spent much time nipping the bottle. They gave me a lantern, a billy club and a whistle.

It was often so cold that even steady walking couldn't keep the chill off. I'd go from one warehouse to another. There was a small shed connected to one of the buildings that gave me some protection from the rain. It didn't have a stove and I grew to understand why night watchmen took a nip. The saloons provided the only warmth.

The wet nights gave me a terrible chest cold that I carried for most of 1903. Rum warmed me. I had acquired a taste for it and against the rules, a small flask accompanied me on my rounds.

I was writing John often, trying to get back on my feet. I had a piece of lumber land my father left me. I might sell it and come home.

DP had not been lucky with the *Ladysmith*. He'd launched her in 1901, ready to capitalise on the Boer War. Luck was not with either of us.

The money I was sending home was less than half what I made on the *Treasurer*. The Seamen's Mission was a threadbare place with dented furniture and scruffy floors. It had the permanent odour of stale beer and stale men.

Letters from my children lifted my spirits. Blanche had married and was expecting her first child. I hadn't been there for her wedding. Daughter Sadie had gone out west with Mary. She was teaching and sounded happy. Mary seldom wrote and James Bernard never did. He was still in Red Deer and Laura said he would probably stay, as there was plenty of work for him.

I started looking for better paying jobs. I would take Blanche or Sadie's letters in my vest pocket to boost my spirits as I made the rounds. When on the waterfront I tried to ignore the empty ships berthed ghost-like in the mist of the East River.

It had rained during the night and the foggy dampness hung in low clouds over the docks. Water dripped off every roof on South Street but the morning air was brisk. I was walking back to the Seamen's Mission when a carriage pulled up alongside of me.

It was him. Hanging out the window holding a cigar and a bottle of spirits in the same hand. His smile was the same insult to the world, cynical and mischievous.

"Well, well. Captain Allan Graham, best you get in before pneumonia gets you."

I had not seen him in several years but his dissipation seemed no greater. I had aged, he had not.

I always resisted kindness from him until I'd tried to humble him in some way.

"I thought you'd be dead by now," I replied.

"It's you who'll be dead, walking around in this foul weather when I'm offering the comfort of my coach."

I didn't want to see him. Didn't want him to see me carrying my lantern. No more a captain, just an old night watchman with a terrible chest cold. But I took a deep breath and stepped inside. The best I could hope for was a good breakfast at his expense.

I was in his carriage before I realised he had two women with him. Why was I surprised? Sisters, they said, laughing drunkenly. Frilly women, past the prime of their youth with too much powder and rouge.

"We're going back to my ship for a little repast," he explained as he winked at me.

"Just drop me off at the mission on State Street," I replied.

Of course he didn't, and I was soon in his cabin drinking dark rum with one of the women fanning me with her wide-brimmed hat. It was repulsive. All of it. I was tired and hungry and the rum burned a path of fire down my throat. He was past sixty years of age and still cavorting with women. Still without a care in the world.

His women did not appeal to me. I had been lonely in New York, but I had been faithful. If not faithful to Laura, at least faithful to myself.

Drinking the last drop, I grabbed my hat and coat and was out the door. It was always that way with him. In some way I was worse off for such an encounter. Three times as far to the mission as I had been when he picked me up. I was lightheaded and angry.

Why is it, I demanded to know, that he still has his ship? He has his command, still has his rum and his women. Why does time not touch him? It made me furious, the unfairness of it all. Water splashed on my pant legs. Maybe I was the small child stomping in the puddles. I didn't care. All the frustrations of my life came pouring out of me. When I got to the mission I was burning up from sweat and my clothes were steamy. It was nearly noon and in a few hours I would have to get up and go back to the warehouses. I was filled with self-pity, sitting on the side of my bed, my head in my hands, feeling utterly defeated.

Noises on the street drew me to my small window. Two old men were huddled on a wet doorstep and a policeman was standing over them, gesturing for them to be on their way. They got up slowly and while I couldn't see their faces I recognised them. They were old sailors who could no longer afford a room at the mission. I knew their faces, grim and weather-beaten. They sauntered down the street in their ill-fitting clothes. Those men were younger than I but had been more beaten by life.

I was damned if I could understand it. Will Thompson still going. What stood between him and those men? What stood between myself and those men? A job as a night watchman? Was there more?

I had a family – a wife, children, brothers and I had lumber land. I had something.

I fell asleep knowing I was more fortunate than many.

A few days later, Will Thompson arrived at the mission and roused me from my sleep. He took me to dinner at Sharp's Steak House where he drank two glasses of rum before ordering his food.

"What the hell happened to you?" He lit a cigar and waited but I did not reply. "You commanded one of the finest ships on the east coast and you end up a night watchman in New York." He blew smoke into the air and waited again.

"Bad luck," I replied.

"Want to sail with me?" he said, catching me off guard.

"No."

He laughed and took another long drink.

"I'm selling some lumber land in Economy," I said. "I may buy shares in a ship and make it my command."

"Hmmm," he replied. "And if you don't?"

"I'll stay here."

"As a night watchman!" He said it sarcastically and laughed when I mentioned honest work. "Guarding the possessions of the wealthy is not work. Being wealthy is the only work of importance."

He was cocky and I know now that was his strength. He told me he'd been in jail, sentenced in New Orleans to two years hard time for stabbing a man. He petitioned the governor, had greased the right palms and was out in six months.

"When those bastards say 'hard labour' they mean it. Look at my hands."

They were scarred and hard; his palms had the calluses of men who swing an axe all day. I noticed his middle finger was crooked. He had broken it himself to get off the chain gang.

"What did you do?"

He waved the smoke away from his face.

"I had a little problem. There was some stolen property aboard my ship. This Norwegian accused me of stealing and one thing led to another until I finally put my knife into his ribs. It shut him up pretty fast. Come with me," he repeated. "I'm bringing the greatest cargo you can bring from the Indies."

"What?" I asked.

"Women," he said with a smile. "Forty, fifty at a time. Good lookers. They all have jobs when they get here. I guarantee it."

"You guarantee it?"

"Yep."

"You find these women jobs."

"Yep, every last one of them."

"Where do you get them work?"

"Everywhere, anywhere. They're not fussy. They sleep in the holds of my ship and lounge around deck in the good weather. Mind you, I have to beat the lads off them but these passengers pay double fare.

Anything to get to New York. I'll make you mate. You can have your pick."

"Where do they get jobs?" I persisted.

"Plenty of places for good-looking women to work in New York."

"Whores?" I said.

He shrugged. "Maybe some, not all. God! One I brought up last year, she's gadding about town with some senator. All done up in furs. The prettiest woman in New York, not much in bed, though. Had her myself but she was dead, you know. No life. Bet she's come alive under the senator." He laughed, "Come on, get out of this place, sign on!"

"No," I said, "I won't deal in women."

His offer was repulsive but yes, attractive too. Maybe I should throw in with him, I thought. He was doing better than I was.

Sitting there at Sharp's I closed my eyes and reflected on all the women I had known in the Indies. Laughing girls in the Kingston market, sultry servants quietly moving amongst the tables in the big halls on the plantations of Montego Bay. The beautiful Havana women with flowers in their hair. I could hear the whores in Trinidad calling to me from their alleys. Willing to be taken right there like animals in the open air. I thought of little Maria Mendoza that night so long ago, when she jumped over the fire. Her screams and later her mother's elegance in grief.

Maria was one of the lucky ones who had gone to private schools to study Shakespeare and Milton. I loved the Indies. Loved the people. No. I would not go with him. I wanted to escape as much as those poor shanty dwellers he was bringing here. But I would not go with him.

It was much to my satisfaction that within months, fate finally caught up with him. Judgement was hard but I dare say just. He was arrested, tried and acquitted but his money had run out and his ship was seized and I admit this also now, a nub of delight burned in my gut.

The next time I saw him we were both back where we had started, living along the shore. We were old and alone. His wife dead, mine in the west. He was dying. I was nearly blind.

It was on my first visit to his bedside that these inquiries began to overtake me. Unjustified feelings mingled with questions I couldn't repress. Maybe there was a certain smugness in me. I could see enough to walk up to his house where I could finally look down on him.

He is dead now and my story is almost finished but not quite.

In May of 1908 I got a note from an agent I didn't know, wanting to see me as soon as possible. He shook my hand heartily.

"An associate of mine is looking for a captain to take a ship to Halifax."

His name was Fletcher. A fat man who lowered his girth into a well-used leather chair. A fat, bald angel come to my rescue.

"The ship is," he picked up a paper and began reading it slowly, "a four hundred ton brig, been sold to T.A. Douglas & Sons of Saint John. But they're refitting her in Halifax for the coastal trade. Back and forth across the Fundy, I suspect. I told them I'd assist finding a captain if I could."

The brig was the *Celeste* and she certainly needed a refit. There was water in her hull ankle deep. Her decking was marred and her booms and yards needed replacing. But she was a sailing ship and I'd have the wind with me again. There was no guarantee I'd be hired permanently as captain, but I'd be going home. Home with the wind. It was enough.

My job was to make the ship sea ready. I supervised the repairs and hired a crew. I couldn't find any good men from the Dominion, they'd long since deserted New York. I settled for two Irish brothers who had worked their away across the Atlantic along with four New Bedford fishermen and a Frenchman I had come to know while I was a night watchman. They were all experienced and Fletcher & Sons was anxious to get the *Celeste* underway.

So was I. My health was deteriorating and so were my eyes. I was looking through fog. All a doctor could find was a touch of pleurisy, which did not account for any weakness in my vision.

I will never forget the morning we left New York. There was a certain lightness in me. I had been a night watchman, a steamer mate, a prospector, a supply ship captain, but what I was more than anything was a man of sail. It was the canvas flapping above me that applauded my work. I could taste the sweetness of it. It had been over forty years since I first sailed into New York. A city that had changed greatly, it had boosted me and ultimately beaten me but I was coming back. I tried to focus on the sails, their thrusts, the telltales running in the breeze. We would have good winds coming into open water.

Of course, I know now I was lying to myself as I had done all my life. Deep within me I knew the truth. My eyes were no longer good enough. But that morning in New York I was part and parcel with the elements around me. The wind and the sails and the sea and myself were together again, old friends lost and reunited. Sea birds darted in front of us. The tugs and steamers and a few old square-riggers were my honour guard as we sailed down the harbour. Sea bound. We passed the jetties and warehouses, horses and freight wagons. Sea bound. I was at the wheel.

My crew was a tough but undisciplined and quarrelsome lot. We had hardly cleared New York when a fight broke out between one of the Irish brothers and one of the sailors from New Bedford. When the mate, another New Bedford fisherman, broke it up he received a broken nose from the elbow of the Irishman named Walsh. I put the Irish youth in chains but released him at midnight when all hands were needed aloft. We were in the teeth of a driving gale.

That was the start of it. The brig pitched and rocked all the way up the coast. She was taking on a lot of water and our pumps were manned constantly. Waves rolled over the deck, taking the feet out from under us. Sailors cursed and got up again before the next one hit us like a driving waterfall.

More and more I gave the wheel to my mate. There were times I couldn't see the topsail and when I was standing by the wheel, the forward mast seemed covered in mist. The wind was slapping hard. The ship was labouring. The man at the wheel needed a good pair of eyes.

We ran through three storms by the time we were off Boston, when we got an S.O.S. A large, fully rigged ship foundered in the distance, her lanterns flashing distress. By the time we drew near, the ship had capsized, we could see men in the water, heads and shoulders just above the brine. Giant waves pounded down on them and there were fewer heads that bobbed up again. They would be there one minute and gone the next. Some reappearing, others disappearing. My lads did their best and came together as a good crew. The waves were high and the water freezing. If you dipped your hand into the sea, you quickly lost the feeling in your fingers. We saved nine of the sixteen who had been on board. Wet wretches, sick and shivering, spewing seawater, then trembling, teeth chattering. I knew what to do.

"Get them up, get them moving."

My young sailors looked at me but did as I ordered.

I had hoped to dock in Halifax within a week to impress the owners. But the storms had delayed our progress. We were in the mouth of the Gulf of Maine when a fog bank set in. I had taken the bearings and kept the ship single reefed. Reading the charts, taking the bearings, just watching the sea were difficult tasks and by then I knew I was finished. My mate, a Yankee named Munro, knew something was wrong. In the middle of the rescue I handed the wheel to him.

At six-ten in the morning on our ninth day at sea the *Celeste* ran aground on a rocky shoal off LaHave, Nova Scotia. I was at the wheel.

It was my ship and my responsibility. The inquiry found it so and I could not argue.

The ironies of life! We fetched up where, thirty-six years earlier, we had seen the light and felt hope that our nightmare on the *Dove* was about to be over. The winds of fate kept bringing me back to this place.

The wrenching sound of ripping wood made the old brig scream as the sharp pinnacles of the shoal thrust deep into the timbers of the bow. The waves pushed her harder up on the black rocks. The ship was solidly fixed on the shoal. I squinted to see the broken timbers, letting on I could make out details I couldn't.

My hopes of a future command were gone. My days at sea were over. What had begun with such hope. I had left New York with the false feeling that I could regain my position as a sailing skipper. My dreams were all dashed on those jagged rocks off LaHave.

It took ten days of humiliation to patch the bow. Carpenters and lumber came out twice by scow but could not get near us. Some fishermen came to watch, keeping their distance. When the patches were finally down, in the highest tide of the year, a big steam tug pulled us off the shoal and took us to Yarmouth.

It was all a nightmare. I was pointed at and whispered about as the captain who put his ship on the rocks. Two days later, a representative from Fletcher & Co. handed me a letter relieving me of my command. An inquiry would be called. They talked of my life. My faultless record as captain. There was testimony about saving the nine sailors.

I went home.

And so it was. I was found negligent and my masters papers suspended. I had little money and yes, I admit it, I was bitter. I was rattling around a house with a wife I hardly knew. It was not a happy time.

Laura's suggestion was for us to go away. "Why not be close to our children?"

"We'd be farther from Blanche," I replied.

It was the grandchildren Laura craved. I wanted to see our children but I didn't want to stay in the west and Laura did.

"What will we do out there?"

"What are we doing here?" she countered. "You're walking around the house grumbling. You can do that out there and I'll be close to the grandchildren. Which I dearly want to be."

In the midst of our debate we were dealt an awful blow. On June 7[th,] 1909 James Bernard was killed. Instantly they said, by an auto in Red Deer. Walking around our house, the gloom reminded me of 1859. When you lose a child you never fully recover.

There was no stopping Laura then. All our children, except Blanche, were in the west. Sadie was in Edson, Alberta, and Mary with her three children lived in Saskatoon. More than ever Laura wanted to be close to them. We left for the west. We were going as Laura said, to be with Mary, Sadie and James.

I couldn't explain to her my reluctance. She had been home a lifetime and I had waited a lifetime to come home. I wanted to live in the house we'd built so many years ago. To be able to cast my weak eyes over the bay every morning. The house, the cove, Economy Mountain behind us, the graves of my sisters, the closeness of my brothers. I had come home, finally returned. Now I was leaving again.

On one point I would not budge. I refused to sell our house. Laura sought a permanent break. She wanted to cut all ties. I would not.

They had a memorial service for James in Five Islands, where they had buried my mother, father and sisters. We left the next day.

It was a long train trip, longer than from Baltimore. Long and lonely. We had little to say to each other. There was no mirth, no enjoyment and no interest in the scenery. Laura knit and through failing eyes I watched the rolling landscape transform from spruce woods to potato fields to granite rocks. Central Canada and wide rivers, Manitoba and scrub brush and finally to a flatness, just miles of level ground.

The farther we moved across the Dominion, the more lost I became. A failed captain whose life's work ended on a black shoal. I was leaving any possibility of spiritual redemption.

The wheat fields of Saskatchewan sent the first stirring through me since we boarded the train. The fields moved, blurry but golden. The ill-defined motion of flaxen water. It was the golden ocean I had dreamed of on the *Dove*. This gilded sea with soft winds. Laura put down her knitting and we both watched the wheat blow back and forth. We didn't see the same thing. She saw grain blowing in the wind and I saw a great golden ocean. It made me immeasurably lonely.

It was an empty land. That's how I described it to George and John on my return. Empty with quiet, determined people. Not only was the land flat, so was the air. Flat, thin and so dry it left you gasping. It was so cold in winter it would freeze your piss and turn your lungs to leather. No wonder people didn't talk much. They were afraid of dying in mid sentence, their lungs filled with the frigid air.

I knew wind. The wind in the west had no soul. It had blown over nothing but dry plain for ten million years.

We rented a house on the outskirts of Saskatoon, as close to Mary as we could get. Laura was revived. Some of her youthful warmth returned. I was happy for her and tried to be happy for both of us. I took our grandchildren for walks and taught them how to whittle. After an hour or so, they had enough of me so I walked on alone. I split wood but my eyes made it slow going, the axe often missing its mark. Once I drove it into my leg. The gash took four months to heal. By then we were deep into winter with great swirls of snow sweeping across the frozen plain. It was lifeless. Not a bird to make a smudge in the empty air, not an animal to put a print in the miles of drifting snow. I sat by the fire and tried to read Dickens. I would nod off and dream he was reading to me as he had done that night in Carlyle, his long fingers stabbing at the air as he read.

The following spring the prairie turned to mud, the roads became swampy rivers of sludge. Horses hauled plows through the fields.

Mary and her husband drove us to Red Deer where we stared at James's tombstone. Laura cried and called him, "My dear little boy."

I hardly knew him. Every time I came home, he was taller and more distant. I had lost him long ago. When Laura was out of earshot, Mary told me James looked unnatural at his funeral, that there was a waxy whiteness making him more unreal than dead. She said his eyes had been sealed to prevent a lid from popping open but they didn't look right. His cheeks were too rosy, his hair combed differently. He was thirty-two years old.

"So young," she said.

"Yes," I replied.

Then she said, "Papa, do you realise how little you and Mother talk to each other?" It was obviously something she had been wanting to say for a long time. Mary was not an impetuous person.

"No," I answered.

"Even around the children you hardly speak to one another. Are you all right, Father? I know this has been a shock. But it's not just James's death. All winter you seem so, so lost."

"I feel I'm somewhere I don't belong."

The comment came before I realised how it would hurt her. I knew by her shocked expression it was like a slap across her face. She had been so excited that Laura and I were close by. Tears welled up in her eyes. We were alone in a little roadside place on the way back to Saskatoon. Laura had gone to the powder room and my son-in-law, Jim Moir, was paying the bill for lunch.

"You don't think you belong here by us? Your daughters, your grandchildren, your flesh and blood? You don't think you belong here near James?"

Her eyes flashed as the hurt turned to anger.

"And what would you do rambling around that big house in Economy? Here at least you have people who love you. It's too bad you can't appreciate it."

"Rambling around that big house," were Laura's words but I knew Mary was right. I loved her, loved all my children but there was something, some part of me, I had left behind somewhere.

"Go home," Laura said. "Go home and drink and mope. Live by yourself."

"You won't come?"

"No, I will not!"

My daughters and their husbands, grim-faced and tense, came to the station. Laura would move in with Mary. She hugged me stiffly.

"Come back when you're ready. Take care of yourself."

She knew I would not be back. Two years alone now, except for that nosey Mrs. Marsh and visits from my brothers and their brood. Little Percy brings my mail. Rosa says he is her last child. Blanche worries and visits when she can. I put on my best show when I'm with her.

Blanche is the one thing Mrs. Marsh has over me. That woman has a touch of larceny in her soul. She threatens to tell Blanche about the empty bottles. Twice she found broken glass on the floor where I've dropped my tumbler.

George disapproves of my rum. He and Rosa disapprove. John is a church deacon who might let a dram pass his lips once a year if that witch of a wife isn't looking. A pity none of them had a still so we could enjoy a repast under the apple trees.

I have four hundred dollars in the bank. The last of my land money. Then I will be destitute. It bothers me sometimes, but not much.

I should have the smugness of a deeply religious man disdaining earthly possessions. I don't. I am coming to the end of things and it is not the ending I imagined as a young man. I am not going out like a lamb into the arms of God but I am going out fighting, struggling to the last breath.

I have no complaints now, just inquiries. That was the purpose of watching Will Thompson. I do not want his death. It is not the bedridden loneliness nor the bloody wheezing that repels me. It is the vacuum. The blackness, the nothingness of him that I fear. The absence of God. The absence of everything. I have lost much that I value – the love of my wife, the life of my son, the affection of my daughters, the respect of my brothers and the esteem of my first captain.

But I have not lost all. There is still a flicker in my soul. There will not be his blackness and for that I am truly grateful.

Epilogue

Captain James Allan Graham died the following fall, on September 24th, 1911. He is buried in the Presbyterian Cemetery in Five Islands, Nova Scotia. Laura returned to their home in Lower Economy during the last months of his life. The two of them were seen walking on the beach again, as they had when they were young. Laura would hold his arm to prevent him from falling. By then, Captain Graham had been diagnosed with diabetes and was almost completely blind. Laura lived until 1936.

Captain Graham went to sea for over forty years. Most of the ships he sailed on were built in Faulkners Cove, Lower Economy, by DP Soley and his partners. The shipyard was on the very beach where Captain Graham and Laura often walked. All traces of the shipyard have disappeared as have the ships themselves. They are memories now. Only in the imagination do such working vessels exist, crewed by men with callused hands and weathered faces, men who could make the block and tackle hum as they raised the sails. With a plug of strong tobacco in their mouths, these men knew the surging power of full sails, pitching decks, dipping bows as their ships plowed the waters of the world.

Now in Faulkners Cove it is sunset and sea gulls fly way out on the bay. There is not a ship in sight.

September 16th, 2002